NOT MY CHILD

An unputdownable psychological thriller
with a breathtaking twist

JANE E. JAMES

JOFFE
BOOKS

Joffe Books, London
www.joffebooks.com

First published in Great Britain in 2023

Cover art by Nick Castle

ISBN: 978-1-83526-049-4

AUTHOR'S NOTE

The subject matter in *Not My Child* is of a very dark nature and I understand that this can be triggering for many readers. One of the reasons I wanted to explore the theme of sexual assault is because it can cause lifelong trauma that never goes away.

The two fictional young women in this story were unable to talk about what happened to them, and, as a result their later lives were deeply affected. For this reason, women have been known to report cases of rape and sexual assault many years after they occurred. It's important for those who have been sexually assaulted to know that it's not their fault, and even if the two women in this story couldn't see that, I wanted to share their story on their behalf. If either of them had felt secure enough to report their attack to the police, the other could have been saved, and this is exactly the kind of torturous and unnecessary self-blame that victims put themselves through when they hear that their rapist has struck again.

The charity Rape Crisis* has reported one in four women being raped or sexually assaulted as an adult and the overall statistics in England and Wales found that 85,000 women experience rape, attempted rape, or sexual assault every year.

Out of that shocking number only one in 100 rapes were reported to the police and resulted in a charge. This means five in six women who are raped don't report it. The reasons they gave for not reporting these crimes were — embarrassment (40%), didn't think the police could help (18%) and 34% said it would be humiliating. Of their rapists — disturbingly, only 6% ever face justice or end up behind bars. Five in six rapes against women are carried out by someone they know.

Worryingly, juvenile rape is on the increase too, and the victims are often teenage girls between the ages of thirteen and fifteen. This is thought to be due to easier access to online pornography, and a combined lack of maturity and sex education on the rapist's part.

For anyone who is affected by this story, Rape Crisis operates a sexual abuse support line. This is open 24 hours a day, 365 days a year, for victims and survivors of any gender.

Specialist staff are there to listen, answer questions and offer emotional support. They can be contacted on 0808 400 2222 or you can visit the website for a live chat option at sexualabusesupport.or.uk.

*Statistics sourced from Rape Crisis (online 2023)

'Only monsters claim not to be monsters, and only hurt people hurt people' — Jane E. James.

THE CHILD

Ryan stands in front of the house where his mother raised her other children, while he grew up in a home among strangers. Kind people. Mostly. But strangers all the same, who didn't know how to love a child that wasn't theirs. The red gloss door should have been *his* front door. Number eighteen. The same age as him.

Until today, the brass door knocker has never known his fingers. It doesn't feel like he's coming home when he lets it drop three times. The sound is like a gun going off. Glancing nervously around, he bunches his fists in his jeans pockets.

The wooden loveseat in the front garden, next to a pot of wilted flowers, is where he should have sat and smoked forbidden cigarettes. His first kiss with a girl would have been snatched pressed up against the garden wall, late at night out of eyeshot of prying eyes. Concerned parents wondering what their teenage boy was up to isn't something he's ever had to worry about.

'Can I help you?'

The man who has opened the door has a tea towel thrown over one shoulder and a burn on his arm that looks as if it will blister. Patches of sweat cover his unbuttoned shirt, displaying a smattering of wiry black chest hair flecked with grey. He's thin and gaunt, and he smells like fried onions. He has chocolate-coloured, regretful eyes, and a too-short haircut with rebellious tight black curls sprouting through it, like spring bulbs. Ryan's first thought, as a psychology student, is that this individual is not comfortable with who he is and that he has secrets.

Ignoring the man's puzzled expression, Ryan peers over his shoulder — they're around the same height — into the hallway behind him, catching snippets of infectious laughter, a bare ankle, and a flash of something squeaky and inflatable as two children spill noisily into the hallway and adjoining rooms. Sensing Ryan's interest, the man partly closes the door, obscuring his view. He's too polite to rush Ryan along. But he makes it plain he's busy. Got heaps going on. Two small children, for one thing.

Smoke from a barbecue curls its way out of the house and into Ryan's nostrils, causing his stomach to flip over with hunger. He hasn't eaten since yesterday. And that was just half of a sandwich somebody left behind on the bus.

They must have been outside in the garden in the middle of a family barbecue when he knocked on the door. There'll be burnt sausages, a blow-up pool, a giant trampoline, sunburnt skin, wasp stings and tears before bedtime. Aren't there always tears before bedtime? Isn't that how it works for unwanted children like Ryan?

His gaze slides back to the man, whose chocolate eyes are waiting for him. His expression indicates that he wants Ryan to go away and is hoping he's knocked on the wrong door. But this is the right door. And he's the right man. His mother's husband. The stepfather who doesn't know Ryan exists. And those are the right children. His half-brother and sister.

CHAPTER 1: DINO

Nine months earlier

They'd had a typical church wedding at his parents' insistence, but Dino and Tara weren't religious people, which was odd for a home-grown Italian Catholic boy like himself. The downside to this was that their kids, Fabio and Bella, had no idea how to behave in church. Their cries and protests hadn't gone unnoticed by the vicar or the respectfully hushed congregation, making Dino feel more of a failure as a father than usual.

His mamma and papà are on hand to make sure the little ones are kept out of mischief during the service, but they're still a handful for his elderly parents, especially Papà who has early-onset Alzheimer's disease. They're not bad kids by any stretch of the imagination, but they can be loud and boisterous. Like him and Tara. Laughing one minute, shouting the next.

Neither he nor Tara had excelled at disciplining their children, something his mamma was super critical of. Italian parents were strict. And didn't Dino know it. Because of this, he and Tara had deliberately distanced themselves from his parents — a cruel move, he realises now. After the last two weeks, he doesn't know what he'd have done without them.

He hadn't always gotten on with his papà. But the severe, unaffectionate man he'd once been so afraid of had taken charge of everything while Dino fell apart, devastated by the sudden loss of his wife Tara, who they're burying today. He still can't bring himself to think about the circumstances of her death. She'd been cruelly mowed down by a hit-and-run driver the police have been unable to trace. Dino now finds himself looking for dents in car bumpers everywhere. At the time of the accident Tara had been crossing a street on the other side of town, somewhere she had no reason to be. If the police couldn't figure out what she was doing there, damned if Dino could.

Looking down at his shoes, the only dark pair he could find to go with his cheap off-the-rail suit, Dino kicks himself for not remembering to polish them. They're as scuffed and neglected as he is. Tara used to say he was the best-looking man she'd ever met, but she wouldn't recognise her dark-haired, dark-eyed, handsome Italian now. He keeps forgetting to eat, as well as brush his teeth, and he's lost over a stone in weight.

Life without Tara, as a single dad, is going to be harder than Dino ever imagined. As if they were a part-time hobby, he'd spent his free time fooling around with the kids. He'd wanted more but Tara was adamant two was enough, and she was the one who kept their family functioning. Shopping. Doctor's appointments. Remembering to pay the bills on time. Sometimes not paying the bills on time so they could enjoy a rare family day out.

It stings him then, like an ice pack slapped on a burn, that Tara would have hated being buried on a Monday. Why hadn't he thought of that before? It was her least favourite day of the week, as it meant going back to work after the weekend and sending the kids back to school. They weren't rich. They didn't own a big house, like Tara's relatives did. They rented privately, and finances were tight. They barely scraped by each month. But they were a close-knit family regardless, needing nobody else.

It had always been Dino and Tara and then, after the kids came along — Dino, Tara, Fabio and Bella, a snug family unit. Tara was his first real love, and he was hers, or so she'd said. He'd believed her . . . until he came across the letter, but after reading it, he wasn't sure what to think. No, strike that. He *is* sure what to think. He just doesn't want to voice those thoughts.

The letter is crumpled and wet with tears from being read too many times. He hasn't even shared the contents with his mamma and they're close. He knows this isn't the right time to be thinking about it, but it's the only thing on his mind. Dino hasn't made up his mind what to do about it yet so it remains in his trouser pocket.

Making decisions was Tara's department. As was everything else. Dino was a husband and father in name only, leaving him unsure of the role he was meant to play. One thing he *is* clear on — as a duped husband, he's meant to read a eulogy for his wife's funeral, which amounts to telling lies. He hadn't wanted to do it but his papà insisted. That's what Dino should be focusing on. Pleasing his papà. Not the letter.

He'd practised reading the eulogy aloud in the downstairs toilet, away from the kids, crying every time he stumbled across the words he'd written down, and then furiously scribbled out — *devoted, loyal, loving, kind.*

Tara had been all of those things. But she was also a liar. A stranger.

The letter brushes against his leg as he strides towards the pulpit. It crackles against his thigh, acting as a reminder that Tara wasn't who he thought she was. For having the courage to speak openly about the loss of his wife, who is more lost to him than she can ever know, he receives a passing pat on the back from his papà, for *being brave.* But Tara was the brave one. *Lead passenger*, he used to call her.

On reaching the podium, the vicar ushers him up three small steps that suddenly appear gigantic. A lump in Dino's throat catches him off guard. He would rather be anywhere else than here. Even at work. Delivering boxes of organic fruit and vegetables to people far richer than him. It's natural for him to feel this way. It's his wife's funeral. Best get the eulogy over with. 'Presto, presto,' as his papà would say.

As Dino's clammy hand closes around the microphone, he wastes seconds pretending to adjust it before allowing his gaze to settle on the mourners who have gathered on this coldest of October days. It strikes him how empty the church is. He does a quick headcount, thirty people. Tara was thirty-three, so that's not even one person for each year she'd lived. He supposes this is the price you pay for being a private person. Although he's angry with Tara, he feels wounded on her behalf. *Where is everybody?* She had no close friends but he'd have thought her work colleagues at least would have shown up.

The funerals he'd been to in Altamura, Puglia, where his parents lived before emigrating to the UK had been packed-out in comparison. Coughing into his hand, Dino's eyes land on the shrunken figures of his mamma and papà in the front pew. Both are in their early sixties but look years older, due to their sun-weathered skin and silver hair. Bella, his ginger-haired toddler, sits on her grandad's lap, playing with his tie while Fabio, his five-year-old son, has his arms crossly folded in front of him because he'd wanted to accompany his dad on the podium but hadn't been allowed.

He reminds Dino so much of Tara at this moment, that he doesn't think he'll be able to continue with the eulogy. *What was he thinking?* He can't do it. Not in front of all these people. Suddenly thirty is a vast number. He's bound to end up in tears and make a fool of himself, causing his papà to tut. Tara could have pulled it off if their roles were reversed, but not Dino. He's never been one for public speaking.

That's when he sees them—

Tara's three older brothers.

And Dino's blood runs cold.

Each has the same pale green eyes, freckled skin, and thick sandy hair that he remembers from the last time he saw them altogether, dancing at his and Tara's wedding ten years ago. The brothers were born years apart, but they look so alike they could be triplets. Sitting closely together in matching seal-grey suits, they remind him of sardines in a tin.

When one of them smiles at Dino — he's not sure if it's Chris, James or David — his mind is made up for him. Without the smile, he would've muttered an apology and called the whole thing off. Walked away. Instead, he takes the letter — not the eulogy he's meant to be reading, out of his pocket and noisily unfolds it under the nose of the microphone.

Clearing his throat, he tugs at his too-tight tie and pauses. Such helplessness would've prompted Tara to storm up here with the intention of rescuing him — just as his son had wanted to do. He uselessly searches for her among the churchgoers, even though he knows she isn't there. As that fact hits home once more, his eyes glaze over with chilly tears.

'I was married to two women. One I knew. And one I didn't,' he announces coldly, eyes hardening. 'Before my wife died, she wrote a letter. In it, she told me things I didn't know about her. Secrets that she kept from me. From all of us.' Dino pauses, ignoring the sharp intakes of breath and shocked murmurings that echo around the church.

'She asked me not to tell anyone what the letter said and begged me to destroy it as soon as I'd read it. But I'm not going to do that.' A jolt of pain pulses in Dino's temple, and he clasps his white-knuckled hands around the stand for support. 'You might think me disloyal for going against Tara's wishes, but I've decided to share the contents anyway.'

Dino pointedly glares at the three brothers who are now uncomfortably shuffling in their seats. 'Starting with lie number one.'

CHAPTER 2: TARA

Aged thirteen

I tell lies. Loads of them. That's me, Tara. The black sheep. The ugly ginger freak with frizzy hair and white skin that burns easily, earning me the nickname of "vampire girl" because I rarely go outside in the sun. My freckles are the talk of the school. Always have been. I'd be a social outcast if I didn't have three good-looking elder brothers to boost my status. As it stands, I'm popular with the girls at school for all the wrong reasons, but I'm also despised. The majority of boys ignore me. That's fine with me.

As a thirteen-year-old girl with no real friends, I spend most of my time alone in my bedroom, which is meant to be my sanctuary, except it isn't, it's more of a hiding place from my mother and brothers. They can't make fun of me, insult me and put me down if I'm not around. Vanishing from rooms they are in has become a party trick of mine, much like a magician. So welcome to my bedroom. It has pink walls, yellow curtains, and a pink heart-print bedspread.

I'm considered an oddity because I'm not into boys, make-up, or clothes, preferring to draft stories in my lined notepad. I carry it with me everywhere in case Mum decides to stick her nose where it isn't wanted, and so that one of my brothers doesn't get the chance to throw it into the bin again, as punishment, knowing how much my scribbling means to me. In reality, Mum isn't sufficiently interested in me to want to find out what I write. She simply sees and hears what she wants to. That's usually not me.

My walls are devoid of boy band posters. Instead, I have photographs of horses. I also don't flip through the glossy pages of teenage girls' magazines that are all about boys, make-up, and fashion. Nope, I read *The Silver Brumby* books by Elyne Mitchell, whom I wish was my biological mother. I have the entire collection, even though I've never sat on a horse.

Thirteen is too old to be fantasising about horses or writing childish, stories but I'm a late developer. Still very much a little girl in a bigger girl's body — I've never kissed a boy, *ew* and haven't begun my period yet. But I don't tell the girls at school that, because who wants to be known as one of the last girls in year nine to become a woman?

There's no air in the bedroom and I can't open the window. Dad was meant to fix it but he died before getting around to it. He was only forty-six when he dropped dead of an aneurysm in Morrisons car park but he looked much older, due to a lifetime's dependency on cigarettes and alcohol. When he was alive, hen-pecked, and put upon, Mum said DIY was the only thing Dad was good at. She's changed her tune since and has transformed him into a saint now that he's dead, after years of threatening to leave him because of his drinking. Mum's convinced that I will turn out just like him, a drunken waste-of-space but I'm determined to prove her wrong. At least he was kind. . . even when paralytic.

We're all waiting for Mum to recover and return to normal. But I don't believe she will. Black suits her. And she loves the attention that grief brings her. We've been given new rules — or at least I have — my older brothers are less affected because they can come and go as they please. Nothing much has changed. Boys are still afforded more freedom than girls, despite the fact that we are less protected in the real world than we've ever been. Mum has ordered that the curtains be shut at all times and there be no more laughing or shouting, and especially no playing outside, because what would the neighbours say when your dad has only recently died? *Who plays outside at my age?* was my first thought on hearing this.

My eldest brother, David, who thinks he's now the man of the house, barks out daily reminders of 'don't bother your mother.' Even his warnings are delivered with pinches to my arms, his slimy green eyes burning into mine, because we're meant to make ourselves invisible. He's Mum's second favourite, but all three of her boys are precious to her. Their good looks, height, green eyes, and sandy hair make them stand out in a crowd, whereas I am noticed for all the wrong reasons.

As Mum's only daughter, you'd think she'd love me at least a little bit but she's never forgiven me for turning out to be another ginger-haired, ugly, freckle-faced freak like her. Plus, I remind her too much of Dad. The side of him she couldn't stand — stubborn, feisty, and hard to control. It aggravates her that I don't like the same things she does. A girl who can't bake, cross-stitch or crochet — all hobbies of hers — and who isn't into clothes isn't what she'd expected when she first found out she was having a girl. As a tomboy who is blunt and socially awkward around people, I'm an embarrassment. To her, I'm the black sheep. An outsider. A troublemaker.

I used to be chatty, pleasant, and outgoing, having opinions all my own. Until I realised that staying quiet was the sensible thing to do. This made me easy to ignore. Being ignored is all I wish for. Things have got so much worse since Dad died. He was the only one who ever defended me from Mum and my brothers, saying they were nothing but bullies.

Living in fear of going home gets in the way of my school lessons. I used to be a straight-A student but now I barely scrape through with a D. You'd think that would trigger all kinds of alarm bells with my teachers but no one recognises my silent cries for help, or asks whether I'm okay. Even if I got into fights and swore at the teachers, they'd put my change of behaviour down to my dad dying and cut me some slack. But slack is not what I need.

I'm too young to leave home but I fantasise about running away all the time. I know I'm not wanted here. But, where would I go? We have no other relatives in the area to whom I can turn and there are no grownups I feel I can trust. I don't even have a favourite teacher. Much less a favourite brother!

We're all close in age, with only two years separating us, so they're not much more than kids themselves. But, if I instinctively know that they're mean behaviour is wrong, why don't they? They're older than I am. Then I ask myself what's wrong with me that my whole family hate me so much. Am I the black sheep everybody makes me out to be? Is it my own fault I get picked on so much?

CHAPTER 3: DINO

The church is extremely cold. The coffin is impossibly small. Tara was tiny for a grown woman, standing five foot two inches tall and weighing just eight stone, but she made up for it with a big heart and a quick temper. A large, purple *MUM* flower tribute, purple being Tara's favourite colour, stands on top of the natural eco coffin that Dino had paid extra for. Or, rather, his parents had. He can't recall why he thought an environmentally friendly send-off was a good idea since Tara wasn't the least bit concerned about the environment. What she cared most about was their family.

And it's her family, the three brothers, who Dino focuses on as he tries to weigh up how he feels about them now that he knows the truth about them and the enormity of what they've done. He'd never liked them any more than Tara had, but he tolerated them at family gatherings for her sake and because family was important to him. He feels duped, even dirty, now that he knows they helped cover up his wife's secrets, that they lied to his face during every interaction he'd ever had with them. The Fountains had tricked him, and they had all turned out to be liars.

'Lie number one will come as no surprise to Tara's brothers, who were actively involved in keeping her secret hidden from me and my family.' His voice booms loud and clear when his feelings towards his wife couldn't be any less so. 'You attended my wedding and laughed and joked with me at our reception knowing that my marriage to Tara was based on a lie, yet you kept it to yourselves. Have you any idea how that makes me feel?' Dino swallows hard. His chest aches. Everything hurts. His pointed finger turns into a fist that he wants to bring crashing down on the brothers' skulls. 'My wife told me that I was her first love, and that she was a virgin when she met me but that was a lie and you knew it.'

'Things like that shouldn't matter today,' argues the tallest of the three brothers. Could this be David, the eldest?

'Oh, you're absolutely right, they shouldn't, and Tara could have had a hundred lovers before me and it wouldn't have made a difference, but it's the fact that she lied, that all of you lied, that hurts the most.'

Out of the corner of Dino's eye, he notices the vicar hurrying towards him, the hem of his white robe dragging on the ground, no doubt intent on removing him from the podium. Dino shakes his head and holds out a forceful palm, shooting the vicar a warning glance.

'It's not the right time or the place, Dino. This is God's house.' The vicar persists but doesn't come any closer.

'It was none of our business,' the eldest brother says in defiance, puffing out his chest.

'But it *was* your business, because all three of you were responsible for bullying a vulnerable underage girl into giving up her baby for adoption when you found out she was pregnant, and then threatened her to keep silent about it so as not to shame the family name. And you did a good job, because she didn't even tell me, *her husband*, about lie number two.' Dino's frown slides off his face onto the brows of the congregation. Gasps. A stunned silence. Murmurings. Rustling.

Each of the brothers look suddenly startled, like terrified pigeons on a rooftop. They look at each other as if they've never seen one another before.

13

People begin to leave. Dino doesn't know what to do. Should he call them back and force them to listen? Or let them go? Although the attack on Tara's brothers feels justified, Dino knows the vicar was right in stating that this was an improper time and place. Today is meant to be about saying goodbye to Tara, not revisiting her shameful past. Dino squares his shoulders and shakes off that thought because the shame was never hers to begin with.

Dino's mamma is halfway down the aisle with the kids in tow, Fabio battling her the entire time, and Dino is determined to do the same. He will not be stopped, no matter how much his papà tuts and shakes his head in disappointment. The kids shouldn't hear about what happened to their mum, though. It's best if they leave church.

The brothers have stood up, as if they too are preparing to leave. Dino can't let that happen. If necessary, he'll lock them in and barricade the doors. Is he overreacting? Probably. Does it matter? Hell, no. Then he notices that they're silently communicating with each other as if trying to work out their best form of defence. Raised eyebrows. Shrugs of the shoulders. Creased brows. The same one who spoke before — Dino's convinced it is David — straightens his tie, undoes a button on his jacket and juts out a chin before addressing the vicar, without even glancing in Dino's direction.

'We're only here to pay our respects to our sister and I can assure you we had nothing to do with convincing Tara to give up her baby, but I can understand why, years later, it might suit her to think that. As there would be less self-blame that way.' David wrinkles his nose as if at a mild inconvenience. 'We don't want to speak ill of the dead in God's house, vicar,' a meaningful dig at Dino, 'but our little sister was, shall we say, inventive at times with the truth. She always did have an overactive imagination.'

Tara had warned Dino in her letter that the brothers would remain stoically loyal to each other because blood was thicker than water in their eyes. That's why, even as an adult, she'd never pointed the finger, knowing they'd gang up on her and that she wouldn't be believed.

Tara had written long jumbled sentences about a black sheep. It didn't make much sense to Dino but he got that Tara was referring to herself, which made him angry. He'd never been a violent man, even during his wayward hormone-fuelled teenage years when he'd got in with the wrong crowd and became a source of concern for his parents, but if he could have five minutes alone with the brothers for what they'd done to Tara, he'd throttle them.

'Bollocks,' Dino shouts so loud his throat burns and his eyes bulge. 'She was only fifteen, for Christ's sake, and you, being older, should have looked out for her.' His hands ball into fists at his sides and rage takes the place of blood in his veins. 'Instead, you blackmailed her into doing the one thing she didn't want to do — give her baby away.'

In a pitiful attempt to get the mourners on his side, the eldest brother casts feeble glances around the church. 'That's not true. She made that up. You didn't know Tara back then. She was a teenage delinquent. An out of control runaway . . .'

CHAPTER 4: TARA

Aged fifteen

I bunk off school. I'm disruptive in class. When Mum isn't looking, I steal her cigarettes and money. I come home late. Some nights I don't come home at all. Sometimes the police are involved. Each time I'm picked up, found, whatever you want to call it, I'm dragged back home, to our semi in Ryhall Road in Stamford and lined up like a traitor about to be shot.

'How can you do this to your mother after all she's been through?'

I don't offer reasons or excuses but wait for the name-calling to begin. *Black sheep. Liar.* I don't react or look at them, them being my brothers, when they say this because being the black sheep of the family means I'm not like them, and that's a good thing.

They want to know where I've been and who I've been doing it with. They're referring to me having underage sex with boys, which is disgusting. As if I'd do that. Boys are the last thing on my mind.

I didn't steal a tenner from Mum's purse or her last packet of cigarettes. I don't know what you're talking about when you accuse me of nicking alcohol from the drink's cabinet.

And of course, I'm not emotionally abused on a daily basis by my unfeeling family, who use me as a scapegoat and tell me I'm useless, just like my dad, so they can feel better about themselves. That would be unthinkable.

Usually, when I want to escape, I take the train from Stamford to Peterborough, using money pocketed from Mum's purse, to hang out in parks with gangs of older kids. No one asks me my name or where I'm from. Most of us are from the same place. Running from the same thing. You can see it in our eyes. We're either unwanted, abused or neglected. Sometimes all three. Unlike the charity appeals on TV for underprivileged children across the world, we have nobody to look out for us. In England's towns, kids like us are invisible.

What about me? I want to scream when I overhear my teachers talking about me when they think I'm not listening. *That Tara is trouble. What are we going to do about Tara? She lies all the time. She won't tell us why. No one else in her family is like this.* Thank God for that, is what I say.

Today is my birthday. I'm fifteen. Mum didn't forget. She got me a card and a shop-bought cake. And a My Pony annual which is intended for readers years younger than me. It doesn't matter. I'd like to be that age again. I wish I were little enough to sleep with Mum in the bed that still smells of Dad.

I'm determined not to spend my special day in a place of fear and shame, so I've filled my pockets with notes stolen from my eldest brother's savings jar and a half bottle of last year's Smirnoff is stuffed inside my hoody. I'll be long gone by the time anybody misses me, on the six o'clock train into Peterborough.

As the front door crashes behind me on my way out I don't think "poor me", but "fuck them".

CHAPTER 5: DINO

It's the wake, and Dino has had too much to drink. *Not a good idea.* That's why he's unable to get his head around how people can eat straight after a funeral. What is it about burying a dead person that makes mourners want to tear into even more dead flesh?

Instead of mingling and making people feel at ease, as his papà expects him to, he casts angry eyes at those who've come to pay their respects. He uses that term loosely. Most have smiles pasted on their faces and pastry crumbs on their black clothing. *Have another sandwich, why don't you? Here's that third cup of tea you asked for.*

Dino knows he's being churlish and unreasonable. It's not like he had to pay for the caterers or the community hall, which is situated smack in the middle of Little Italy — otherwise known as Stanground — an area of Peterborough that's home to one of the largest populations of Italian immigrants in the UK. His parents are well-respected here, but although they've lived in England longer than they haven't, his papà still struggles with spoken English. They're hardly wealthy but what they do have they lavish on Dino and the children. Dino's lucky to have them. He hasn't always thought so.

His children are enjoying all the adult attention. Fabio practises handshakes with grown-ups while his sister basks in over-the-top compliments about her ginger curls and freckles. Dino's thankful he doesn't have to worry about them today. His mind's elsewhere. He can't believe *they're* still here. The brothers. Or that his parents are speaking to them.

Dino sits alone at the bar, his hand curled around a large glass of Rioja. He has no idea that his hostile expression and wine-stained lips are putting people off from approaching him. From across the room, he watches the brothers. Dino's papà had overruled him outside the church before the internment of Tara's body, insisting that the brothers be allowed to attend the funeral reception out of respect for Tara and to reassure the rest of the mourners that all was well. Dino wanted to spit when he heard that. *How could things ever be well again*? David is apparently doing the talking for all three of them because the other two's lips don't move. They're nodding and shaking hands with people, but they avoid smiling as if they know this will be frowned upon after the accusations that got thrown around in church.

What he'd accused the Brothers Grimm of, in the eyes of those present, is less important than the uncomfortable embarrassment they'd been made to suffer because of it. In a church too! Oversharing of that magnitude is unacceptable in the eyes of people like his papà, who do not believe in airing their dirty laundry in public. Dino sighs into his glass, understanding that the brothers have won the sympathy vote for today and he's been cast as the bad guy. Nothing new there.

Eighteen years ago, he'd gotten mixed up with a bad crowd and became a different person for a while. Somebody his family didn't recognise, or like. He'd drank too much. Smoked too much. Swore too much. The group of lads he'd hung around with had progressed to stealing cars, minor theft, and intimidation. Dino had done a lot of things in his youth that he wasn't proud of. But at the time he'd thought he was cool and unafraid. A handsome Italian stud with the gift of the gab. People around here have long memories and they won't have forgotten. Dino will always be the De Rosa boy to them. His father's good-for-nothing wayward son. He squirms on the barstool in shame thinking about it.

And look how that ended! The humiliation of being rescued by his parents, while his mates were still banged up behind bars, isn't something he's likely to forget. Because he'd never been in trouble with the law before, the police, give them their due, agreed not to charge young Dino for taking a ride in a stolen car, as long as the De Rosas promised to keep him out of trouble in future. His papà, as angry as Dino had ever seen him, agreed to those terms and sealed the deal with a handshake. It helped that the sergeant on duty was Italian.

On the drive home his mamma wouldn't stop crying, while his papà would every so often turn around in his seat to cuff Dino across the back of the head. Knowing he deserved it, Dino tried not to hold the beatings against his papà. Things were different in those days but he couldn't imagine ever raising a hand to his own children.

All these years later and he still hasn't earned his papà's respect. Without Tara by his side, he's not sure it's even possible. Although his papà never voiced his feelings, because that's not what De Rosa men do, Dino's certain his papà thought Tara was too good for him. He used to say that Tara had all the passion his son lacked and that he, Dino, was more English than she was. That's why his papà loved Tara so much.

Not his mamma though. She was all about her boys. Dino first. Then Papà. It must have been galling for him to know that his wife's affections had been irreversibly transferred to their son. But he had Tara in a way that Dino did not. Theirs was a unique friendship based on mutual love and respect that often left Dino feeling excluded. 'Shared values', Papà would say, as if that explained everything. Dino had been told many times that he wasn't deep or reflective enough to believe it, so it meant little to him.

Most outsiders thought he and Tara had grown up together, as she was so in tune with his family. *More one of them than Dino*, he'd heard said a hundred times before, and each time it grated. Yet they had grown up sixteen miles apart, he in the city and she in a small market town. He hadn't met his future wife until he was twenty-five and she twenty-two.

Nodding to the bartender to refill his glass, Dino avoids looking in his papà's direction knowing he will have been horrified by his son's emotional outburst in church and the outpouring of grief that followed. His gaze slides once more over the three brothers who look like seals in their grey winter coats.

Dino wants to lash out and punch things. He has so much repressed fury, his bones ache from holding it in. His anger is directed towards Tara one minute, because he wants more than anything for her to take back the things, she said in the letter about not being a virgin when they first met, the baby she had adopted and her emotionally abusive childhood, then at the brothers, for obvious reasons. His papà for tutting at him in church. His mamma for being worried sick about him when he can't bear the extra responsibility right now. Jesus, he can't bear any of it. He wasn't cut out to be a single dad. How is he going to do this on his own without Tara?

He wants to give up. Admit defeat. Go for a drive in his car and never return, leaving his parents with the responsibility of the children. Dino knows this is cowardly thinking but if a widower can't indulge in a little fantasy, then who can? Especially after a bottle of wine. He's been stumbling around in a daze since Tara died, not knowing if it's day or night. People who don't matter keep telling him he needs to be "strong for the children's sake if nothing else" and he opts for the nothing else part every time. The children will be fine. They're resilient. Isn't that what Tara's mum and brothers must have said about her when they forced her into an adoption she didn't want?

21

Tara might be a liar, as the brothers were quick to point out, but Dino doesn't doubt what she said about her family for one minute. He feels the truth of it in his gut. Finding out about the baby was a huge shock though. He could kill her for not telling him. As for lie number three . . .

'Tara, how could you?' he wants to rage. But he's been told that as a man, as a De Rosa, he must keep it together. So that's what he must do. If he wants to be a man. Like his papà.

Dino had felt like a man until he came across the letter. He discovered the innocent-looking cream envelope three days after Tara's death, in a memory box that contained precious memories of their lives together. The letter exploded, like a grenade, in his hand when he opened it. *Dearest, Darling Dino*, it read . . . and the rest as they say is history.

CHAPTER 6: TARA

The birthday girl

I wear an oversized hoody to cover my mass of frizzy, ginger curls that no comb can tame. It partly hides my face too, which I know is gaunt and pale. My pea-green eyes, which everybody says fire up with electricity when I laugh — which isn't often — have dark shadows under them, yet I'm only fifteen. I dig my hands deep in my pockets, and I strike a boyish attitude, hoping to blend in without drawing too much notice for being a girl.

We're at Ferry Meadows, a local beauty spot in the centre of Peterborough that's surrounded by lakes and woodland. During the daytime, when the park appears safe and unspoilt, families bring their kids here to play. But it takes on a darker tone at night when druggies, drunks, vandals, and teenage delinquents emerge from the shadows.

People come to die here as well. Mostly alcoholics and the homeless. Corpses are not uncommon. We're standing in a wooded area known as Fox Play, beneath a wobbly bridge where passers-by won't notice us. One of the large lakes is creepily lit up by the moon behind us. It's pitch black and everyone relies on their phone lights to find their way around.

I've not hung around with this gang before. Three boys and two girls. Aged between twelve and seventeen, I'd say. As the outsider, I have to prove my worth. It's not easy approaching an established group of kids but it helps that I've brought several packs of cigarettes and a half bottle of vodka. I have only until they run out for them to decide if I get to stay or not. If I'm not accepted, they'll call me names and threaten to throw me in the water, and I'll know where I stand. Adults think they know what it's like to be a kid. But they have no idea.

I've made myself as invisible as I can, but the two girls' noses are out of joint, simply because I'm another girl. They slide jealous eyes my way, letting me know that this is their territory. One of them is a big girl, and by that, I mean really big, as in fifteen stone or more. She laughs at the boys' jokes as if they were hilarious. They're not. They're quiet and sullen, and, like most teenage boys, they can barely string a sentence together.

'Do you want to see my tits?' she asks each one, in turn, flapping her jacket open as if ready to whip them out at a moment's notice.

The boys shake their heads and mutter something unintelligible before turning away from her. That's when she flings her cigarette end at my trainer as if it's my fault nobody wants to look at her tits.

'Watch it,' I warn, as I step on the dog end, extinguishing its bright orange tip. Big girl backs off but her friend, who is much taller than me, gets in my face.

'Or what?' she demands.

I can't make out her features in the dark, but she has large, pouting lips, reeks of cheap perfume and is chewing gum. Her white teeth flash at me as she stickily opens and closes her mouth, a ball of gum bunched in her cheek. Chew, chew, ew.

'Leave her alone. She's all right.'

This comes from the older boy. The one with intense eyes who looks around seventeen. His name is Sean. That's

24

all I know about him. That, and the fact he has a wad of cash and a ton of crack cocaine stuffed up his trouser leg. He'll show it to anyone who asks to see it. Except, of course, the police. He believes he's doing me a favour, sticking up for me, but he doesn't understand teenage girls as I do. They'll definitely want me gone now. But they'll do it subtly. Not out in the open in case the boys call them out for being bitches. It's easy to imagine what they'd do to me if we were alone. I can feel their slaps and hear their name-calling in my head. Nothing I haven't been called before. *Ginger freak. Slag.*

Knowing that my time is up, I decide to slouch off before I'm forced to. With a bit of luck, I'll catch Pauline, Troy, Sam, and Carl smoking cannabis over by the Badger play area. This gang all live in the same care home and I'm surprised they're allowed out at all because their clothes stink of weed, like all the time. I don't dabble as I like to keep my wits about me. Nor do I drink any of the alcohol I steal. For the same reason.

Although my friends weren't there earlier, they may have returned by now. Us teenagers are sensible enough to know that it's safer to hang out in groups in the park at night. Kids, especially older ones, might name call, give you a kicking for fun, steal your cash even, but it's the adults we fear. You never know who's going to creep up on you when you're alone.

'Catch you later, guys. I'm off.'

Sean grunts in recognition as I raise a hand in farewell. The other boys don't say a word, but I can feel the bitchy eyes of the girls burning into my back as I walk away. My step has a bounce to it, but only because I don't want them to think they've beaten me.

I'm holding my phone out in front of me with the torchlight on full beam so I don't trip up in the dark. I've been walking about three minutes when I hear faint footsteps behind me. Trainers crunching on the bark-lined woodland trail. Freezing in fear, I swing my mobile phone around in a full circle, trying to identify who's there. I know it's time to run when I pick out a moving shadow circling me like a wary wolf.

I'm fast. But not as fast as he is. I know it's a *he*, and not a she, because he laughs and breathlessly calls out for me to 'Wait. Don't run. Come back.'

I stumble, aware that my ankle has caught against something and suddenly I'm falling. Like in proper slow motion. One leg goes from under me. Then the other. My splayed hand sneaks out to protect my head on the way down. Bracing myself for the fierce crack of bone or twisted limb, I hit the ground and my forehead scrapes against something sharp, throwing me into an instant daze. Everything around me is spinning. But through the brain fog, I can make out a blurred face above me. The smiling, laughing face of a boy I don't know.

His greedy searching hands and hot, wet mouth are on me, tearing at my clothes. At the waistband of my jeans. I writhe beneath him, unable to scream since his mouth is sloshing against mine. The sensation of being unable to breathe is terrifying. His breath, a mix of fags, weed and vodka, makes me want to puke. There's no air. My head throbs. My legs spasm, sending shockwaves of pain through my body. When his burrowing hands brush against my naked skin, I claw my fingernails through the dirt, searching for a rock, a stick, or anything else to hit him with but find nothing. His insistent hands are tugging at my jeans, and I feel the cold air on my thighs. Suddenly, there's a heavy weight pressing down on me.

I try to make eye contact but it's too dark. The moon is too far away. Like me, the boy wears a dark hoody to hide his teenage angst. Then, something sharp and terrible enters me. I gasp and cry out. The boy moans and tells me, 'It's good. You'll like it. All girls do.'

My ribs feel like they're breaking under the strain of his weight. He's slight and tall, as far as I can tell, but the lack of oxygen is causing my lungs to explode. I can smell urine close by and feel dampness on my bare backside. I think we're lying in dog piss. At last, it's over and a new salty smell enters my nostrils. Semen. Then he's rolling off me, pulling his pants and jeans back up and searching for an unfinished joint in his back pocket.

I turn away from him, pull up my own jeans and stagger to my feet. I shoot off in the direction of the lake as soon as I realise that I can walk without falling.

'Hey.'

The boy is calling out to me in the dark but this time he doesn't attempt to follow, not now that he's gotten what he wanted. He sounds surprised. As if he wasn't expecting me to take off like that as soon as it was over. I have no phone. It got left behind. So, I run without knowing where I'm heading, conscious that I could easily trip and fall again. But I don't let that stop me. I'll keep on running as long as my heart keeps on pounding. As my feet hit the ground, the same words play havoc in my head.

Happy birthday to me. Happy birthday to me. Happy birthday, dear Tara . . .

CHAPTER 7: DINO

What kind of husband watches porn and masturbates on the day of his wife's funeral? *A deceived one*, Dino reflects angrily, as he gazes down at his semi-erect penis. Bring on the Catholic boy's guilt, it might make him feel something other than a sense of betrayal that he couldn't, *wouldn't* forgive. Jerking off in the marital bed is a two-fingered salute to Tara for putting Dino through the agony of knowing she'd had a baby without telling him about it. *Lie number two*.

But he's kidding himself if he thinks he can ejaculate. His bravado is exactly that, bravado. Rather than ogling the two dark-haired beauties soaping each other in a bathtub on his iPad, he feels an overwhelming urge to see Tara. Dead or alive, it doesn't matter. Just to have her face in front of him would be enough. He was a fool for refusing to go to the morgue and sit with her, as his papà had done. He'd wanted to but his pride wouldn't let him. All he could think about at the time was that she'd lied to him.

Why hadn't she trusted him enough to tell him what happened to her when she was alive? The brothers. The emotional abuse. The baby. Not to mention who the father of her child was. She hadn't alluded to that in her letter. How come he'd never noticed Tara's body had already gone through childbirth when they first met? It wasn't as if he didn't know his way around it. She had a few stretch marks on her breasts and thighs but nothing out of the ordinary. Her stomach was as flat as a boy's and she was super tight down there.

When Dino is being logical, which is hard to do in his current state of mind, he understands that Tara never deliberately set out to hurt him, but she *was* guilty of not telling him the truth. He could argue, like the brothers had done, that her past was none of his business, but that wasn't who they'd been as a couple. He'd assumed they told each other everything. He feels betrayed. But then again, Dino has to accept that he's being a hypocrite on that score because he hadn't told her everything either.

Sighing, he closes the iPad and reaches over to turn on the night light, illuminating the chaos of the bedroom. Tara's clothes are everywhere. Dino had decided getting rid of everything of hers and donating it back to the charity shops where most of it came from would be healing. It wasn't. His mamma had warned him more harm than good would come of it and she was right. Tara's ghost is everywhere. In the purple, fur-lined hooded jacket, the piles of petite size eight skinny jeans and the pairs of unsexy black CAT boots. He's more aware of her than ever before, her presence almost stronger now than even when she was alive, and wonders if this is true for all widowers.

Dino lights up a cigarette from the comfort of his bed and inhales. He wouldn't get away with this if Tara were alive. She disliked him smoking, even though he did it rarely, a leftover from his rebellious teenage years. His wife didn't smoke or drink and was completely immersed in their family. She was the perfect wife and mother. But what about Dino? What of the women who frequently came on to him? The wealthy women he met on his delivery rounds who were smitten by his Italian good looks, easy charm, and flirty smile. He never mentioned them to Tara. She'd have cut off his balls if he'd done that.

Those women looked after themselves. Facials. Highlights. The gym. Healthy, organic, yoga-infused lifestyles. They had it all — fantastic careers, or husbands with fantastic careers, and big houses, yet they were drawn to Dino. Most were married or had too much time on their hands. They did not have to clean or shop as his wife did. One of them told Dino that she felt attracted to him because he reminded her of her first boyfriend. She'd commented on his cheeky personality and fit body. Dino had never cheated on Tara, though, no matter how much he was tempted. Not even once. He couldn't bring himself to do it. She was his girl. Always had been. They were soul mates. Twin flames. Besties.

They'd met at the Peterborough speedway track where Dino was a reserve motorbike rider. If one of the team got injured then Dino would replace him, racing around the track and overtaking at high speeds. With everything to prove, he took more risks than he should, earning him a reputation and the nickname of Dino the Daring, which the crowd, and especially the girls, loved. The East of England showground became his regular hang-out for a while, for once earning his papà's approval, and he practised often in the hope of one day making it as an official Peterborough Panthers rider. But he never did. The competition was fierce and the wealthier boys who didn't have to work had all the time in the world to train whereas, he, Dino, worked sixty hours a week as a forklift truck driver.

He'd seen Tara around the track a few times even though she didn't seem interested in the sport and hung out with a crowd he was unfamiliar with. She wasn't Dino's usual type. He leaned towards the leggy, aloof blondes that were both fans and girlfriends of the drivers. But there was something about the smallness of Tara that appealed to him, making him feel protective towards her. She was cute in a girl-next-door kind of way, except when he finally plucked up the courage to talk to her, he discovered she was as potty-mouthed as they come. She also had this really loud, rude-sounding belly laugh. Knowing his papà would disapprove, Dino made up his mind to start a conversation with her the next time he saw her.

'You're lying,' Tara had accused, looking gobsmacked, when Dino told her that the bikes racing noisily around the track at 50MPH did not have brakes.

'It's true. I swear.' He'd laughed.

'You'd have to be fucking stupid to ride a bike without brakes.' She'd told him bluntly. When the penny dropped, she had blushed in a really sweet way which made Dino's heart turn over. He'd never understood what the expression meant until that moment. She seemed so familiar, as if she'd been put together just for him. The small hands with chipped purple nail polish. Gorgeous red hair with natural curls. And lashings of cider-coloured freckles dotted across her nose and cheeks.

'Oh, I get it. You're one of them. The riders,' she'd said with less interest than before.

'You're not a fan then?' Dino felt crushed and suddenly awkward. For some reason, he wanted, *needed*, to impress this girl.

'The noise must send you deaf,' she'd grumbled distractedly, glancing around, to trace the whereabouts of her friends. Dino's only thought was that he couldn't let her go. Not now he'd found her. He resisted the urge to put out a restraining hand to stop her from leaving.

'I could take you for a ride around the track sometime if you like.'

'Nah. I'm not into spoilt rich boys.'

Dino's initial reaction was to walk away. There were prettier, keener girls wherever he looked, but he was besotted by her in a way he'd never been before. He felt like he knew her. Really knew her. And acting on his emotions came naturally to him as an Italian.

'The name's Dino the Daring,' he'd offered his hand in a very grown-up gesture that didn't entirely suit their age group or interests. 'And I can assure you I'm neither rich nor spoilt. Far from it, in fact.'

She'd appraised him then from beneath her bouncy fringe, one eye on him, the other on her group of friends who were moving further away. When both lime-green eyes settled on him, he experienced a jolt of electricity that felt powerful enough to throw him in the air.

'Well, Dino the Daring, meet Tara the Terrible,' she'd laughed dirtily, flashing a set of perfectly imperfect uneven teeth at him. Dino was captured from that moment on.

One year later they were married. Everybody assumed they were pregnant. Except they weren't. But they were desperate to leave home and start their new life together and if that meant giving in to Dino's parents' wishes for a traditional, church wedding then so be it.

Tara was harder to persuade. She'd wanted a quiet registry office wedding but his mamma would never have forgiven Tara for that, so Dino shamelessly pressured her into it. This was the one time he'd ever bullied Tara into doing something she didn't want to do. Dino had only been married for five minutes when he realised that she was going to be the boss from then on.

'I am your wife, Dino De Rosa,' she'd said when they were alone together after exchanging vows. 'Not your mother. Not your girlfriend. Your wife. And one day I'll be your children's mother. The most important promise you can make to me today is to always respect that.'

That was something he'd never forgotten. Nor made the mistake that many married men make, by treating his wife as if she were his mother. Tara might be small but she was a giant in spirit. As tough as old boots and brutally honest to the point of being hurtful. She wasn't cruel, but she could be harsh. Dino had a softer, more forgiving nature but get on the wrong side of Tara and you'd know about it. She was a pocket rocket. A firecracker.

Dino had never fully understood the strained relationship Tara had with her mother but he knew not to push it, otherwise, that volatile temper of hers would turn on him. Liv Fountain had lived only ten miles away from her daughter but she seldom visited as she became increasingly reclusive over the years, rarely leaving the house. Tara likewise refused to visit her mother in Stamford, severing all ties with the town. This meant that the mother and daughter only saw each other on special occasions, such as Christmas or one of the kids' birthdays. Now he knows what happened to Tara as a child living in the house on Ryhall Road, he gets why she never went back and why she nursed a grudge against her mother, for allowing the bullying to go unchecked under her roof. *Jesus*.

And the blackmail.

When Dino thinks about how he would react if anything like that happened to his daughter, he wants to bulldoze the house down with Tara's brothers inside it. But when Liv died four years ago the family home was sold and each of the Fountain children inherited equal shares in the sale. Everyone except Tara, that is, who somehow got forgotten about. Dino had given Tara a hard time for not challenging the will. They were hard up, nothing much has changed since then, and the money would have allowed them to put a deposit down on their own home instead of having to rent. But she wouldn't budge on her decision, saying the fight wasn't worth it, so, in the end, Dino gave up. That was his go-to solution for all things Tara-related.

Dino is plagued by the knowledge that the brothers had invested that money wisely, including Tara's share, in a joint family business, Fountain & Sons, which went on to become hugely successful. It nags away at him like an infected ulcer waiting to burst. If they hadn't coerced Liv Fountain into writing Tara out of her will, he'd like to think the De Rosas could have made something of their lives too — maybe not on the same scale as the brothers who were owners and directors of a multi-million-pound logistics and warehousing company, but Tara could have gone back to college, as she'd always said she wanted to do.

Instead, Tara spent her life packing organic fruit and vegetables into boxes in a cold warehouse while Dino delivered them. Working for the same company, Nene Organic Vegetables, had its advantages as it allowed them to see each other both inside and out of work. They also received plenty of free graded-out wonky fruit and veg which kept their small family going.

Tara, unlike the girls Dino dated before meeting her, didn't play hard to get. She didn't say things she didn't mean or feel in order to keep him guessing. But he now realises that she fostered dark secrets rather than being the woman he thought he knew, inside and out, for better or for worse. It bothers Dino that he can't recall a single time when he'd caught her out, deep in thought, as if she might want to confide something to him. It makes him think he really hadn't known her at all.

He'd told her countless times throughout their marriage that he wished he'd known her when she was a young girl but she'd pierce him with those green eyes of hers, pull a freckly face and remark, 'You'd have hated me. I was awkward and ugly.'

'I absolutely would have adored you,' he remembers reassuring her, only for her to turn angrily on him.

'Well, I wouldn't have wanted you to.'

She'd been curt and had hurt his feelings. Push, pull. Push, pull. That was Tara. He was always kept on his toes. That is how they kept their passion for one another alive. Of course, they argued like any other couple but he was usually the first to back down, wanting to be friends again. Not Tara. She could go days without speaking to him. 'The silent treatment,' his mamma would say, claiming it was toxic behaviour. Well, she would, wouldn't she? Dino's mamma was fiercely protective of her only son. Most Italian mothers he knows are the same.

Although he never said so, Dino hadn't agreed with his mother since no matter how upset Tara was with him, she'd go to great lengths to reassure him, stating in a tight voice, 'Look, we're okay. We're safe. I'm not leaving you and we'll get through this but I also fucking hate your guts right now and want to punch you hard in the face.'

Later, while folding the laundry or preparing his packed lunch for the next day — a cheese sandwich with a slice of salted tomato on top just the way he liked it — she'd weakly smile his way and say, 'Everyone has a right to feel safe and I want that for you and our kids always.'

Had she been trying to tell him what happened to her when she delivered emotionally charged speeches like that? That she hadn't felt safe? Her whole fucking childhood had been one massive betrayal after another. Instead of receiving the love and protection that every child deserves, she had been ignored and mistreated by her family, the people she should have been able to trust the most. It's no surprise she couldn't trust anyone to divulge her secrets, especially her husband, who would have reacted negatively and made everything about himself — his betrayal and anger at being lied to. He knew that now.

Dino is no longer a husband, but a widower with two small children, to whom he has no idea how to be a parent.

CHAPTER 8: TARA

Pregnant

'I'm going to be a fucking mother at fifteen,' I seethe, narrowing my eyes at my reflection in the mirror, but especially at the naked and exposed bump above the top of the ever-tightening waistband of my pyjamas. I'm four months gone and I can't hide *it*, or the multiple blue lines on the multiple pregnancy test kits ordered from Amazon, any longer.

For the first two months after being attacked in the park, I lived in a state of fear, denial and increased anxiety waiting for my period to start. I had convinced myself that it was impossible to become pregnant after having sex only once, especially if it was the result of rape. Nobody was that unlucky, surely. It turned out I was wrong. I *am* that unlucky. Haven't I always known this? Who else would end up getting attacked and raped on their fifteenth birthday?

Everyone wants to know what's going on with me and why I'm biting people's heads off. Mum. Teachers. Schoolfriends. Christ, even Mrs Lundy who walks her dog past my house three times a day is demanding to know why I won't pet poor Pongo any longer. I'm going to have to tell Mum the truth soon. Today, in fact. I can't go on starving myself the way I've been doing in an attempt to keep the weight off. The baby needs nourishment.

The fact that I've finally referred to it, the bump, the thing that happened to me, as a living breathing baby makes me want to throw up again. I bolt out of my bedroom, and into the bathroom just in time. When I'm done being sick, for the third time this morning, I glance up, red-eyed and weary-bodied, to see my youngest brother, Chris, standing on the landing gawping at me. Before he can accuse me of anything, I slam the door on his bug-eyed face and bolt it shut. Despite being a fifteen-year-old girl who needs her privacy and personal space, I'm not allowed a lock on my bedroom door but Mum has made sure there's one on the bathroom so that the boys can piss in peace. I don't know who I hate more at this moment. Her or my brothers.

'Fuck off,' I scream from the other side of the locked door. 'Fuck right off.' And then I pound my fists against the cold, hard cistern until they ache. Something tells me that I no longer need to be concerned about telling Mum my secret. He'll beat me to it if she hasn't heard the noise already. I burst out laughing as I recall his look of shock and disgust when he saw my protruding belly, as he grasped what was going on with me and my body.

I've been racking my brain for months now trying to figure out what triggered the attack that night in the park. *Who was the unidentified boy and where did he come from?* I suspect it could have been intense-eyed Sean. He was the only one that night to show any interest in me, which would make the baby's father a known drug dealer. But it could just as easily have been one of the other boys. Or someone else entirely.

Whoever it was, they had followed me after I left the group. The weird thing about the attack was that my rapist acted as if I wanted it as much as he did. What was wrong with him to make him think that? Did this have something to do with the way another girl had acted towards him? Had he mistaken me for the large girl who offered to get her tits out?

Later on that night, I'd stood outside Thorpe Wood Police Station, with an unfamiliar wet patch in my knickers watching police officers come and go in the blue blur of the outside light, unsure of what to do. Should I report it? I wasn't even meant to be out, let alone hanging out in parks with older kids and druggies. My brothers would kill me if they found out. Besides, the police might think I was more experienced sexually than I was letting on.

And what of Mum when she finds out I'm pregnant? She'll make it all about her. Her pain. Her suffering. And my brothers will accuse me of being a dirty slag. It was their favourite word, aimed at most of the girls they knew, even the plain, academic ones who never harmed anyone. I'll never understand why Mum allowed this language to go unpunished.

When I eventually crawled into bed at 3 a.m. that morning, I knew that reporting what had happened to me was out of the question. I'd be grounded forever. Or put in a home far away from here. Mum would disown me. In any case, I had no idea who my attacker was. Just a suspicion that it might have been Sean.

'*You must have been asking for it,*' I could hear Mum's voice in my head.

As I wipe sick from my mouth, I find myself growing curious about the bump. If I don't connect it to the boy who attacked me, then I feel a surge of protectiveness inside. The baby is fifty-fifty mine. I've never had a younger brother or sister, nor have I had much experience with babies in general, so I'm not sure if I have maternal feelings, but I've researched pregnancy and know exactly what's happening inside me. By now the foetus will have formed eyelids, eyebrows, eyelashes, nails, and hair and it may even be sucking its thumb and yawning.

To be honest, I'm not sure how I feel about any of this. All I know is that I'm overwhelmed and feel unprepared for the world of parenting when I'm still a child myself. I'm surprised when I run my hands over the tightness of my swollen belly and I feel a sharp, quick movement inside, as an angry little kick bumps against the palm of my hand, and a wave of instantaneous all-consuming love washes over me.

When I hear my mother's voice on the other side of the door I'm thrown back into the horrible present and my newfound courage deserts me.

'Tara Fountain, you come out of there this minute. Do you hear?'

When I don't respond, except to draw breath and prepare myself for the inevitable attack, she raps a bony knuckle on the door. I know she won't be alone. My brothers will be there with her as a backup. I feel sick to my stomach but my hand won't budge from my small bump. There are two of us now as opposed to one. My odds against the four of them have improved.

'Right now.' Mum's voice goes up a notch. 'And I mean it. I know what you've been up to, my girl.'

When I hear the danger and menace in her voice I cower. There's to be no trial then. Or pity for the delinquent runaway. I've already been found guilty. Of what I can only guess. In their eyes I won't be a vulnerable teenage girl, someone who's been exploited and abused. I'm the black sheep. Older than my years. And I'll be accused of having led the boy on, so I'll only have myself to blame. As usual, everything will be my fault.

'You've always been the black sheep of this family, so you only have yourself to blame,' my mother yells in my face the second I open the door.

'That's not true. It takes two to have a baby. You should know that. But in your case, Mum, giving birth didn't make you a mother, did it? Not to me, at any rate.' I cut her down with a sense of superiority I didn't know I possessed.

Mum, seeing her sharp words are not having the desired effect on me, immediately switches on the waterworks.

'How could you, Tara?'

My brothers shake their heads in synchronised despair and my eyes shift to the three of them, who are lined up like a firing squad in a hierarchal line of power and authority. Oldest to youngest. Tallest to smallest.

'Now look what you've done,' all three Fountain boys complain at the same time.

CHAPTER 9: DINO

Dino finds himself blowing up balloons for his daughter's birthday just three weeks after his wife's funeral, which feels kind of wrong to him. He hates that they're throwing a party for a three-year-old, who won't remember it in years to come, when his life, as he knows it, has ended. His mamma had insisted though, claiming Tara wouldn't want her family to miss milestones.

Dino couldn't care less what Tara would have wanted as her opinion no longer matters, but he gets the impression his mamma intends to use his late wife's name at every opportunity if it means getting her way with the children. At some point in the future, he knows he'll have to take back responsibility for Fabio and Bella, but he's not ready yet.

Fabio is sprawled on the rug in the middle of the living room floor playing with his collection of toy soldiers. Bella is in the kitchen with her nonna, helping to bake her birthday cake. Dino doesn't need to ask what sort of cake they're making. It will be made out of sponge and raspberry jam and decorated in pink unicorns. His papà is out in the garden clearing leaves and doing the other odd jobs that Dino can't bring himself to do.

His enthusiasm for fixing up the home he and Tara lived in for most of their married life had died the moment the hit-and-run driver mowed her down. He feels bad leaving everything to his papà, whose memory is deteriorating by the day. Only this morning he asked Dino three times in a row where he kept his drill bits. It was all Dino could do not to scream at him, 'in the tin on the shelf in the garage'.

The art deco house they rent on London Road in Fletton is run down and badly in need of repair, but Dino couldn't afford to buy it even in its current state. He and Tara only earned £45K a year between them, and that was before tax stoppages. Now there's only one wage coming in, he has no idea how he'll survive. Although the rent is low, factoring in the state of the semi-detached three-bedroomed property, it costs a fortune to heat in the winter due to not being properly insulated or double-glazed.

Their landlord is an old family friend who doesn't have the money to fix up the house, and even if he did, the rent increase would be too much for the De Rosas to afford. But, despite everything, Dino considers himself lucky to be able to live in such a large house in a safe, pleasant area of town.

He's due to receive a payout of twice Tara's average salary from her employer's death-in-service scheme soon, but this won't last long. He has yet to repay his parents for covering the cost of the funeral and nearly had a heart attack when he found out the bill came in at just under £9K.

Nene Organic Vegetables has been generous, extending his compassionate leave twice, but on Monday he's due to go back full time. He's dreading it. Tara, having worked there much longer than Dino, will be everywhere. Her ghost will be in the packhouse, grading vegetables into boxes. Or on a break in the canteen bitching about Jo in accounts, whom Tara couldn't stand because Dino once commented that he thought she was pretty. Even Jo will be a painful reminder of Tara to him now.

Having blown up the final pink and white unicorn balloon, Dino is out of breath. He's unfit and needs to get back to the gym. Even there, sympathetic eyes wait for him. Feeling as he does, angry all the time, he cannot cope with the condolences, man-hugs and offers of help. He knows he comes across as fake when trying to say the right thing, so he'd rather avoid these situations altogether. Another good reason for not having a child's birthday party! He wonders if he can get out of it. Go for a walk instead. He's sure his mamma would understand. But his papà, not so much.

Deciding there's no time like the present to find out, he strolls into the kitchen, trying to act all casual but his mamma instantly sees through him.

'No, Dino. Not today, son. Your friends want to see you. They're worried about you.'

So much for misreading his mamma, Dino thinks. But then again, apparently he didn't know the first thing about his wife either, despite being married to her for ten years.

'Mamma. I can't. It's too much. Too soon.' Dino's eyes fill with tears at the thought of being surrounded by his and Tara's joint acquaintances, who have since crawled out of the woodwork with offers of help and support, but Dino cannot forgive them for failing to attend her funeral. Their claims that it was announced as a private service, which Dino knew nothing of, fell on deaf ears and is one of the reasons why he can no longer be himself around them. And the expectation that he will put on a brave face for the sake of his daughter, and be equally nice to her friends, even going as far as to tease and play with them, makes his stomach churn.

'Let the boy do what he needs to do,' His papà barks, entering noisily through the back door and trailing muddy footprints across the freshly washed floor which lets Dino off the hook in more ways than one because his mamma's focus is now on the dirt and not on him.

'Thanks, Papà.' Dino throws him a grateful smile, grabs his jacket off the back of the chair and slips it on over his tired shoulders. Remembering to kiss his daughter and calling out to Fabio to be good, he's out of the house in seconds. The cold November air revives him as he pounds the pavement. Every second he puts distance between himself and the threat of having to mingle with a house full of people, and he's flooded with relief.

He has no idea where he's going until he arrives at the gated driveway belonging to Holywell House, a Georgian Grade II listed townhouse on Cherry Orton Road in Orton Longville, which is on the other side of town to his house and a good three miles away. Despite being out of shape, he'd completed the walk in less than thirty-five minutes.

This is where it happened. Where Tara died. It's not the first time Dino has visited the scene. It won't be the last. His grief draws him back to it repeatedly. Her blood might have been washed away but her DNA would still be detectable under a microscope. She died almost instantly, they'd said. *Almost*. This meant she hadn't died on impact as he'd initially been led to believe. She'd have been conscious for a few more minutes and might even have been aware of what was going on around her. Did she see the driver? The person who did this to her? Would her last thoughts have been of the children and Dino? Or was it her secretive past that accompanied her on her journey into the next life?

Although Dino isn't a practising Catholic, he can't entirely shake off his religious upbringing, but he doesn't share his mamma's belief that he will find solace in the church and not at the bottom of a bottle. Dino has cut down on his drinking, for the sake of his children, but it's not enough to satisfy his mamma. She's a teetotaller and is of the opinion that alcohol is the root of all evil. She's convinced that the person who drove into Tara had been under the influence of alcohol at the time and that's why they didn't stop to help her. Dino doesn't disagree and his blood boils at the cowardice of their actions.

The police have stopped calling with updates as they're no closer to finding out who did this. There were no witnesses. Anybody who was at home in any of the nearby houses that day heard nothing. All they've got to go on is a standard shade of fuji-white paint, found on Tara's clothing and identified as code LRC867 which is commonly used on Land Rovers, of which there are many thousands in the UK. Even after analysis, there's been no breakthrough in the car model, although the vehicle itself is estimated to be less than five years old.

Somewhere out there is a white car with severe front bumper damage where it hit Tara's right leg, breaking it in five places, before flipping her onto the bonnet, causing yet more damage to her and the bodywork. Tara had then bounced off the car onto the road where she was lucky not to have been run over again as the vehicle took off at speed, leaving skid marks behind that the police were unable to trace, as well as the broken, bloodied body of his wife.

If it were just numerous broken bones, she'd have survived the accident and may even have walked again, but a fractured rib had pierced one of her lungs causing massive internal bleeding. So despite all the circumstantial evidence and the public appeals for information, the car has still not been found. The police believe it's long gone by now; sold through a dodgy dealer and shipped under a false plate overseas.

Dino doesn't go along with this theory. The chances are that whoever caused Tara's death by dangerous driving wasn't a criminal, and therefore wouldn't have a clue how to dispose of a wanted vehicle. That doesn't explain what they were doing driving through the exclusive Cherry Orton Road residential area if they didn't live there.

They're far more likely to have stashed the car somewhere safe in the hope that the police will eventually stop searching for it. It takes money to pull something like that off, so whoever is responsible is not without means. Dino will never stop keeping an eye out for it. As far as white Land Rovers go, he's become quite the expert. He knows his Defenders from his Sports.

And what of the couple who live beyond these gates, in the impressive mansion that boasts an orangery, five bedrooms and a separate annexe? He doesn't know their first names, only their surname: Grant. The police informed him that the wife had been very distressed when she found out that Tara had died outside their home and that they planned to sell up at the earliest possibility. Yet there's no for-sale board outside so he assumes they've since changed their mind. They'd sent flowers to the funeral home, which his mum had said was very kind, but all it said was "In deepest sympathy from the Grants".

What were you doing here, Tara? He asks for the hundredth time. She had no business being here that day. They didn't know anyone who lived on this side of Peterborough. The houses are in a very secluded position and she would have had to go out of her way to walk down here. Besides, she was supposed to have been shopping in the city centre. That's what she'd told him that morning before he left for the gym. *Lie number three.* He'd kissed her on the cheek as usual and she'd smiled in that sexy way of hers which made him think he was on to a promise for later. She hadn't given anything away. Why had she lied? If she'd taken the bus into town as she was meant to have done, like she did most Saturdays so she could hunt out bargains in charity shops, a favourite pastime of hers, she'd still be alive.

Who or what was in Cherry Orton Road that he didn't know about? And what was it about this particular address that had fascinated her?

CHAPTER 10: TARA

Roommates

There are two beds in the small side room on the Lilac ward. The bed nearest the door is occupied by my massive belly, there's no room for anything else, while the other is empty, the blanket pulled to one side because the girl it's been assigned to has nipped to the loo. Again. The walls are a soothing lilac and daylight streams in through the window, through which I can see the other side of the contemporary tower block building. It has many floors and a myriad glass windows.

Room four, which has an "engaged" sign on the door, is accessed behind the midwives' station and nobody other than staff or approved visitors is allowed in, due to us being given "age-appropriate status" on account of us, meaning the other girl and I, being underage. Most expectant mums are in the main wards. I caught a glimpse of them as I was wheeled past by a hospital porter who smelled strongly of spices and curry. They are much older than me and my roommate, despite the fact that they're only in their late twenties and early thirties. They can be heard moaning, and being told to "relax", "take it easy", and "breathe" by their birth partners and husbands.

The maternity unit at Peterborough City Hospital is bigger on the inside than it looks and the gathering of midwives around beds as well as the sound of curtains being tugged closed to allow for routine vaginal examinations makes me nervous.

I've been told that none of us will give birth in any of these side wards but will be moved to a delivery suite after our cervixes are fully dilated and when contractions are coming in at a rate of three every ten minutes. All of this sounds terrifying even though I've researched every aspect of giving birth, so I'll know what to expect. Reading about it is not the same as experiencing it, though, and I never imagined labour would be this awful. Knowing that I might have to endure hours more of this, and that the pain is only going to worsen, makes me sick with fear. No matter how nice everybody is, I still have to go through this alone.

Mum refused to accompany me, blaming her agoraphobia, and it was my older brother, David, who reluctantly called for a taxi to pick me up, but only after my waters had broken because they wouldn't let me on the ward until that happened. This was the first time I'd been allowed out of the house in weeks, having been home-schooled for the last five months of my pregnancy. Although everyone blamed this on my excessive morning sickness, diagnosed as hyperemesis gravidarum, which can cause hospitalisation, I knew that I was a distraction and a disappointment that no one wanted to bump into in the school corridor on a daily basis. My classmates were curious about the baby but their mothers saw me as a threat, a reminder that this could happen to their daughters.

When the door bangs open and my roommate comes back in, I'm glad of the distraction. My back is killing me and I'm having to move around a lot to keep comfortable. I'm sitting up, breathing through a contraction one minute, squatting the next, then resting on my side, wincing at the sheer weight of my belly. My arms and legs remain stick thin, thanks to throwing up for months at a time, but the baby weight has gone straight to my belly and my bones ache constantly from the pressure.

'How are you doing?' my roommate asks.

'Dying slowly,' I joke, except it isn't funny and my eyes suddenly well up with tears.

'You're doing better than you think.'

As I exhale during another contraction she comes over and massages my back. I swear they're coming faster than the midwives have predicted.

'Thanks,' I say, glancing around to look at her properly for the first time. She has long curly hair like mine, only hers is black and held back in a patterned headscarf in a style that's too old for her. 'What's your name?'

'Brianna,' she grins, placing both hands on her smaller-than-mine bump. 'You?' she wants to know.

'Tara. I'm fifteen. How about you?'

'Same.'

Brianna high-fives me and pulls up a chair next to my bed. She's also wearing a hospital gown like me, with an unattractive slit up the back, but she looks so much better in it than I do. This girl, who seems carefree, fun-loving, and as bright as popping candy, is on her way to being stunningly beautiful but doesn't seem to realise it. I feel uglier than ever next to her.

'I love your hair,' she tells me.

'You're kidding, right?' I run a hand through my unruly, loose curls that refuse to be restrained in a ponytail. 'I love yours,' I gush, desperate for her approval.

'What are you in for?' Brianna giggles.

'A baby.' I frown, not getting her humour straightaway.

'Natural delivery or section?'

'Natural,' I grimace, 'if anything about childbirth can be called natural.'

She laughs again. 'You're funny, Tara.'

She's fifteen and pregnant. The same as me. Yet, unlike me she's made up her mind to be happy and seems to want to feel joy in everything. Add to that she's stunningly beautiful and kind too. *Can this girl be for real?* I wonder, wanting to be just like her.

'I'm having a section,' Brianna tells me, making a slicing knife motion with her hand.

'Poor you. Do you know when?'

'Nine thirty. But I don't mind. My mum had me the same way and she said it was a doddle.'

I start to question if I should have asked for a caesarean section, but I'd been urged to have a natural birth because recovery is meant to be quicker for both mother and baby. My mum hadn't advised me either way. She'd shown no further interest in me or her future grandchild since learning of my pregnancy. She hadn't even tried to get to the bottom of who the father was, assuming, I think, that the black sheep was guilty of sleeping with lots of boys. 'A slut,' she called me.

Mum might not be responsible for my being raped but she has failed to keep me safe. Being betrayed by my brothers, who insisted I kept my disgusting big belly at home out of sight was one thing but when your mother fails to protect you, that's crippling. It's another childhood trauma I have to carry around with me and it's even more of a burden than an eight-pound baby.

'Have you done a poo yet?'

Brianna's words cut through my thoughts and I find myself back in the room. None of my problems have gone away. The baby is still inside me. The imminent birth is unavoidable.

'That's all anyone talks about in here.'

'I know, it's gross. Don't they understand teenage girls at all? We can talk about blow jobs, hand jobs and anal sex even, but mention our poo and we turn into Disney princesses.'

I screw up my nose to demonstrate that I'm in agreement. 'Do you know what you're having?

'A girl.' Brianna's smile takes up her whole face, which is glossy with sweat, making her appear even more radiant. She is experiencing pregnancy in a way that I am not which makes me feel sad.

'I'm going to call her Dana, after my Jamaican grandmother.'

'That's nice,' I smile at her because she deserves to be congratulated on her baby's name, but it doesn't reach my eyes and she's quick to notice.

'What about you? Boy or girl?'

'I wanted to keep it a surprise,' I say, shrugging my shoulders as if it doesn't matter.

'It's a boy, I can tell,' Brianna squeals excitedly.

'How?'

'Because your bump is all up front, unlike mine. That's what my mum reckons anyway.'

I'm curious whether she's right and if I'm carrying a boy. If so, will he be a replica of his father? Then I remember that I'll never know because I'm not keeping my baby. Everyone including Mum had insisted it was for the best and I didn't argue. It was easy to convince myself that I couldn't love a rapist's baby anyway. Besides, I was only fifteen. How would I cope without any support? Mum has told me that if I keep "it" I'll have to go into social care as she won't have me in the house. Apparently, I'm a disgrace and I bring shame on her and everyone else. My brothers back her up, so there's no chance she'll see things differently and soften.

I've been told that I'll be able to nurse my baby for an hour but afterwards, he or she will be handed over to social services and given to a new family who has already signed the paperwork. I've seen their squiggle on the document, next to mine.

'Do you have a birth partner?' I ask, wanting to know why this gorgeous, well-meaning girl, who is loved by her family, is here alone.

'My mum's not well,' Brianna's smile plummets. 'She's having chemo downstairs in the cancer ward.'

'I'm so sorry,' I take her hand in mine and pat it. This is the most adult thing I've ever done. I want to grieve for her but instead, I try to mirror her bravery.

'What about the father?' I ask tentatively, worried that my nosiness may ruin our promising friendship. A mask comes down on her pretty features and I realise I'm not the only one hiding a secret. Perhaps the dad in question doesn't want anything to do with the baby but she doesn't want to admit this.

'He can't stand the sight of blood,' she pulls a face. 'What about you?'

'Oh, same,' I grin, rolling my eyes.

CHAPTER 11: DINO

Dino stares at the blood splatters on his reflection in the bathroom mirror. He hasn't shaved since before the funeral and last night Bella refused to kiss him before going to bed, complaining his scruffy beard scratched her face and made it itch, so he had finally cut most of the black, peppered with grey facial hair off this morning, followed by a cut-throat shave with a brand-new razor that he swears has taken half of his skin off.

Bella and Fabio were shipped off to their nonna and nonno's last night and will return on Sunday afternoon. They have a packed weekend planned. Fabio is excited about catching the train to London to visit the Hyde Park Winter Wonderland. Christmas has come early for his kids, although in reality, December 25th is not far away. His parents are not typically overindulgent as a rule, but they make an exception for their grandchildren. *Someone has to*, Dino reflects bitterly. He just hopes that all of the excitement doesn't exhaust his papà too much.

Getting rid of the beard has made him feel better. Lighter somehow. It's been seven weeks since Tara died and he went to the gym for the first time last night. Two hours of lifting weights gave him a burst of endorphins which was exactly what he had needed. Tomorrow he'll follow up with a long run. Going into the bedroom, he pulls out a clean shirt and slips it on over faded black jeans which he needs to wear with a belt due to his weight loss.

He avoids looking at the black rubbish bags full of Tara's clothes. He'd bagged them up weeks ago but hadn't been able to face returning them to the charity shops until today. The stark reality of seeing all her possessions disposed of in such a clinical way makes him nervous. Is he doing the right thing? Is it still too soon, as his mamma had warned?

He's kept hold of Tara's wedding ring, of course, which he plans to give to Bella one day, but it's out of sight, out of mind for the time being. He can't bring himself to look at it, because he knows it was forcibly removed from her finger by a pathologist soon after she died. Dino had to remove his own wedding ring two days before the funeral because it had become loose and was at risk of slipping off his finger. The two gold bands are kept together in the same memory box where Tara's letter was discovered. He doesn't want to think about it right now, but memories of her handwriting crawl across his brain until he can see the words in front of him.

'I can't bear the thought of leaving you without telling you the truth,' she'd written, 'and I don't want you to feel ashamed or embarrassed if any of this comes out after I've gone.'

Nobody knows exactly when Tara wrote the letter. There were no clues to suggest whether it had been penned one month before she died, or six, or twelve months ago. Dino has experienced many different emotions since Tara passed away but embarrassment is not one of them. Even now, remembering the words she'd used to describe how she felt about her abusive family makes his blood boil.

'I don't want to leave this world without having told one single person about what happened to me in the house on Ryhall Road. I was fifteen years old and pregnant at the time, and my family kept me locked up for the whole of my pregnancy, only allowing me out to attend medical appointments under the watchful eye of one of my brothers as I was a known runaway and an embarrassment to them. They claimed they intended to minimise damage, so I was to keep the pregnancy as private as possible, meaning only those who needed to know knew. I tried telling them that the world had changed and that nobody cared about such things anymore because there were many school-aged mothers around these days, but they wouldn't listen. Mum refused to even look at me, let alone speak to me. I desperately wanted to keep my baby, but my brothers insisted it was not possible.

'I suspected Mum was having second thoughts near the end of my pregnancy. I'd catch her eyeing my baby belly occasionally with a sympathetic glance, and she'd bring me a cup of tea in the mornings, knowing how much it helped with my morning sickness, which I'd suffered terribly from. I began to hope that she might reconsider and allow me to keep the baby, but then I heard my brothers arguing with her, so I went to stand at the door and listened. I wish I hadn't because it makes me so angry to think about it now. It turned out that I was correct, and Mum was warming to the notion of letting me have the baby at home. But my brothers couldn't handle having a delinquent, sluttish teenager, and a baby in the house, which they said I would likely neglect anyway, leaving it to them and Mum to care for so I could go out and do what I do best, i.e., sleep around with boys. It wasn't fair to them, they claimed, so Mum had no choice but to give in to their demands. I've never hated my brothers more than I did at that moment.

'I'm so sorry, Dino, that I didn't tell you about the baby, but I just couldn't. I'd buried the memory of it. I had no choice. As for lying about being a virgin and letting you think you were my first lover, please don't be angry at me for this, as you were my first in every sense of the word.

'Just before Mum died, I sort of forgave her for her role in what happened. After all, she was mentally ill for most of my life, but for whatever reason, she never received the necessary treatment, and I believe she was largely influenced by my spiteful, uncaring brothers.

'Obviously, they were instrumental in getting me written out of the will as well, saying I didn't deserve a single penny, and Mum was too weak to argue with them by that point. We've all moved on with our lives since then and had children of our own and I maintained my secret for years because I didn't want to embarrass my family, until it became sort of impossible to talk about it, even with you. But now that I'm an adult with my own children, I realise it was wrong of them to make me feel this way and that I shouldn't have been forced to give up my baby, nor be made to keep quiet about it. Not for anyone. I was only a child at the time, and I had no one to guide and advise me other than my family, so I gradually grew to accept the things they said about me over time — that I was a black sheep and would have made a terrible mother. They said the baby was better off without me and who was I to argue? At fifteen, I assumed they knew best. It's only now, that I'm mum to Fabio and Bella, that I realise how toxic my family were. Mum didn't know how to love us and my brothers were wrong about me being a bad mother. I would die for all three of my children.'

Dino is enraged by the way Tara was treated. And that she'd had to tolerate her brothers continued presence in her life because he, Dino, had insisted, since family was important to him. That must have irritated the hell out of her. He now regrets challenging them that day in church. He knows he was out of order bringing up his wife's past at her funeral, and that was never his intention, but seeing the brothers standing there in their sharp suits, looking like model citizens and loving brothers, caused his blood to boil and he'd seen red. He still doesn't see why she couldn't have told him about the baby. Maybe not right away, but certainly before they married and had children of their own! It wasn't as if he were a monster! He wouldn't have given her a hard time over it.

But is he certain of that? Hadn't he always prided himself on marrying a virgin, an untouched girl? Was Tara right to be afraid? Not wanting to consider that possibility, Dino directs his thoughts to the question of why she doesn't ever say anything about her child's father. That strikes him as particularly strange. Even if the boy was young, as Tara was, his parents could have perhaps supported her through the pregnancy, as her own family clearly weren't about to. Who knows, perhaps the father was a loser.

Dino is out of the door an hour later, fortified by a bacon and egg fry-up; the boot of their scruffy, beat-up Ford Kuga run-around stuffed with the black bags. Being a born and bred Peterboroughian, he knows his way around the city centre, but finding car parking for each shop is going to be a problem.

The Sue Ryder Vintage and Retro shop on Bridge Street is the first one he visits. It's not what he was expecting and he can't picture Tara in here. The style of clothing isn't to her taste. The shop itself, described as a "vintage emporium full of curiosities" sells all kinds of memorabilia, vinyl and 1940s collectables. When he finally drums up the courage to approach the shop assistant with Marilyn Monroe curls who's wearing a vintage floral tea dress, he's told the items in the bags are not acceptable.

'What do you mean they're not acceptable?' Dino growls offended because a charity shop has refused to take his late wife's clothing.

'No offence,' Martha says, he knows that's her name because she has it pinned to her dress, 'but it's just not our style.'

'How can it not be your style when they were bought from here?'

'I don't think so,' Martha says, chewing her lip and taking another look. 'No, I'm afraid not. We wouldn't have stocked these items. Are you sure you've got the right shop?'

'Not anymore,' Dino puzzles. 'But my wife came in here every week for months on end. Every Saturday without fail she bought something.'

'There are quite a few other charity shops in Peterborough.' Martha then looks beyond Dino to the small queue forming behind him.

'Yes, I know and my wife visited them all. She was really into second-hand stuff.'

'What was her name? I might know her,' Martha volunteers helpfully.

Dino doesn't say what's on his mind, which is that this girl, who he'd guess to be aged between nineteen and twenty-three, would've had nothing in common with Tara. 'I can do better than that,' Dino takes out his battered wallet and pulls out a photo of Tara and the kids taken at a picnic a couple of years ago. If he's being truthful, she looks miserable as sin in it. He'd surprised her with a day out at a local beauty spot but she'd been in a foul mood the entire day and in the end they'd left early.

He points to her. 'That's Tara.'

'No. I've never seen her before. Sorry.' Martha shakes her head and this time when she glances up and peers over his shoulder at the queue, he knows he's being dismissed.

It's the same in the next four charity shops, including the one near his parents' house, where Tara was supposed to have volunteered on occasion. They didn't recognise any of the clothes or Tara's picture. The British Heart Foundation on Bridge Street, Cancer Research UK in Westgate, Scope at Hereward Cross, and Barnardo's in Stanground — were all places she'd mentioned frequently but no one remembered seeing her there.

Where was Tara getting her clothes from if not the charity shops? More importantly, what was she doing with her Saturdays if she wasn't shopping? *Was this another lie?*

CHAPTER 12: TARA

The child

The delivery suite has an elongated odd-shaped bed in it, which is supposed to allow me to give birth in whichever position I'm most comfortable with. I wanted to punch someone when I first heard that. Since entering the latter stages of labour, I've become annoyed by everything. Even the partner's chair next to the bed, which I won't be needing, infuriates me.

My only hope is that the IV pole next to the bed contains a cocktail of all the pain relief drugs I've read about over the last few months but still can't pronounce; opioids such as pethidine, diamorphine, meptid and remifentanil, as well as gas and air, otherwise known as Entonox. When I told the midwife I needed all of them to "make me comfortable", she smiled. She'd obviously heard the joke a hundred times. But I was being serious.

The lights are dimmed and fairy lights are strung up on one wall but I can't see the point in them. This is no party. In case something goes wrong there's a baby station as well as other medical contraptions I can't name lurking in the background. The midwife has pointed out the ensuite shower room several times already but I refuse to stand under the hot water to relieve the agony in my back because I don't want her to see me naked.

As far as midwives and adults go, Michelle is lovely. I suspect she was chosen for me because she's nearer my age than the others. She's also petite, again like me, with tiny hands that make vaginal exams less intrusive. Michelle, like Brianna, is concerned about my bowel movements.

'When it comes time to push you might accidentally poo yourself if you haven't done one already,' she warns, quickly adding, 'It's quite normal if you do, so don't worry about it.'

Determined not to shit myself in front of a stranger, I grumpily take myself off to the ensuite shower room and spend the next fifteen minutes trying to empty my bowels but fail miserably. The contractions are getting longer and stronger, and I'm finding it difficult to breathe through them the way I've been taught. It seems to me that Mum must have had a backbone after all, having given birth to four babies. Kudos to her. I will never put myself through this again though. Not for anybody. Never, ever.

When I waddle back into the room, Michelle places her hands on her hips and purses her lips. 'Well? Did you go?'

'All sorted,' I fib, wondering why I lie when it's not even necessary. Has it become a habit? Am I a psychopath?

Looking pleased, Michelle pats the bed and passes me a mouthpiece, saying, 'The gas and air will help with the contractions. Just remember to take slow, deep breaths when they start up again.'

I'm so grateful I want to cry. And I wish, once again, that I hadn't lied. She deserves better. I deserve better.

Twenty minutes later, I'm pushing so hard and screaming so loudly I don't give a shit that I've shit myself twice and that poor Michelle has had to clear it up both times.

'You're doing great, Tara,' Michelle murmurs from between my legs. I also don't care that she's seen more of my genitals than I ever will. My embarrassment has ended up in the bin along with my excrement and the rest of the clinical waste.

'Am I fully dilated yet?' I ask, hoping that it will soon be over so I can go back to being a school kid who doesn't know what these terms mean.

'Yes. Everything looks promising. You can go for it whenever you feel ready.'

When I glance down, I am startled to see splashes of blood on my thighs and lower calves. 'Is that normal?' I want to know, strangely more anxious about the baby than I am for myself.

'Absolutely,' Michelle confirms.

I know she's telling the truth because she's smiling in a genuine way. The kind of smile that doesn't fade away quickly. I can spot a liar from a mile off. It takes one to know one.

As another contraction takes hold, I screw my face up in agony, and I let out a guttural scream. When I press down, my legs spread wide of their own accord. This is the worst pain yet.

'Good girl.' Michelle encourages.

'Is it too late for an epidural?' I beg.

'Nice try, Tara,' Michelle laughs, 'but it's not necessary. Labour is much easier for girls your age.'

'Are you saying this is the easy option?' I grind out as my body bucks with another torturous contraction. I then fall back on the pillows and wait for the pain to subside.

'I can't do this anymore, Michelle. I can't.'

'You can, my lovely. I know it doesn't feel like it and you're exhausted, but believe me, you can.'

'I want my mum,' I sob into my hands.

'I know you do, honey, and for what it's worth you deserve a much better mum than the one you have.'

That makes my ears prick up and I wonder what she knows about my situation. Obviously, more than I think. I watch her fussing with the baby's heart monitor which is strapped to my belly. She doesn't seem concerned about anything so I assume the baby is okay. *But what if it isn't?* I sit up, suddenly on high alert. She's right. I can do this. *I have to.*

As the next contraction grips me, I let out a low, cow-like moan. It feels like I'm about to take the world's biggest dump.

'The head. I can see its head,' Michelle exclaims. 'Lots of dark hair.'

My first thought on hearing this is that Sean, the druggie, has dark hair. Does that make him the father? The rapist? I wouldn't have a clue about the other two boys' hair colouring.

'Blow. Blow. Blow,' Michelle orders, when I want to give up again.

I'm tempted to scream, 'I am fucking blowing,' but I lack the energy. Then, in the next minute the baby unexpectedly slides out of me in a liquid whoosh and I no longer feel anything. The pain is quickly forgotten.

'It's a boy,' Michelle gushes. 'A healthy baby boy.'

She doesn't attempt to clean him up before placing him on my bare stomach. He's crimson, wrinkled, and shiny, like a slab of meat in a butcher's shop window. Except he's very much alive and wriggling in my arms which aren't sure what to do with a newborn.

'He's perfect,' Michelle purrs. Then, dropping her professional demeanour, she kisses me on the forehead in a way which I think is meant to make up for the fact that I've had to go through this alone without a mother or a birthing partner.

'Perfect,' I repeat, staring down at my son, whose tiny, pearly-pink fingernails are wrapped around my thumb. His dark, intense eyes are open, resting on my face as if I were the most important person in the world to him. As he is to me, unexpectedly. The umbilical cord is still attached, which means we remain connected for now. But not for much longer.

CHAPTER 13: DINO

Dino disposes of the bin bags full of clothes at the recycling bank at the Cash for Clothes depot in Fengate. When he'd accidentally ripped one open and Tara's purple faux fur-hooded jacket spilt out, like an unwanted body part, he thought he'd be sick. He scooped it back up and added it to the large metal container but he felt like an arsehole afterwards. Although hard up, he told the guy on duty that he didn't want a penny for the clothing and to donate what they were worth to charity.

'What charity?' the guy with the Eastern European accent had insisted on knowing.

'Any. I don't know, how about Save the Children?' Dino had barked as if everything was this guy's fault. After that, he'd slinked off, ashamed of himself for his outburst.

His day is going from bad to worse. As if he didn't have enough on his plate already, he's now haunted by the suspicion that Tara was having an affair. Why else would she lie to him about her whereabouts every Saturday? He's already established she wasn't shopping for bargains in charity shops, so it's unlikely she was catching the bus into town either.

He's torn between going to the pub and getting pissed, which would ruin all of last night's efforts at the gym, and going home to ransack the house to see if he'd missed any-thing of significance that might provide him with an answer. Apart from the letter, had Tara left behind any other clues as to what she'd been up to and with whom?

Dino slams into his car and bangs his fist on the steering wheel. Red Bull cans roll about on the floor. His son's school jumper has been left on the passenger seat. It has a runny egg stain on it. Dino had intended to take it in the house and wash it but never got around to it. One of Bella's dolls glares at him from the child's seat in the back, as if to remind him of his parental obligations. There is mess and chaos everywhere he looks. Tara hasn't been gone two months and already they're falling to pieces.

Dino notices that a small piece of white card has slipped through one of the air vents on the front dash and he digs it out with a chewed pen he finds in the glove department. As soon as it's in his hand he recognises it as a parking permit. It must have been there for a long time because it's caked in dust. He gazes at the ticket absently and sits up straight in his seat when he realises it's for a car park at Orton Meadows that he's never used before. It's dated September 3rd, three weeks before Tara died. He pulls his phone from his pocket and looks up dates.

A Saturday.

Entry 11.30 a.m. Payment was made in advance. Parking for two hours had cost £5.60.

He'd been working that day and had finished around 2 p.m., going straight to the gym afterwards. He remembers because football was on the big screen and Italy had won. When he got home around 4 p.m. the car was in the driveway and Tara had ordered them a takeaway to celebrate the win. They'd even slept together that night. He recalls the details because the kids had spent the day at his parents' house and when they called to ask if they could keep them overnight, Tara had said yes for once. When he asked her what she'd done all day by herself, she told him she'd caught the bus into town and had gone shopping. She rarely took the car, claiming she didn't want to be ripped off by paying extortionate parking fees.

He pulls up at the Orton Meadows car park fifteen minutes later. There are more popular parking spots at Ferry Meadows, but this one is quiet. The bins don't appear to have been emptied in weeks. Litter spills out of them and weeds have grown up through the concrete. What a dump. The only positive aspect is that the parking bays are shaded by tall, green trees, giving the area a deceptively woodland feel.

Dino suspects that mostly dog walkers and weirdos use it. He has no idea why his wife would have parked here for more than two hours. They have no friends or family on this side of town and there are no shops nearby. Tara was afraid of dogs so it was unlikely she'd have done a friend a favour by taking their dog for a walk out here. Besides, knowing he'd always wanted a family dog, she'd have suggested they go together.

He doesn't get out of his car to look around because there is dog crap everywhere and he doesn't want to step in any of it. He's got enough shit going on in his life as it is. Something buried in his subconscious niggles at him as he sets off again, this time for home. He's certain he's missed something. A clue that's staring him in the face.

He hasn't gone far, only half a mile, when he notices a familiar road sign. *That's it. I knew there was something off about this.* Braking harder than he should, Dino pulls over, throws the car into a severe three-point turn in the middle of the road, earning him several blasts of the horn and an up-yours sign from another driver, and points the car in the direction of Cherry Orton Road. He was last at Holywell House two weeks ago.

Because they're wide open, he doesn't linger outside the gates this time, instead marching straight through them and up the elegant block-paved driveway. There's a swanky, grey, Volvo hybrid estate parked in front of a double garage. The formal grounds are immaculate. There isn't a single leaf or blade of grass out of place. Dino would like to bet that the Grants employ a gardener and a cleaner, whom they claim to treat like family. He knows the type. He's met enough of them on his delivery round.

Dino takes a deep breath as he presses a finger three times on the doorbell in quick succession. It's deadly quiet. There are no sounds of children running around screaming or a TV on loud like in his house. He's beginning to think there's no one at home when he sees the shadow of a woman approaching through the glass in the double doors.

She's tall, elegant, and extremely attractive, with a knock-out figure, but when she sees Dino on her doorstep her smile freezes. He can feel her recoil as if he had spat in her face.

'Hi. I'm sorry to bother you but I was wondering if you might be able to help me.' Dino tries out his best cheeky boy grin on her but she's as cold as ice.

'I very much doubt that,' she answers curtly, glancing behind her as if hoping someone will come to rescue her from having to talk to Dino.

'You don't know what it is yet.' Dino cracks a joke, then feels stupid and awkward as she stares frostily at him, waiting for him to continue.

'Look, it's best if I come clean,' Dino sighs. 'It's Grant, isn't it?'

'Mrs Grant, yes.' She corrects him.

'My name is Dino De Rosa and . . .'

'I know who you are.'

Dino is taken aback by the savagery of her reply. 'You do?'

'I saw your picture in the paper,' she shrugs, unwilling to help him out.

'In which case,' Dino clears his throat and nervously swallows, 'you'll know that my wife, Tara, died outside your house. Just over there.' He turns to point in the direction of the gates and the adjacent road.

'I'm perfectly aware of where it happened. The police were here for days.'

Wow. What a bitch. 'You make it sound like an inconvenience.' Dino is on the attack now.

'What is it you want?' she barks, folding her arms.

'Actually, I was wondering whether your husband was in?'

'My husband! What do you want him for?'

Dino observes how her eyes widen with fear at the mention of her husband. He wonders if he beats her and that's why she's so hostile.

'Is he in?' Dino asks again.

'No. I'm afraid not.' Another look back over her shoulder as if she's terrified someone is going to catch her out in something.

'And will he be back soon?' Dino persists before she can shut the door on him.

'That depends on what you want him for.'

'I believe he may have known my wife.' Dino can hardly bring himself to say the words, *I think they might have been having an affair,* because once said they can't be unsaid.

'That's impossible,' she states authoritatively, yet there's a smirk on her face that somehow suggests, *Is that all you've got?* He can't figure her out.

'Why is it impossible?'

'Look, I'm sorry for your loss, Mr De Rosa,' she says this in such a way that Dino doubts it very much, 'but neither I nor my husband can help you.'

And with that, the stuck-up bitch slams the door in his face.

CHAPTER 14: TARA

Teenage mothers

Brianna looks more rested after undergoing major surgery than I do from pushing an eight-pound baby out of my vagina. Even though I'm told eight hours of labour is nothing compared to what some women go through, I want to complain that I'm still a child and haven't acclimatised to pain yet. Period cramps and toothache were the worst things I'd experienced before falling pregnant. For the moment, I push all memories of the rape out of my mind. I don't want my baby anywhere near those thoughts.

Brianna's baby is dressed in a pink onesie with elephants on it and is suckling noisily at her mum's purple nipple, which to my eyes, looks as big as a saucer. So far, my baby boy, who is dressed in a blue flannelette hospital issued gown, hasn't latched on to my nipple, which has remained a girly pink, despite being told it would turn brown during pregnancy. Even when he did manage to get his mouth over it, milk shot out of my breast like a firehose, dosing my poor boy's face. After that, he lost interest and the midwife is now preparing a bottle to start him off, saying that not all babies take to the breast.

Watching Brianna nurse her baby as if it were her fourth or fifth child makes me feel like a failure. I wanted to give my son the best start by ensuring he received the colostrum in my milk immediately after birth, which I'm told contains vital nutrients that boost the baby's immune system and protects them from illness in their first few months. That was meant to be my parting gift to him. Instead, he's to have substitute milk as well as a substitute mother.

'I was awake the whole time because of the epidural. It was scary but exciting.' Brianna is looking at me, eyes wide with awe. 'I kept imagining that I could feel them cutting me open, the knife and everything. The surgeon nearly pissed himself when I said that.'

Despite feeling down in the dumps, I burst out laughing. The next minute, I'm crying. My emotions are all over the place. I look at the sleeping baby in my arms and howl some more.

'I'm sorry you're not getting to keep your baby,' Briana tells me, gently.

'Who told you?' I ask.

She shrugs as if it doesn't matter and I suppose it doesn't. One way or another everyone's going to see me walk out of the ward empty-handed.

'What are you going to call him?'

'I won't, I mean, there's no point. They'll be here soon to take him away.'

'You should name him anyway. He's your son. Nobody can take that away from you. '

'You think so?' I flinch as a fresh wave of pain washes over my stomach. After effects of childbirth. A bit like the fallout of when a volcano erupts.

'And if he decides to come looking for you when he's eighteen, you can tell him what his real name is.'

I hadn't thought of that and I'm touched that she suggested it.

'Ryan,' I say decisively. 'After Ryan Reynolds.'

'Nice,' Brianna nods in approval.

'Shall we keep in touch after, I mean if you want to.' I grimace at how desperate I sound but being in Brianna's company makes me feel safe in a way I haven't experienced before.

'Sure, let's exchange numbers. Read yours out and I'll prank you.'

Once this is done, I feel better. Brianna is the only link I have to my baby. Once we're out of the hospital, we can meet up and I can talk to her about him. I've only known her for a few hours but I'm certain I love her. Not in a romantic way, even though she is gorgeous. It's just that I've never had a proper friend before. Not like this. Without her I have nothing.

'You will stay in touch, won't you, Brianna?' I plead, swiping away yet more tears.

'Of course,' she wipes milk from Dana's mouth and coos at her. 'We're besties now. I mean how many fifteen-year-olds do you know who have babies on the same day?'

We both burst into laughter at this, as if we were hanging out after school.

'You can be godmother to Dana if you like,' she offers shyly.

'Seriously? I'd love that.'

'It's settled then.'

'Does it matter that I'm not a Christian or that I don't go to church?'

'I won't mention it if you don't,' Brianna winks. 'I'll tell the vicar you're an angel, which you are by the way. You'll get to meet my mum too, hopefully.'

'Is she? I mean, how long? Have they said?' I stumble on my words because saying the right thing is unfamiliar territory to me.

'Nobody mentions it,' Brianna bites her lip and looks away. 'All I know is that she's sick a lot of the time. But she can't wait to meet Dana. She's going to love her.'

I fall silent after that. I'm happy that Brianna has a close relationship with her mother but her situation only highlights how different mine is. My mother doesn't love me fiercely in the way Brianna's mum appears to. When I return home, she'll be as distant as ever and won't enter into any discussions about my pregnancy or the baby. As far as my brothers are concerned, I'm an embarrassment. Their slutty younger sister who got herself knocked up at fifteen and had to give her baby away.

When we hear the thump of multiple feet approaching and the scrape of a trolley on the floor outside the door, my heart leaps into my mouth and I lurch up in bed on high alert.

'That's them,' I say to Brianna. 'They're coming for Ryan.'

I can't bear to see her tortured expression, nor gaze down on my baby boy's innocent face, so I turn my head into the wall and loosen my hold on him, letting him go before I need to.

CHAPTER 15: DINO

'Slow down. One step at a time, man,' Detective Inspector Christian Banks warns Dino, pushing a glass of water across the table at him as if he thinks that will calm him down.

Dino has met Banks several times on account of him being the lead detective investigating Tara's death, but he has a laid-back attitude that frustrates Dino no end. The prick acts like he's Dino's best mate as if they're drinking buddies or something. Dino couldn't imagine anything worse than going to a pub with the man who couldn't find his wife's killer.

'I'm telling you there was something off about her. The way she acted when I asked to see her husband. And she spoke to me as if I were a piece of shit at the end of her shoe. She's hiding something. I know it.'

'Assuming you're right,' Banks leans back in his chair and puts his hands behind his head in an all-too masculine gesture Dino is familiar with, 'what do you think that is?'

'I've found out that Tara wasn't where she was meant to be most Saturdays. Instead, of catching a bus into town and going shopping like she was meant to, she'd taken to driving over to a car park near the Grant's house.' Dino swallows, realising how pathetic he sounds. He can't provide the detective with any logical argument for what he's about to say next and Banks knows it.

'That's hardly against the law, is it, Dino? Besides, you know what women are like, acting all mysterious and unavailable from time to time in order to keep their man keen.'

'No, I don't. Tara wasn't like that.' Dino has no idea anymore if that's true or not. 'I think she knew Mr Grant and that they were intimate. I also think Mrs Grant had become aware of the affair and that's why she acted how she did when I rocked up at her house today.'

'That's an awful lot of thinking.' Banks lurches forward, letting his tilted mid-air chair crash to the floor. 'So, let me get this straight. You think Tara was visiting Mr Grant at his home and that somehow the wife got wind of the affair, or caught them at it, and then what? I'm not sure I like where you're going with this.'

Interview room four at Thorpe Wood Police Station is small and claustrophobic. There's no window. Dino can't breathe. He's reminded of the time he got banged up for helping to steal a car. Grasping the glass of water in his shaky hand, he slugs it back in one go.

'I don't like where I'm going with this either but I think one of them ran Tara over.'

'You realise what you're accusing them of, Mr De Rosa?'

Banks is observing Dino in a way that makes him uncomfortable. It occurs to Dino that the camaraderie and masculinity are an act and underneath the testosterone-fuelled exterior is a smart man. Banks is not the idiot Dino mistook him for which he finds reassuring.

'So, I'm Mr De Rosa now, am I?' Dino grins.

'You are when you accuse someone of murder.'

'I'm not saying for sure that I think that's what happened. But something's not right. Tara has visited that house more than once and there's got to be a reason for it.'

'And you don't like that reason?'

'I don't like that reason,' Dino confirms.

Dino wrings his hands and pulls at the collar of his shirt. He can smell sweat on his clothes. 'Can you get a warrant and check out their garage, see if they've got a white Land Rover tucked away somewhere?'

'I can't get a warrant without any sort of proof,' Banks says, scrunching up his dark eyes.

'Well, can you at least go round there and ask him if he knew Tara? Find out what was going on?'

Banks stares unblinkingly at Dino as if memorising his face in case he needs to come back to it in the future. Under such scrutiny, Dino feels guilty as hell and he's done nothing wrong. He can't help thinking that this is a guy who knows how to catch out criminals. And one who looks like he's always just had sex. The lucky dog.

'Leave it with me.' Banks says, getting to his feet.

'So, you'll go around there and talk to them?' Dino isn't moving from his seat until he gets the answer he wants. Banks sighs because he knows this.

'As I said, leave it with me.'

That's good enough for Dino for now so he also gets to his feet.

'You know, Dino, I struggle to sleep at night when I can't solve a case like your wife's nor yet find a shred of evidence to put away whoever did it. I'm married too in case you didn't know and, just like you, I have a boy and a girl, so don't think I'm not on your side but I can't go around arresting people without a good reason.'

'Fair enough,' Dino nods, thinking how unfairly he'd judged Banks before.

They shake hands and hold each other's eye. Dino wishes he could take him out for a drink.

CHAPTER 16: TARA

The black sheep

They say time heals everything but that's another lie adults make up to give you false hope. I don't take anyone's advice anymore. I've finally toughened up. I'm definitely not the girl I used to be. Stupid. Naive. Too nice for my own good. A people pleaser. Nope, I'm pleased to say that I've become what everybody said I was all along — the black sheep.

It's been nine months since I gave my baby away. Ironic to think that I could have had another one by now had I wanted to, which I don't. Since then, I've turned sixteen and dropped out of school. Nobody knows what to do with me, least of all my mother. The school has given up trying to force me to attend classes. They continue to send letters to the house, threatening mum with legal action, but nobody reads them. I surprise everyone by not turning to drugs, drink, and boys. I have enough darkness inside me already. I don't quite fit the stereotype that everyone expects of me, and that makes me even more of a disappointment.

At home, I'm silent and moody, talking to no one, least of all my brothers, who go on, as usual, ignoring me right back. If Mum insists on getting my attention, I sometimes oblige her with a grunt and a shrug. That's all she's ever going to get out of me. I don't recognise myself anymore. It's not that I've become mean or anything, but there's this massive emptiness inside me that nobody can fill. It's destroying me. What makes matters worse is that Brianna didn't keep her promise to stay in touch. I'm still gutted by this. Broken, in fact.

After leaving the hospital, I'd waited three days before texting her and when she didn't answer straight away, I wasn't worried. Not at first. I just assumed she was busy with Dana and her mum. I understood that she had a lot going on but would make time for me when she could. Except she didn't. I rang and texted dozens of times but never got a response. I've beaten myself up over it ever since. *Why? What did I do wrong? What changed? Why doesn't she want to talk to me?* The not knowing was horrible. I quite literally wanted to crawl into a hole, the hole being my bedroom, and never come out again.

The only answer I could come up with was that her mum must have died. But as it's now been nine months since the day we said goodbye to each other in the maternity ward, I have to accept that, for whatever reason, Brianna doesn't want to see me. She probably never wanted to be friends with me in the first place and who can blame her? I was the horrid ugly girl who gave her baby away, and Brianna was like a beautiful Disney princess, who was kind and loved her baby to bits. It's no wonder she didn't want to have anything to do with me.

I didn't have a surname to go on, nor yet an address, otherwise I'd have gone round to her house demanding to know what I'd done wrong and begging to be given another chance. She said she lived in Werrington, which is in another part of Peterborough but it's massive. I've walked its streets a few times but it's like looking for a needle in a haystack. She never told me what school she went to or if she planned to go back there or finish her education at home so she could be with her baby. Turns out I didn't know much about my friend at all. I knew I had to give her up though. Forget about her. Or I'd become obsessed.

Instead, I took to fantasising about other people's babies. I even put a postcard up in the local shop advertising myself as a babysitter, but of course, nobody wanted to hire me to take care of their babies. I was a dropout with no experience. Besides, wasn't I the kid who got pregnant at fifteen and gave her baby away? What would make them think I'd look after theirs any better? I know my pregnancy was supposed to be a secret, but who did my brothers think we were fooling? Word gets out in a small town like Stamford. It's not like Peterborough where you can become invisible.

When I see a cute baby in a buggy, I linger in the hope of striking up a conversation with its mother. I want so much to hold a newborn again. To feel its warmth in my arms. Don't get me wrong, I've never thought about stealing anyone's baby. I'm not that crazy. I wouldn't do something like that because I know exactly how it feels to lose a child.

I'm at an all-time low yet I'm too weak to contemplate suicide. The thought of dying scares me half to death. What if Ryan decided to come and find his real mum when he came of age, only to be told she'd topped herself? What would that do to him? No. I can't do that to my son.

On the advice of a social worker, I'd written a letter to my baby which would be placed in the care of his adoptive parents, who I'd been told were in their forties, so really quite old. They have promised to hand over the letter, which was short and to the point, to Ryan when he is eighteen. In it, I informed Ryan of his real name and gave him my contact details.

I never expected to feel such longing for my baby. Didn't know I had such powerful emotions. Most of my life has been spent avoiding feelings.

CHAPTER 17: DINO

The female receptionist at their local GP's surgery reminds Dino of Tara, or maybe he's just looking for her everywhere in other people. She has shoulder-length dark blonde, naturally curly hair and is petite but when she smiles, revealing a set of perfectly white, straight, and even teeth, he's disappointed because Tara's teeth were wonky, uneven, and less than perfect, mainly because she hated the dentist. She didn't even like brushing her teeth, complaining it hurt, as she had sensitive gums.

Sometimes, Tara's personal hygiene was not up to scratch and he would have to get on at her. She could go days without showering, claiming that baby wipes did a good enough job. Was that behaviour normal for a woman? Or did it smack of unresolved childhood trauma and depression?

Years ago, he'd convinced himself he was into tall leggy blondes, the kind his mates favoured, but that was him rebelling against his Italian roots. He's since reverted to type. Tara's his type. He likes petite women with long curly hair. Natural. Not too much make-up. Tara wasn't Italian but she looked it, even with the red hair. Subconsciously, this must have been why Dino was attracted to her. That never changed in the ten years they were together. He'd thought she had felt the same, but now he's not so sure. Even after finding out that she'd repeatedly lied to him, he had never imagined she might also have been unfaithful. He still doesn't know this for certain, but he's starting to think he was a fool for trusting Tara as he did.

He wonders if all women are the same. The receptionist sitting in front of him, behind the glass screen, could be married but secretly be having an affair with someone at work. One of the doctors perhaps. When he glances up to find her smiling kindly at him as if she understands what he's going through he feels bad for having such thoughts. She's nice. He likes her.

'I'm so sorry, Mr De Rosa,' she says hanging up the phone, 'but I've been told that I can't release your late wife's medical records to you.'

'Why not?'

'You have to apply in writing to the record holder.'

'Who might that be?

'They've been passed to the PCSE.'

'And I'm supposed to know who that is?' He tries out a smile on her, convinced she's able to do more for him than she's making out. So far, she's bent over backwards to assist him.

'Sorry. Primary Care Support England. You'll have to fill out an access to health records request form on their website.'

'She was my wife. Don't I automatically get to see them?'

'Sorry.' She pulls a face before lowering her voice in a conspiratorial tone. 'And I'll be honest with you, Mr De Rosa—'

'Dino.'

'Dino,' she takes a sip of tea from the mug in her hand. 'You'll only be granted access if it's relevant to a claim relating to the death of your wife.'

'Tara. Her name was Tara.' He insists, wondering what the receptionist would say if he asked her out for a drink. She'd be horrified, of course. His wife has only been dead for a few months. It's not like Dino wants to date her or anyone else for that matter but he's still punishing Tara in his head. All those years he'd spent resisting women's advances makes him mad as hell now, when it turns out she might have been cheating on him all along. That suspicion and the letter are playing on his mind. He wishes he'd never found it in the first place. What was Tara thinking to write it? It was so unlike her. Normally, she was in charge of her emotions. He liked that about her.

Is that why she didn't open up to him? Is it his fault?

'Here's a pen in case you want to write down the name of the website.' As she hands the Biro to Dino, they both experience a jolt of electricity as their skin makes contact. She laughs awkwardly before tucking her hand away. Is it so wrong of him to like her when she so obviously likes him back? Dino's always been exceptionally good at reading women.

'I just want to find out more about the baby Tara had before she met me. Her records might provide information about the father.'

'I'm sorry, but I'm not allowed to release any of your wife's details. They are confidential.' She says this as though reading from a script meant to appease irate patients.

'Are you married?' He blurts out, wanting her to treat him like a human being not a member of the public.

'That's a very personal question,' she blushes shyly.

'I just thought if you were married, you'd understand where I was coming from. Someone like you must be taken.' No way did he mean to come out with that. The words just fell out of his mouth.

'I'm sorry, I can't help you.' The smile has disappeared from her face. She looks uncomfortable.

'That came out wrong. Not how I wanted it to sound at all. It's just that you're incredibly attractive, so I assumed you'd be married or at least engaged. Shit, I'm making things ten times worse.' He tries out a smile on her but her expression does not soften. *Harsh.*

She's more business-like now, moving things around on her desk and avoiding his gaze, letting him know he's overstepped the mark. It's too soon for him to be thinking of other women. Even the ones who like him. She'll be thinking he can't keep it in his pants.

'I didn't know about the baby.' He admits, deciding on a more truthful approach. 'She kept it hidden from me all the time we were married.'

She throws him a wary, but sympathetic look. 'She never mentioned that she'd had a baby before the two of you got together?'

'No. That's why she wrote the letter.'

'Don't you think that's odd?'

'That she wrote the letter?'

'No. That she never confided in the one person she was meant to share everything with.'

Dino crumples. 'I think it's hurtful rather than odd.'

'Even when she went on to have,' she pauses to glance at her computer screen, 'two other children.'

He can only shake his head, knowing that she, a stranger, is, right now, accessing Tara's medical information, when he, the duped husband, cannot.

'You'd have thought she'd have needed to tell you then in case it came out. The first pregnancy is clearly on her medical records,' she unknowingly divulges this snippet of confidential information. Dino isn't sure how much more he can wrangle out of her but he'll give it his best shot.

'Can't you quickly tell me if the father's name is on there' he implores, gesturing with his eyes to the computer screen that contains all the information he needs. 'Nobody else need know.'

'I'd lose my position if I did that,' she says quickly, before rushing on, something obviously having piqued her interest. 'Why do you think she never told you?'

'I honestly don't know.' Dino is getting annoyed. At her, at Tara. At himself for not realising sooner that the receptionist is more interested in gossip than helping him. He doesn't want her to see him cry, so he gets angry instead, demanding—

'Are you implying that it's my fault my wife lied to me?'

CHAPTER 18: TARA

The best day of her life

It's my wedding day. The happiest day of my life. I'm standing in the four-poster bridal suite of the Bull Hotel in Peterborough having just slipped my wedding dress on. My mum is not here to zip me up. She cannot leave the house due to her agoraphobia. For once, it saddens her. She'd have loved all the attention her mother of the bride status would have given her.

I have no sister or close friend to help me get ready so I do it alone. Strange that I should think of Brianna after all this time. She was the closest thing I had to a friend, yet we only knew each other for a few hours.

I prefer to keep myself to myself anyway. When you're as damaged as I am, it's for the best. It's one of the reasons I don't drink. I've heard so many people divulge their secrets once they get into a drunken state and I can't allow that to happen to me. Although Dino enjoys a drink, he's proud of me for not touching a drop. He feels that as the future mother of his children, it wouldn't be okay for me to get drunk.

He's old-fashioned in that way, perhaps because of his Italian Catholic upbringing, but I'm okay with that. What

I'm not okay with is when he comes home smelling of other women's perfume. Dino is faithful to me and I trust him. It's the other women I don't trust. That's what happens when you marry a gorgeous guy like Dino. He's like Tom Cruise, only better looking, but unlike Tom, Dino is unaware of the effect he has on the opposite sex.

When I first met Dino at the speedway track, I couldn't keep my eyes off him. He ended up being the only reason I kept going back. I certainly wasn't interested in the racing. I remember feeling so nervous when he first spoke to me that I tried to play it all cool and casual like I wasn't interested in him — when I couldn't be more so. I was so ordinary compared to him that I felt I had to up my game by being mysterious. Anything to keep him keen. Yet Dino was the one who spoke of his feelings first which made him so different to the other boys I knew, in particular my three emotionally unavailable brothers. Dino claimed to be the lucky one when I agreed to go out with him and told all his friends that I was out of his league which was hugely embarrassing because they could see I wasn't.

He genuinely believed it though. He still does. That's one of the things I love about my husband-to-be, he's so humble. Another reason women can't resist him. I will have to watch out for that in our future life together, but not today. For one day only I get to be the most beautiful woman in the room because I'm a bride.

Dino's parents were not exactly over the moon when we got engaged after only three months of dating, nor when we announced our plans to wed shortly afterwards. We're marrying on our anniversary as it's exactly one year ago to the day that we met. That was Dino's doing. He's so romantic, unlike me. At first, everyone thought I must be pregnant, *which I'm not*, and then warned us it was too soon and that we should wait a while. By everyone, I mean Dino's mamma and papà but Dino put his foot down, which is quite rare for him.

Convinced that we were right, we refused to delay the wedding. We both wanted the same thing. A happy home. Children. A best friend to come home to. Someone who had your back. And Dino was so handsome, funny, and outgoing I'd be a fool not to snatch him up and take him off the market. What people fail to understand about me is that I've been a grown-up for a long time and that I've been making my own decisions and mistakes since I was fifteen. I'm only twenty-three, but I feel like I've experienced more of life's knocks than people twice my age.

Moving over to the dressing table which boasts a beautiful white bouquet, a gift from the hotel addressed to Mr and Mrs De Rosa, I sit down on the cushioned stool, careful not to crease my floor-length ivory lace gown. Dino's mamma wanted me to wear white, but it drained me of colour. I might not be the ginger I was, as my hair has faded to a strawberry blonde, but I've still got the pale skin and freckles.

I move around items of make-up in preparation for doing my face, not a task I relish as I'm not very good at it. Wondering if I can get away with not wearing any make-up at all, which is how Dino prefers me, I stare at my reflection in the mirror. I think I look prettier than I've ever done before but I'm still not in Dino's league. He's far more attractive than me. Whereas I'm a four or a five, he's an eight. I read once that men and women should expect to marry partners of equal attractiveness or move up and down by one digit, but I have exceeded my number by double. I hope that's not a bad omen.

I hate my hair and freckles and wake up every morning to a cloud of tight curls that wasn't there when I went to bed. Dino calls me his "furball" which is why I keep my hair up most days. I get up early for work and don't have time to straighten it. Like many a ginger before me, my freckles have babies when I go out in the sun so there'll be no foreign holidays for us. I burn easily, which is why we're going to Jersey for our honeymoon. It'll be the first time I've travelled outside England, although Dino has been in and out of Italy since he was a boy.

I hope I don't pass on any of my uglier traits to our children. By that I mean my hair, skin, and freckles, but I could just as easily be talking about my past toxic behaviour. I want our kids to be exactly like Dino. I've wished it many times over. Even at Christmas over the turkey wishbone, which I'd fought for possession of, I closed my eyes and repeated in my head, 'I wish for our children to look exactly like Dino and nothing like me.'

My past has made me what I am and I've become good at making decisions and sticking to them, setting boundaries too, which is just as well because Dino is useless. He struggles to make up his mind or stick to one thing which makes his papà angry. And that's the last thing Dino wants even though he doesn't realise it. Babbo, as I call him — and I'm the only one allowed to do so — tuts at everyone except me. But at Dino most of all.

Dino's mamma worships the ground her only son walks on. Sometimes it's a bit much. We've clashed a few times already. Babbo claims his son is lazy and disorganised and Dino reckons his papà has never forgiven him for going off the rails when he was younger. I say nothing when Dino alludes to these troubled teenage years because who am I to talk? If my life hadn't turned out as it did, I might have made something of myself, gone to university and secured a decent job, as an accountant perhaps as I was always good at maths. What would my life have been like without all the emotional abuse, I wonder? Or if I hadn't been pressured into giving up my baby? He'd be eight years old by now.

I tell myself that I shouldn't be bringing up the past on my wedding day. It isn't fair to Dino. And there lies the problem because I'm being more than unfair, I'm lying to Dino. Keeping him in the dark because I'm terrified that he'll refuse to marry me if I tell him the truth about the baby I gave up when I was fifteen. Like me, Dino has always wanted lots of children. He's never made this a secret. Coming from an Italian Catholic family, who were only blessed with one child, he has a lot to prove to his papà, whom I suspect he secretly worships even though he would never admit this.

Dino's desire to settle down and raise a family is what I want too. Another of the reasons I'm marrying my handsome

Italian Stallion is so he can give me lots of dark-eyed, dark-haired babies. But the truth is I already have a child. One he doesn't know about. It would kill him to know that I kept something as important as that from him. Unfortunately, that's not the only secret I've kept from him. He doesn't know about my shameful childhood either. Mum's mental health issues. The emotional and sometimes physical abuse I suffered at the hands of my three elder brothers, who are only here today because Dino insisted on inviting them.

CHAPTER 19: DINO

Dino enjoys the freedom his delivery driver job gives him. He's his own boss, deciding which route to take and how long to spend chatting with customers. He's lived in Peterborough all his life, so he knows which shortcuts to take around the city centre to avoid traffic jams and peak travel times. This job is a piece of piss compared to his old one as a forklift truck driver. He's never had it so easy. Except in every other aspect of his life.

The downside is that his van is covered in a bright purple livery of assorted fruit and vegetables and is therefore instantly recognisable so he has to be on his best behaviour at all times. It doesn't help that the office number is printed all over it in big bold digits, acting as a magnet for all the Karens in the world to ring up and complain.

This means no sticking his fingers up at arsehole drivers and no whistling at women in the street. Not that he would. But he doesn't even dare look anymore for fear of being reported. That wouldn't go down well at an ethical company like Nene Organic Vegetables which prides itself on being inclusive and valuing its diverse workforce. *Blah. Blah. Blah.* Dino gets it. Women should be respected in the workplace and viewed as equals. He's good at staying out of trouble and he's not an angry white van driver either but he sometimes feels the world is too politically correct. You can't even have a bit of banter anymore . . .

He's got time to kill so he swings by Cherry Orton Road and parks at the other end of the street from the Grant's house. Killing the engine, he takes out his phone and holds it to his ear, pretending to be on a call. This will throw any nosey neighbours off the scent. Not that they were paying attention the day his wife was run over and left for dead in their street.

Each house is unique in design but all are impressive. The Grant's house is the grandest of them all. Its pale yellow brickwork makes it stand out as a blonde bombshell among a street full of brunettes. There's no car parked in the driveway today, Dino notices, but when a man comes out of the house and gets into a black Audi parked three doors down the road, he wonders if this is the elusive Mr Grant and if he should try and have a word with him. He can't see any harm in it.

He's still debating whether or not this is a wise thing to do when the Audi pulls up alongside him. Dino slides his side window down expecting to have to face an irate Mr Grant who must have recognised him, or the van. Part of him welcomes the possibility of conflict with this man who may or may not have been Tara's lover, and he feels his muscles tense in anticipation. Working out at the gym has done him the world of good.

When the Audi's electric window rolls down, and the driver's face is revealed, Dino is shocked to find DI Christian Banks staring back at him. The detective wears oversized shades and a black jacket, very *Men in Black*, and grins at Dino in a *gotcha* kind of way.

'You delivering something down here, Dino?'

'I could be,' Dino swallows nervously. *How much bad luck can a man have?*

'And I *could* have some news for you, but I don't talk to stalkers.'

Dino comes clean: 'I'm sorry. I know I shouldn't be here. But it's hard, you know. And it's been three days since we spoke, so I thought—'

'You'd do some investigating of your own?' The detective shakes his head. 'Not a good idea.'

'I won't do it again.'

'You got any leftover fruit knocking around in the back?' DI Banks removes his sunglasses to eye up the van.

'I could rustle some up.' Dino grins now that he knows he's off the hook.

'Meet me round the corner, away from the house.' DI Banks glances over his shoulder, back at the Grant's driveway, 'I'll give you an update.'

'Okay.' Dino waits for Banks to drive past and then turns the van around in the street so he can follow him. Once he's parked up behind the black Audi, he goes to the back of the van and takes out a box of bananas, apples, oranges, and grapes that was intended for one of his customers and takes it to the detective's car.

Banks gestures to the passenger seat. 'Get in.'

Dino sinks into the shiny chrome and black leather interior and puts the box of fruit on the floor.

'Thanks for that,' Banks nods at the box. 'The kids can't get enough of the stuff. Me? I'm more of a carnivore.'

Dino's not sure he believes him. DI Banks is tall, lean, and good looking, not unlike himself. He'd had him down as an athlete, a runner maybe.

'Mine are the same.' Dino trains his gaze on the dash, not wanting to make eye contact.

He wants to be here and he doesn't. Wants DI Banks to tell him his latest news and what he's found out from the Grants. But doesn't. His stomach is in knots. This is what it's like to live a life full of dread. His whole existence has been obliterated. The future, as he knew it, has disappeared. The only certainty in his life is more uncertainty. *Will he get through it?*

'I don't know if what I'm about to tell you is good news or bad, but the fact is Edward Grant was not having an affair with your wife, which means we're back to square one as far as her death is concerned, with zero suspects and no leads to go on.'

Dino lets the first bit of news sink in. *Tara wasn't cheating on him.* Thank God. He may have lost her forever, but knowing she'd remained faithful to him returns a small part of her back to him. Certainty re-enters his life, allowing him to relax for the first time in weeks. Perhaps because of this, he's slow to interpret the second half of DI Bank's statement. When his brain eventually processes it, he immediately stiffens.

'You mean you're not going to get a warrant to inspect the garage?'

'I don't need to.'

'What do you mean, you don't need to? How can you find out if they're hiding a white Land Rover in there without looking inside.'

'Because they let me look without a warrant,' Banks breaks the news flatly. 'Look, Dino, I want to find whoever did this to Tara as much as you do—'

'I doubt that very much,' Dino grinds out, feeling suddenly angry like he wants to lash out.

'Okay, I take that back, but I can assure you the Grants do not have a white Land Rover in their garage.'

Dino frowns. 'I still think they're hiding something. I've got this feeling.'

'Feelings don't cut it, I'm afraid, not in police work,' Banks says, not unkindly.

'Wait a minute, how do you know for sure that this Edward Grant guy wasn't seeing Tara? I mean, he's bound to lie in front of his wife, isn't he? He's not a fool. And wouldn't want to get found out. Was she there with him when you spoke to him? I bet she was.' Dino's clutching at straws and he knows it but can't stop himself.

'He was out of the country on September 3rd, the day Tara got the parking ticket and again on the day she died. What's more, he can prove it. He travels a lot for work, business class all the way. I'm sorry, Dino, but Edward Grant is not our man.'

'It still could have been her, Mrs Grant,' Dino insists. 'She was there that day, you said, when Tara died, except she conveniently didn't hear anything.'

'What possible motive could she have for hurting Tara?'

'I don't know, because she's a bitch,' Dino half-smiles without wanting to and then has a sudden unexpected thought that causes his heart to twist in his chest. 'What if Tara wasn't having an affair with a man at all, but a woman? Mrs Grant? It makes sense. I can't believe I never thought of it before. Why else would Tara persist in going around there when the husband was away and keep those visits secret from me?'

Dino can't stand the pitiful way DI Banks is looking at him but he digs himself in deeper anyway. 'That would give Mrs Grant a motive, wouldn't it?'

CHAPTER 20: TARA

The past catches up with her

It's my wedding day. The happiest day of my life. That's what I was thinking earlier, while getting ready for the ceremony in the hotel's bridal suite. But no sooner had I married Dino than my world came crashing down. My past has finally caught up with me, and I'm scared that my new life as Mrs De Rosa will be ruined before it even begins.

It's Brianna. She's back. After eight long years. Here at my wedding reception! I caught a glimpse of her in the hotel foyer an hour ago and recognised her straight away. She's more beautiful than I remembered, dressed in a stunning blood orange one-shoulder maxi dress with a split up the side. Her long black hair was perfectly straightened and she towered over the man she was with, who I didn't recognise. She has the appearance of a model. Everybody was staring, which means Dino will have noticed her too. If he should get to talk to her — and he's bound to want to because she's drop-dead gorgeous — does that mean my secret is about to be discovered?

I've often thought about Brianna throughout the years and longed to see her. It would have been a dream come true to run into her and go for a coffee and a chat somewhere. But, not on my wedding day. What is she doing here? Who could have invited her?

Dino expects me to mingle with our guests, but I can't concentrate. I'm acting like a scared mouse by my new husband's side, which isn't like me at all. Dino notices and keeps giving me 'Are you okay?' looks. I'm not okay, but I can't show it.

Where has Brianna gone? is all I can think. She's no longer anywhere to be seen. Knowing I won't be able to enjoy myself until I locate her and find out what she's doing here, and what her intentions are, I mouth the words, 'I'll be back in five,' to Dino and hold up five fingers in case he can't hear me. The room is loud with chatter and music. Over one hundred guests have gathered, including Dino's extended Italian family, whom I met for the first time this afternoon.

Our reception is being hosted in the Broadway Suite, a spacious classically themed room with traditional paintings, elaborate mirrors, and elegant chandeliers. It takes me ages to cross the room because everyone wants to stop and tell me how lovely I look, which is nice, but not quite accurate. Some people compliment my dress, which is a sore subject for me because it isn't the one that I wanted. My heart had been set on a tight-fitting off-the-shoulder gown, but because we'd opted for a Catholic church wedding, Dino's mamma had advised me that it wouldn't be suitable. If someone else had told me that, I would have taken it less personally, but coming from her it felt like an attack.

When it was suggested to me that I wear Dino's mamma's wedding dress I flatly refused. It wasn't ugly, but it was out of date and had turned yellow with age. Dino tried everything he could to encourage me to give it a go, promising that it could be fixed, mended, and dry-cleaned to near perfection, but I didn't want something old or borrowed. I wanted something new. To suit my new life, which is now under threat because of Brianna. The girl who got to keep her baby when I could not. The girl who promised friendship and then betrayed me, just like everyone else in my life had at that time. The girl who is now a woman will never know how much she hurt me back then.

Brianna isn't in the foyer where I initially saw her. Nor is she in the reception area, where we'd eaten our three-course meal and drank champagne. This room is now empty, the guests have moved into the one that I've just left, where the disco will soon begin. The tables haven't been cleared yet, but it still looks lovely. There is a luminous Mr and Mrs sign which flashes soft blue and pink. Each chair has a big bow on it. The linen table-cloths had been shaped into swans, but most are now flat. The cutlery is silver and the glasses have diamond cuts etched into them. I can still hear the laughter from earlier when Dino's best man, Tony, cracked a few obscene but expected jokes, leading Dino's papà to tut.

Babbo had given me away, which felt like a great honour. I adore him. He's extremely sweet and wise. I wish Dino could see that he only ever wants to help and advise him.

Where are you, Brianna? I can feel myself frowning. Not something a bride should do on her wedding day. Then my heart lurches in my chest when I notice an orange flash out of the corner of my eye. Brianna is in a different room entirely. The Penthouse Suite. When we first looked around the hotel, we had considered this room for our reception but soon disregarded it as being too small for our wedding party.

I move closer to the entrance, not wanting her to notice me just yet, and peer in through the open door. A group of around thirty people are sitting in the room, all facing a sort of stage where the man I saw Brianna with earlier is speaking through a microphone.

He's attractive and well-dressed in a suit and tie, but he's much older than she is. By a good ten years I'd say. I'm not sure if they're in a relationship or not, but the way she watches him, as if proud of his accomplishments, leads me to believe they are. Perhaps even married? She stands to one side, but far enough away from the podium to avoid dis-tracting him. He's supposed to be the main attraction, but with her nearby, it must be impossible. Many of the men and women in the audience are staring at her, but she seems unconscious of this.

He's not only well-spoken and confident, but he's talking about entrepreneurs, practical strategies, and financial freedom, all of which I'm unfamiliar with. I'm sure Brianna did well by marrying him because money flows off the couple, in their clothes and attitudes, but those kinds of monologues bore me to tears. Give me my straightforward, down-to-earth Dino any day. Brianna had a wicked sense of humour when I knew her. I can't see her being content with someone as dull as this man, yet she looks to be.

She looks like everything I want to be. Confident. Gorgeous. Sophisticated. Her life appears vastly different to mine. She's made something of herself whereas Dino and I haven't two pennies to rub together. As it is, his parents are having to pay for our wedding which is embarrassing to have to admit. As I watch her basking in her partner's glory, I wonder what my life would have been like had I been allowed to keep my baby.

Some people could argue that I chose to give him up, but I was only fifteen at the time, and I was one of those girls that everyone had given up on, even my family. I was the black sheep. Hadn't I caused enough trouble for everybody, especially mum who was still grieving for dad? Ryan is much better off without me but I still miss him and think of him all the time. I'm consumed with the hope that he'll try to find me one day. I desperately want this, but I'm also frightened of what a disaster it could be for my life. For Dino.

I'm curious about Brianna's baby too, Dana, who shares my son's birthday. Does she resemble her mother? Is she also lovely? Talented? Funny? Kind? I'll never forget the pink elephant onesie she wore.

Brianna's gaze is fixed on her partner, and she doesn't look my way once, so I grow bolder and move further into the room. My shoulders relax as I realise her being in the hotel is coincidental and has nothing to do with me. She has no idea I'm here.

My eyes must have wandered away from Brianna's for a second because the next thing I know, hers are scorching into mine. Is it just me, or do I see fear in her eyes? The Brianna I knew was not afraid of anything or anyone. Then when I see her cast a frightened glance at her partner, who is still droning on about performance and growth, I realise it's him she's afraid of. Their earlier "ideal couple" parade was just an act. I feel outraged on her behalf as I see her wrestle with her emotions, wringing her hands and bowing her head as if in shame. If he mistreats her, he doesn't deserve her. I loved her once. I'm certain I could love her again. I won't let anything bad happen to her. I'll be her friend for life if she'll have me, even if she did let me down badly before.

I try to capture her attention with a modest wave of my hand, deciding to make myself known to her in case she hasn't recognised me, but I know she has. She scowls in return and appears to sigh. I watch her shoulders sag one inch. Then she's on her way over. Her gaze is fixed on me as she strides across the room.

I open my mouth and arms to greet her, but she storms right past me, leaving me with no choice but to brush off my surprise and follow her into the ladies' restroom. She doesn't hold the door open for me, instead allowing it to close in my face, but I'm close behind her the whole time. In comparison to her Amazonian stature, I feel small and insignificant beside her.

'Did you want something?' She stands with her back to one of the white, contemporary sinks, hands on hips, attitude all over her face. 'You've been staring at me.'

'Brianna, it's me, Tara,' I excitedly tell her.

'I'm sorry, but I don't know you.'

'You must remember me; I haven't changed that much.' All three toilet cubicles are empty and there's no one else at the sinks but I lower my voice anyway in case one of my wedding party guests should come in. 'We met at the maternity ward.'

'I think you've got me mixed up with someone else,' she says coldly, examining her tangerine nail polish as if that was of more interest than me.

'No, I haven't,' I feel my eyes well with tears as I remember her rejection from the first time around. Have I been wrong about her all this time? Perhaps she was never nice or kind.

'We had our babies on the same day. You had Dana and I had Ryan.'

'I have no idea what you're talking about. My name is not Brianna and I don't have a daughter called Dana.'

She's looking at me as if I'm insane and I take a step back from her because I'm starting to think she's the one who has mental health problems.

'That's not possible,' I insist. 'It is you, Brianna. I'd know you anywhere. Why are you lying?' Then, remembering what I saw earlier, I ask, 'Is it something to do with your husband? Are you afraid of him? If he's abusive, you can tell me.'

'You're one crazy lady. Acting as if you know me when you don't know a goddam thing about me.' She lets out a cruel, sarcastic laugh, 'You should be worrying about *your* husband, not mine. I saw the groom in the foyer earlier eyeing up all the women, including me.'

'That's not true.' I gasp. 'Dino wouldn't do that. He's a wonderful man and I'm lucky to have him.'

Brianna crosses her arms and glares at me. Suddenly, her shoulders fall and her voice softens. 'If I did know you, Tara, I'd warn you that he could never expect to deserve you.'

She turns her back on me then and washes her hands with such force that I believe she is attempting to wash me out of her life for good. I'm frozen in silence. By her words and actions. *It is Brianna. I know it is.* She couldn't say anything to convince me otherwise.

'Now I'm going back to the room to support my husband and I don't expect to bump into you anymore this evening. Or ever again,' she warns, fixing her large brown eyes on me.

When she's gone, I take her position by the sink and splash cold water on my face, but it doesn't stop me from crying. I want to chase after Brianna and force her to tell the truth, acknowledge that she does know me, but I can't risk alerting Dino to her existence in case she reveals my secret.

Instead, I must obey her request and leave her alone. Return to my end of the hotel and my new husband who is bound to be searching for me by now, and then meet my brothers, whose faces I can't look at without seeing my younger damaged self, reflected back at me in their green eyes.

Preparing myself for what's to come, I take a deep breath and confront my pale freckled face in the mirror before exiting the restroom.

I had no idea then that it would be another ten years before I saw Brianna again. I wouldn't let her get away so easily next time.

CHAPTER 21: DINO

The more Dino thinks about the possibility of Tara having an affair with Mrs Grant rather than the husband, the more it makes sense. He realises this may be wishful thinking on his part, because, strangely, he can forgive a fling with another woman considerably more easily than an affair with a man. It's a masculine thing. He can't rationalise it. Or fight his feelings.

Only another bloke would get where Dino's coming from, but Tara having sex with a woman would hardly be a betrayal. He could accept that and not hate her for it. But the thought of her having sex with another man sickens him. While he doesn't recall Tara showing any lesbian tendencies while they were together, she also wasn't especially interested in men. Tara was concerned about her children and Dino. Nobody else came close.

If he's right, he wonders what went wrong between the two women, because obviously something had. One of them might have wanted to break things off and the other hadn't. Did Tara threaten to tell Mrs Grant's husband? That would certainly have given her a motive for wanting Tara out of the way. Or was it the other way around, and Tara decided the relationship wasn't worth ruining her marriage? Was Mrs

Grant the one who refused to accept it was over? If so, what might she have done to get her own back on Tara? Would she go as far as to hurt her?

DI Banks had warned Dino that he was barking up the wrong tree and to stay away from the Grants. Or else. But Dino couldn't help himself. He had to know. This is why he's dressed all in black and armed with a crowbar because he's determined to get into that garage tonight so he can find out for himself what they're hiding. He doesn't doubt DI Banks' version of events, but the Grants could have been forewarned of his arrival and stashed the Land Rover elsewhere in the meantime. Anything was possible.

He'd waited until after dark before heading on foot to the Grant's end of town. It's a cold December night with Christmas just around the corner and Dino has to jog to keep warm. Even so, white puffs of breath, like patches of fog, escape from his mouth. The whole of Cherry Orton Road is illuminated with shimmering lights, threatening to expose Dino who'd been depending on the unlit pavements to conceal his movements.

No expense has been spared in this neck of the woods. There are curtains of lights at the windows. Snowflakes light up massive trees. Front gardens boast fancy sledges. In Fletton, where he comes from, there are just as many Christmas decorations but they are cheap and tacky in comparison.

The gates to the Grant's driveway have been closed for the night so Dino has to climb over them. When his jogging bottoms catch on a metal crook, causing him to dangle precariously, he has to yank himself free. The tearing sound is like a weak cry for help, causing Dino to grimace beneath the black balaclava he's wearing. It's Fabio's, and too small for him, but it's elastic, so it just about fits. It does, however, pull at the flesh surrounding his face, causing his mouth to tighten into a hidden sneer.

When he had glanced at himself in the mirror before leaving the house, he was surprised by how deadly and intimidating he looked. He wouldn't want to run into someone like him in the middle of the night. He hopes Edward Grant doesn't have a gun. But this isn't the United States. Except for farmers, does anyone in England own a firearm?

Amber lights flood half the downstairs rooms, so someone's in. Unless they have the lights set on a timer, like the kid in the movie *Home Alone* did when he was defending his home from intruders. Dino, on the other hand, is not a thief. But he is trespassing. And if he's caught, he could end up getting arrested. He dreads to think what DI Banks would say then. He'd throw the book at him most probably. But Dino has no intention of getting caught.

He shrinks as he crosses the driveway, stooping low and hunching his back. A wave of adrenaline propels him quicker than he expected, and he nearly impales himself on a giant potted olive tree in his haste. He takes a deep breath as he approaches the brick wall of the kitchen. He had underestimated how terrifying it would be to intrude on someone else's property. He's definitely not cut out for a life of crime, he thinks. His heartbeat is so loud in his chest that he's afraid the Grants will hear it through the wall.

When he musters the nerve to glance through one of the windows, he is surprised to see them sitting at a large, gleaming kitchen island, eating food, and sipping wine, as if Tara hadn't died outside their house just a few months ago, which allegedly saddened Mrs Grant so much that she told the police she was planning to sell their family home. There's no sign of any distress now on either of their faces, Dino observes bitterly. Edward Grant refills their glasses with white wine while ignoring his plate of food. Mrs Grant focuses her attention on her dinner, a fork partially lifted to her mouth.

He's dressed in a roll-neck sweater, dark jeans, and a pair of trendy reading glasses dangle on a chain around his neck, giving him a studious look, whereas she's dressed like a hooker in a tight, body-sculpting vampire-red dress and stilettos with a distinctive, red-bottomed Louboutin heel. Dino frequently encounters wealthy couples like this on his delivery rounds. Knowing how other people dress for dinner in their own homes used to amuse him and Tara. They'd never done anything like it before, thinking it a waste of time. Tara's first thought when she got home from work was to rip off her bra and change into her PJs and slippers. Dino wasn't all that different. They only made an effort when they went to his parents' house for Sunday lunch or at Christmas, when they all wore matching jumpers.

The kitchen/breakfast room, which has bifold doors leading onto an open BBQ area at the back of the property, is as far away from the front driveway as it can be. He's about to walk over to the garage now that he knows where the Grants are. They won't hear his efforts to break in from here unless it's hooked up to a burglar alarm. But then another person enters the room, bringing a certain attitude with her. Dino estimates her age to be eighteen or nineteen, and she's extremely attractive. He wonders if this is the Grant's daughter. She looks just like her mother, after all, tall with the same eyes, but she is nothing like her father.

He had no idea they had a child. But why would he? He doesn't know them. The girl seems to add tension to the room. Mrs Grant pushes her plate away and slams her fork down, as Edward Grant pours himself another drink. He does not refill his wife's glass this time. It's as though he realises their peace has come to an end. It's obvious to Dino that they're continuing a row that they'd parked earlier in the evening.

Mrs Grant is on her feet, remonstrating with her daughter who shrugs her shoulders and postures defiantly, shaking her head from side to side. When Edward Grant jabs a finger in her direction, careful not to spill his wine, mother and daughter turn their eyes on him coldly and then the daughter storms out of the room, closely pursued by the mother, who's hard on her heels, screaming after her. Through the glass, Dino can make out a few broken sentences—

'I thought we'd agreed that you were to have nothing more to do with that boy.' This from the mother.

'Agreed? Dictated to more like.'

'It's for the best. You know that.'

'It's not fair when he's done nothing wrong. This is all your fault, Mum.'

'How dare you say that to me, after everything I've been through.'

'You? That's a joke. It's Dad I feel sorry for. Having to put up with you!'

'And you're to stay away from the rest of his family.'

Dino makes his way back to the driveway, using the building's walls as a guide, as if it were a maze he was trying to escape. He's about to leave, deciding to return another night when the Grants are asleep, when he hears a pipping sound followed by the whir of automated doors opening. He crawls under a darkened window to hide as light floods the driveway. He gets a clear view of the garage doors, which are slowly opening and notices movement inside. He's aware of loud voices and believes it's the mother and daughter continuing their argument.

Car headlights come on to blind Dino and he's forced to remain where he is for now, under the window in a patch of the garden filled with thorny rose bushes which tear at his already worn jogging bottoms. He watches a car reverse wildly out of the right-hand door of the garage. The daughter is at the wheel, tears spilling down her cheeks as she angrily revs the engine. Dino quickly clocks the make and model. It's not what he was hoping for. Instead of a white Land Rover, she's driving a brand new, top of the range Mini Cooper, barely a year-old judging by its number plate.

The car takes off at speed, heading towards the automated gates at the end of the driveway which open just in time, leading Dino to wonder if she would have had the courage to drive straight into them if they hadn't.

The thorns cling to him like bad luck, drawing blood, but he can't move or release them from his skin because Mrs Grant has emerged from the garage and is standing in the driveway, watching after the car with her daughter inside as it disappears. Dino, grimacing in pain, watches her shake her head from side to side, echoing her daughter's earlier gesture.

She then looks about the garden and adjacent places, as if startled, appearing to sense that someone is watching her. Dino becomes immobile. He's afraid to breathe for fear of giving himself away. He'd be in big trouble then. Mrs Grant finally returns inside and Dino jumps out of his hiding spot as soon as he hears the whir of the electronic doors start up again. He only has one chance to find out if there's a white Land Rover inside it before the lights go out and the garage doors close.

And he's not going to squander it.

CHAPTER 22: TARA

The first dance

Dino twirls me around in his arms as I adjust my sparkly tiara, which tilts to one side like a crooked princess's crown. I'm barefoot, having flung my painful pointy-toe sandals beneath a table somewhere. I'm sure the bottoms of my heels are now black with grime.

It's the first dance of the evening, and we're the only ones on the dancefloor, with everyone else gazing and smiling at us. The lights have been dimmed, and a spotlight controlled by the DJ, follows our movements across the room as we sway to Michael Bublé's *Everything*.

Dino chose the song. I'd wanted *I Believe In A Thing Called Love* by the Darkness, which is a bit more rock and roll but he claimed it wasn't romantic enough. And because he's had a couple of drinks, not too many, he's loudly humming the Bublé lyrics into my ear. One thing my husband does not do well is singing and I don't have the heart to tell him that he keeps getting the words wrong. I just want his lips to remain on the skin of my neck. Forever.

I'm still upset about Brianna and I'm wondering if they've moved on by now. To a trendy wine bar in town perhaps. My heart is both full and broken, and while I'm gazing adoringly at my husband, I'm crying on the inside. I lean towards Dino's chest for comfort, enjoying his familiar, reassuring scent. I can't get enough of the combination of citrus and woody earthiness, with a sprinkling of what always reminds me of new car fragrance thrown in. I want to crawl inside him. His smell is tailor-made for me, and I inhale it like a drug.

Girlish, romantic thoughts like these are not my style at all and make me cringe. Because so few people in my life have brought me peace and happiness, I cling to those who have drip-fed breadcrumbs of love. Take Brianna for instance. She has rejected me twice now but I still have feelings for her. A therapist would probably claim that I have an anxious attachment style, which is characterised by clinginess and hyper-vigilance about the behaviours and reactions of those I care about. But I can also distance myself from the most toxic people when I have to.

On that thought I ask myself: *do I miss my mother?* The answer is a surprising and telling *no*. As it's my wedding day, I miss a maternal presence, yes. I mean, what girl doesn't want her parents there on her big day? But I'm not missing the one I have. I carry too much childhood trauma around with me, like the heaviest of school satchels, to ever forgive her totally.

I can't wait to be alone with my new husband later tonight. Dino is much better at socialising than I am. I'm more at ease in smaller, more intimate gatherings, among friends and co-workers. I hate being the centre of attention. Being hugged by strangers who act as if they've known me my entire life makes me nervous. The worst part is Dino's enormous contingent of family who have flown in for our wedding. Shouldn't they ask for my permission before dragging me in for tight cuddles?

Dino reassures me that it's their way of welcoming me into the family but he knows how awkward I am with strangers, especially in public. Because of my past, I dislike people pawing me. Dino sympathises but doesn't understand where I'm coming from as he values family more than I do. This is not surprising given that he is unaware of my ugly upbringing. I can't bring myself to tell him about my emotionally abusive childhood. I don't want him to look at me with pity, or worse, shame or embarrassment.

We've never discussed our thoughts on rape, and why would we? Don't we lead perfectly normal, healthy lives? It's not that I don't trust Dino, but I don't want to drag the old Tara into my new life. She can rot in her teenage bedroom with the yellow curtains, heart-print duvet, and broken window for all I care.

Dino's mum sobbed throughout the wedding ceremony as a way of making it all about her. I swear she gets more attention than I do and I'm the bride. She does it on purpose, of course. Her outfit is so awful people can't help but stare. It's dusky grey in colour, and so deliberately dark, she could be mistaken for being in mourning for the son I've taken from her. That's all she keeps telling anyone who'll listen and there are plenty of Italians here willing to do just that. 'He's my boy no longer,' she cries, casting venomous glances my way.

I adore my father-in-law but my relationship with Dino's mother is a difficult one. I'll do everything I can to get along with her for Dino's sake because he loves his mamma, but her love can be overpowering and she's prone to interfering. I suspect she wants to rule us all and it isn't in my nature to allow this. I've had enough of others meddling in my life and wrecking it. Even for Dino's sake, I'm not going down that road again.

Belatedly, I notice my three brothers discreetly observing me and I sigh in anticipating of having to greet them. Their awful wives are around somewhere.

'Do I really need to talk to them?' I'd jested previously to Dino and he'd seemed mildly astonished, telling me, 'Of course you do, they're family.'

Because family is everything to Dino, even if that wasn't the case when he was a troubled adolescent who shattered his mamma's heart by getting into trouble with the police, he expects me to embrace mine. He's learned the hard way that's not going to happen. Ever. Even if my family were open to the idea, which they're not, I wouldn't entertain it.

My relationship with my mother is more strained than ever. She hardly leaves the house anymore and is a pale shell of her former self. Now that her boys have flown the nest and she's on her own, I had thought that she'd have an epiphany and realise the value of having a daughter, someone to take care of her and keep her company in her old age, but I was wrong. Her loneliness didn't make her want me anymore. In fact, the exact reverse was true. She's become accustomed to being alone. And she seems to live only for the infrequent visits of her three handsome sons, of whom she is extremely proud because 'haven't they done well?'

I nearly choked when she came out with that. 'How so?' I'd been curious because I couldn't see it myself. One was a lorry driver, another worked in a warehouse, and the eldest, David, held the grandest job title of all — a mere clerk in a logistics company. All are married to miserable women, which is something to celebrate, I suppose.

Speaking of my brothers, I tear my eyes away from them now and notice a pregnant woman sitting alone at a table. She is much nicer to look at and I find myself smiling at her.

I was introduced to her earlier but can't remember her name. She's married to one of Dino's mates and has a huge bump that the Italian family are trying to get their hands on. I hope they don't do that to me when I'm pregnant, because I won't tolerate it. The thought of someone placing their hands on my unborn child stirs up feelings of fierce protectiveness.

I can't wait to be pregnant with Dino's child and plan on being the best mother and wife, even though I have a temper, a strong need to control and a sulky nature. Dino gets irritated when I withdraw and go completely silent on him. And vice versa if he overdrinks, which he does on occasion. But there is a strong bond between us. I once read that "hurt people hurt people", and while I have no wish to hurt the man I love, I have enough emotional intelligence to recognise that you can't endure what I've been through without being damaged, all of which affect your personal life.

As a new wife, I want to satisfy my husband in every way possible, including sexually, but when I ask myself if I truly desire Dino as a woman should a man, the answer is a shocking no. This hurts me more than Dino could ever know because I couldn't adore him more if I tried. But sex is a disgusting and unwelcome act for me. I know this is due to my past, and as a result, I hate the man who raped me, whom I've come to think of as *my rapist* in an almost possessive manner, more than I've ever done before.

It's his fault I have to fake desire for my own husband. How could I have known rape would impair every part of my life, like a disease slowly devouring me? I put on a good show pretending to enjoy intimacy, not just for Dino's sake but also for mine. *Fake it till you make it* has become my motto. I hope to experience an actual orgasm one day, but every time we have sex, all I can feel is my rapist's hands crawling over my body, not Dino's. And what should appear next but his dark, hidden face and the scents associated with that night? Sweat. Semen. Grass. Cigarettes. Alcohol. Weed. Dog piss.

I lean in closer to Dino, wanting those memories and odours to fade. *Please, please, please make them go away.* Today is my wedding day. Why can't I be happy for once? My brothers are still standing on the side of the dance floor, watching us. They are dressed in identical three-piece grey suits. Each right hand holds a glass of beer. They look so alike that it's uncanny. People "ooh" and "aah" over them, thinking they're triplets, which they are not. They dress alike on purpose because they enjoy the attention. They've inherited that trait from Mum. What can I say? We're a narcissistic family.

'It's our turn to dance with the bride next,' they joke, smiling at me as if I were their favourite, most cherished sister. But I'm neither of those things. I'm their only sister and they despise me. They won't let me forget that I've always been the black sheep, yet I know they will never reveal my secret, especially to Dino, because family loyalty is everything to them. That extends to anyone outside our immediate family. I doubt even their wives are aware of the baby that I had to give up, because of them. What goes on inside the Fountain household is and always has been top secret. Mum's mental health. My pregnancy. The adoption. Dad's alcoholism. We never discuss things as a family. We pretended they didn't exist.

Dino and I lean back to stare into each other's eyes. His are expressive and lovely, a dark chocolate colour to match his olive skin.

'My handsome Italian Stallion,' I remark, my face expressionless.

'Why so serious?' Dino chuckles. 'Today is our wedding day, Mrs De Rosa, and I love you.'

'Right back at you,' I tell him because I don't find it as easy to express myself as he does. Not in the presence of other people. If I said that aloud Dino would quickly pick me up on it, saying, 'They're not other people, Tara. They're family.'

We're so different in that regard, and I'm sure he hopes I'll come to accept his family as if they were my own. I adore his papà in the same way as I did my own father, but his mother talks solely to Dino, ignoring anything I say. She'd prefer a quieter, more ladylike daughter-in-law, but it's not my fault Dino chose me. I try not to swear around her, but now and then a *shit* or a *bugger* comes out, and she looks at me in horror.

As our song ends, I feel a tap on my shoulder and glance up to see my eldest brother, David, standing there. His open arms are waiting to engulf me. Dino seems to think it's a great idea and that it's natural for me to dance with my brother so he doesn't try to rescue me. I have no choice but to stumble into his hateful embrace, stiff as a board, trying to avoid any skin or eye contact. Everyone watching us will believe that my brother must genuinely love me, but this is simply another way for him to exert control over me.

If Mum had been here, she'd have loved watching this spectacle. I can almost hear her clapping and saying, 'Oh, that's so sweet of him. How lovely.'

When it's finally over, and I've danced with all three of my brothers in quick succession, and I'm able to make my excuses and leave the dance floor, people stop to tell me how lucky I am to have three older brothers who look out for me. Overcome with rage, irritation, and a slew of other emotions, I fight back tears and return to the loos, hoping for a miracle such as finding Brianna inside, realising she made a mistake before and wanting to apologise. I imagine us laughing and hugging afterwards, promising to be best friends forever. But when I do eventually enter the room, it's as empty as my heart.

CHAPTER 23: DINO

Dino remembers Tara going missing at their wedding reception. She hadn't been seen in ages and their guests were wondering where she was. His mamma was annoyed. Papà concerned. Someone said they'd last seen her going into the toilets so Dino went to look for her. And found her crying her eyes out in one of the cubicles, her dress a puffed-up cloud around her waist. She was a mess. Head in hands. Mascara ran down her cheeks.

He recalls how surprised he was, not only because Tara rarely cried but also because she didn't normally wear make-up. He liked her natural look. High-maintenance women who had Botox, lip fillers, tattooed eyebrows and fake eyelashes bored him to tears. Tara didn't even wear perfume as a rule, sticking to body spray and deodorant. He loved that about her.

Tara claimed that she'd become overemotional as a result of the stress and build-up to the wedding over the last few months and he'd believed her at the time, because he didn't know any different. He'd trusted her. But he'd also secretly worried that his mamma might have said something to upset Tara. Without meaning to, she could be a bit sharp at times.

Afterwards, Tara expressed deep embarrassment at being discovered in such a state on her wedding day and made him promise not to tell anyone, especially his mamma.

'I wanted everything to be perfect and now I've gone and ruined it,' she'd said, bursting into more tears.

'No, you haven't,' he'd taken hold of her hands and wiped away the black streaks on her face until she was his Tara again. 'And everything *is* perfect, Tara. Because *you're* perfect.'

Tara was always telling him that she could tell he loved her by the way he looked at her. She said if that look ever disappeared from his face then she'd know it was over between them. When all his pleas for her to come out of the toilets and re-join their wedding party failed, he used this look against her, blackmailing her effectively by asking, 'Do it for me then.'

And she had, but at what cost? If he had known then what he knows now, he wouldn't have forced her to come out and confront what must have been a truly painful situation for her.

Because of course, everything makes perfect sense now when he looks back and remembers that Tara had been dancing with her brothers before going AWOL. It had to have been the memory of how they'd treated her during her pregnancy, forcing her to give up the baby, that caused her to become so distraught. What else would have made her so upset?

He feels as stumped now as he did on his wedding day because he'd found nothing in the Grant's garage except for the usual sort of stuff you'd expect to see, tools, and a lawn-mower, a ride-on in the Grant's case. He's gutted not to have found a speck of white paint or a sliver of loose bumper. He'd felt certain of finding something. Evidence that they owned a white Land Rover or any other clue that might lead to Mrs Grant's arrest.

He's home now and has showered off his fear of being discovered hiding in the bushes but something about his visit to Holywell House still feels off. The kids will be back soon and he needs to be in single dad, responsible adult mode, but he can't put it to bed. The grey Volvo was there as usual, locked away in the garage this time, and the daughter's Mini Cooper was long gone. But where was Mrs Grant's car? Surely, she must drive too. They're rich enough to own as many cars as they'd like. The daughter's car is brand new. If Mrs Grant drives and doesn't own a car, he doesn't buy it. There's only one way of finding out, by paying DI Banks a visit.

But first, he has to tackle the housework before his parents get back with the kids. It's not until he's picking up toys from the floor that he realises how much he's missed them. He even gets teary-eyed when he puts the toys back in the space known as the play area which is little more than a mountain of brightly coloured plastic. Dolls and soft cuddly animals for Bella. Guns, tanks, and soldiers for Fabio. It bothers him sometimes that his little girl is being brought up as a stereotypical, all-pink, feminine girl. Tara was never like that. She was much more boyish. He's surprised she ever allowed it. But then again, Bella has a will of her own. He can't handle the notion of his gorgeous, ginger-haired, freckle-faced daughter, who resembles her mother so much, growing up and having boyfriends. The thought depresses him. It doesn't enter his head to mind that his son is being brought up to embrace violence because, to him, boys are different.

He's shovelling a pile of dirty clothes into the washing machine when he hears a knock at the front door. His parents, who never used to enter the house without knocking because Tara insisted on her privacy, have got into the habit of walking straight in now that she's no longer around, so he assumes they must have forgotten their key. Dino doesn't consider it disrespectful of them to come in unannounced. Never has. As far as he's concerned, they can come and go whenever they want. Tara doesn't make the rules anymore. Dino couldn't manage without their help with the children. If it weren't for them, he wouldn't even be able to go to work.

God knows he needs that outlet and the money. If he had to stay home all day with the kids it would drive him insane.

When Dino throws open the door, he's shocked to find none other than DI Banks on his doorstep. And he isn't alone. This time he's accompanied by a uniformed police officer. Dino's heart rate quickens. He feels sick. Several thoughts bounce around in his head at once.

They've found Tara's killer. They know who it is. Or Dino's been captured on camera at the Grant's house and they're here to give him a bollocking.

'Dino De Rosa,' DI Banks says calmly, 'I'm arresting you on charges of sexual assault.'

CHAPTER 24: TARA

The bump

Giving birth the second time around was a completely different experience, even though I'd been on edge throughout my pregnancy, afraid that one of the doctors or nurses would reveal to Dino that this wasn't my first baby. My first pregnancy was, of course, documented on my medical records but Dino had no access to them. In the end, I became so fearful of being found out that I discouraged him from attending antenatal classes, even though he wanted to accompany me. His mamma, being old-fashioned, didn't think he needed to attend either and if Dino listened to anyone it was his mamma.

Although we'd chosen not to have our baby's sex revealed during the scan, I was convinced I was carrying a girl because I'd gained weight everywhere and didn't suffer from morning sickness as I had with Ryan. Brianna's mother's advice about guessing whether a baby would be a boy or girl based on the size and shape of the bump had stuck with me. That's why I was so shocked when I delivered another baby boy. Fabio was heavier and had more hair than Ryan, but the presence of my new baby reminded me of my firstborn child even more.

When I was able to breastfeed Fabio, at least until my milk ran out, I was devastated that I hadn't been able to do the same for Ryan. I sobbed as I held Fabio, promising to protect him for the rest of his life because I couldn't protect my other child. In my mind, the two babies were merged into one, and I felt that by being the best mother I could to Fabio, I might finally atone for abandoning Ryan. And for hiding him from my husband.

I'm now twenty-eight and Dino and I were married for five long years before we fell pregnant. Those first years hadn't been as happy as they could have been because I expected to get pregnant straight away. When that didn't happen, I convinced myself it was punishment for giving away my first baby and I beat myself up over it every day. Dino took it in his stride, declining to be examined by a doctor because he believed it would happen when the time was right. But I knew *I* was fertile and that I could get pregnant at the drop of a hat so I began to suspect that Dino wasn't.

This knowledge ate away at me until it made me question my relationship with Dino. Did I want to remain married to somebody who couldn't give me a child? He on the other hand, despite wanting kids of his own, said that if it didn't happen, we could always adopt, not considering for one minute the biological mother behind any adoption. That made me mad as hell and, as a result, I didn't speak to Dino for three days.

'I can't understand why you won't talk to me. All I'm trying to do is be supportive,' he'd complained.

But I was also furious with myself as I'd already disposed of my infertile husband in my head, whereas he had shown loyalty to me, never once considering giving me up and seeking a fertile new wife. His mother didn't seem to feel the same. I'd catch her staring at me, chewing her lip as if she were mulling over something important. By the third year of our marriage, she'd given up knitting baby cardigans and was instead mentioning the names of single Italian women she met at church.

Dino might have been blind to her manipulation but I was not. So much for my hopes of being accepted as a daughter. Babbo, on the other hand, was always on my side which annoyed his wife no end. In the end though, it turns out Dino was right because we did eventually become pregnant and our marriage has improved as a result. My mother-in-law has since forgiven me and I her, because if Dino had been my only child and my only chance to have a grandchild, perhaps I'd have felt the same way.

With Fabio being just a few weeks old, I'm still overly protective of him and, possibly because of my past, I hate having to hand him over into the arms of someone else. Every time I'm forced to do this my eyes well up. Dino is proving himself to be a doting dad but he doesn't seem to be as aware of the dangers to our child's safety as I am. I wonder if it's a gender thing. The female of the species gives birth for a reason.

When Dino bottle feeds his son, he gives the milk all at once, rather than resting and winding him every few minutes which causes him to projectile vomit. I can't witness this without breaking out into a cold sweat. *What if he chokes? What if he dies?* And the way Dino casually carries him around the house in one arm makes me nervous that the baby's head will flop to one side and inflict an injury. Because I don't fully trust Dino, his bathing the baby unsupervised is simply out of the question even though he whines about this. Even in the arms of Fabio's capable De Rosa grandmother, who I do trust, my stomach churns.

As for my own mother, who hasn't visited once, due to her anxiety, mental health issues and agoraphobia, which grow increasingly worse, I was forced to take the baby to her. I waited until Dino was at work before going over because I didn't want to risk him being there and Mum letting slip any comments about the grandson that was given away.

* * *

It was bad enough being back in the house where I grew up, due to all the distressing memories that reside there, like a bad tempered ghost, but when I found out that she'd invited my brothers to tea as well I was fuming. This meant I had to sit through a whole hour of my baby being handed around the room like a game of pass the parcel. I should have expected this because Fabio was the first baby born to the Fountain household, at least that was allowed to stay in the family.

'He looks exactly like Dino,' my middle brother's wife, Shelley exclaimed in surprise.

'Well, he would, wouldn't he? Him being the father,' I'd replied bitchily.

It occurred to me that the stupid girl with the stupid pig-tails, *she wasn't a schoolgirl or a Viking for Christ's sake*, probably thought I was cheap and slept around. She'd have heard that from my brother James no doubt. But I was surprised by how gentle he was when it was his turn to hold his nephew. He seemed quite moved. I watched him reach out for Shelley's hand as if he hoped they'd have a child of their own one day.

'I suppose this is as good a time as any to tell you that grandchild number two is on its way,' he announced unexpectedly, shattering my world. He said this while grinning at Mum and Shelley, who was wriggling in her seat, unable to contain her excitement.

I'll never forgive him for upstaging me at a moment of my life when everything should have been about me and Fabio. It felt deliberate.

'That's great news,' Mum gushed in a way she hadn't when I told her I was expecting Fabio. 'How many weeks?' She was all over him and Shelley, and Fabio, who was now back in my arms, had been completely forgotten.

'Do you know what you're going to have?' Mum continued to sip tea from a floral bone china cup. 'Is it a boy or a girl?'

She hadn't bothered to ask me these questions. That knowledge kept me smiling since I couldn't let my brothers know how difficult all of this was for me.

'Another boy,' Shelley answered, looking sickeningly innocent, as if she weren't entirely sure how she got pregnant in the first place.

'And we've already decided on a name,' my brother casually dropped into the conversation, not looking me in the eye.

'What?' another brother asked.

'Ryan,' Shelley beamed.

'You can't call him that,' I object in horror.

'Why not?' Shelley demands clearly offended.

'Just because,' I stutter, thinking it's my boy's name. For the life of me, I can't imagine why James would let Shelley choose the same name for his baby that I did for the child I had adopted.

'Why ever not?' Mum snapped. 'They can call him whatever they like. They don't need your permission.'

It was so cruel of her to defend him, but then again, I knew she would. Glancing around the room at all their expressions, I could tell that everyone was against me. They thought it mean of me to question their choice of name. They could be right. Besides, Mum was not well, and I didn't want to upset her if I could avoid it, not that she ever spared my feelings.

She hadn't revealed what was actually wrong with her but it had to be something worse than the tension headaches caused by her anxiety. She's as thin as a corpse and has a weird odour about her, as if something is rotting on the inside. I wouldn't find out she had breast cancer until many weeks later. Mum might have survived had she visited her doctor for an earlier diagnosis but, as usual, she refused to leave the house.

Rather than participate in the conversation that was now all about my brother and Shelley's unborn child, I withdrew into myself and decided that they didn't matter. I had my Fabio and that was all that counted.

* * *

Years ago, I'd wished for my babies to look like Dino and God had clearly been listening for once, because Fabio was the spitting image of him and nothing like me, thank goodness. If I didn't know for sure that he was mine I'd have thought I'd had nothing to do with the eighteen-hour long labour he put me through before finally making an appearance. Michelle, who was my midwife when I gave birth to Ryan, was right about childbirth being so much easier when you're young. This time around, I'd needed stitches, which are still uncomfortable even now.

'No sex for at least six weeks,' the doctor had advised, which meant I was off the hook for the first time in my married life.

It feels like a well-deserved holiday and I'm making the most of it because Dino is a red-blooded male who loves sex. If I let him, he'd have it twice a day, which I don't, because who's got time for that? We both have jobs. Or at least I did, until I went on maternity leave, but I'll be going back when my pay runs out.

That decision opened a whole new can of worms because Dino's mamma is insistent upon looking after Fabio full time whereas I want to send him to a registered childminder who won't spoil him or go against my wishes, as my interfering mother-in-law is already doing, undermining me at every opportunity because *she* knows best.

We can't afford to live without both wages coming in and Dino's mamma is well aware of this. That's why she claimed it made sense for her to look after Fabio as her services were free, which meant we wouldn't be throwing our hard-earned money away. She's as manipulative as ever, but I know I'll lose the argument in the end because childminders don't come cheap.

'I've already raised one healthy boy,' she liked to boast. 'And look at how well he turned out.'

I remember cringing when she said that, not because I disagreed with her, but because of the way she looked at my husband at the time, as if she could eat him up. *Ew.*

While she bragged about Dino and exaggerated all his achievements, I watched Dino's papà flinch, as if he couldn't be less proud of his son. Something was going on between these two men that I couldn't figure out.

Babbo would do anything for me but I sensed that he felt a deep, underlying dislike for his only son. I couldn't understand it. Babbo has a good heart and Dino, on the whole, has been a good son. Yes, he'd got into trouble when he was younger, but who hadn't? It was wrong of Babbo to hold this against Dino, who, thankfully, due to having a healthy level of self-esteem, typically didn't notice.

CHAPTER 25: DINO

Dino is back in the same interview room he was in before, but this time he's not free to leave. DI Banks had cut him some slack by not handcuffing him as he was marched from his home to the police car but the detective stayed mute during the drive to Thorpe Wood Police Station, even though Dino begged from the backseat for more information about why he was being arrested. Now that Dino's been filled in, he can understand why Banks had looked at him the way he did, as if he were dog shit at the bottom of his shoe. Shit. He wouldn't want to talk to himself either if he was guilty of the charges he's being accused of.

'Are we clear now, Dino, on what sexual assault is?' Banks is asking.

'I didn't do anything. I wouldn't.' Dino covers his head with his hands.

'The legal definition of sexual assault in England under The Sexual Offences Act 2003 is when someone intentionally sexually touches another person without their consent.'

'But it wasn't like that.'

'Are you saying Caroline Roberts is a liar?' Banks does that thing where he leans back in his seat, the chair legs dangling in mid-air.

'No, of course not. I thought we were friends,' Dino says.

'Friends with a customer?' DI Banks raises his eyebrows.

'Well, *friendly*. I've been delivering to her house for a couple of years.'

Dino had believed he'd hit rock bottom when he lost Tara but now, he knows otherwise. He could end up going to prison for this. The thought is terrifying. He'd lose everything. His kids. The house. His job. His only chance is to convince DI Banks that he's innocent.

'I wouldn't class touching a woman's breasts through her clothing or deliberately pressing up against her body as particularly friendly,' Banks says coldly, adding, 'You could get ten years just for that.'

'Look, I swear to you I never touched her in the way you're describing. I wouldn't.'

'You think she made it up?'

'Who knows why women behave the way they do? Maybe she wanted to make her husband jealous or something but it got out of hand.'

'Why would she do that?'

'Why would I?' Dino protests. He's on the verge of tears but he doesn't want to cry in front of DI Banks who has got it together in a way that Dino has not. A mortgage. A nice car. A decent job. A wife.

'You tell me, Dino.' Banks glances at his Apple watch as if he's got somewhere more important to be. 'Why don't you walk me through what happened?'

'You mean my version?' Dino raises his head to meet DI Banks' gaze. He wishes he could read the other man's mind. Does Banks really think Dino could do something like that?

'We had a bit of banter together, that's all,' Dino admits.

'What do you mean by banter?'

'The usual. You know.'

'No, I don't.'

'Joking around. A bit of flirting at most.'

'You mean the kind of banter you should only have with your wife.'

'I guess.' Dino lowers his head again. 'I know it sounds bad—'

'You're right, Dino, it does.'

'But unlike you, I no longer have a wife. Anyway, I never meant anything by it. I thought she was up for it as much as I was.'

'Up for what, sex?'

'No. Not that. Just—'

'Banter,' Banks completes Dino's sentence.

'I never touched her.' Dino is angry now. 'Or any of my other customers. And that's the truth. But the women, well, they sometimes . . . I mean, they like me.'

'So, you're saying they, meaning Mrs Roberts, came onto you?'

'Not physically,' Dino groans, 'but she liked to have a laugh and a chat, and sometimes when her husband wasn't around, she'd flirt with me.'

DI Banks flips through his small black notepad. 'According to Caroline Roberts' statement, she claims that you've been inappropriate in the past, telling sexually charged jokes that she didn't like.'

'She said that?' Dino is gobsmacked. 'But why would she laugh at them if she didn't like them?'

'So, you did tell her dirty jokes?'

'Not exactly. Nothing really rude. I thought everyone enjoyed my jokes.' Dino is devastated by the picture that the seemingly perfect, politically correct Banks is painting of him. 'I wasn't going to say so but she's left me with no choice,' he continues, feeling cornered, 'she was the one that came on to me.'

'Caroline Roberts?' Banks is sceptical.

'I turned her down months ago when Tara was still alive. I didn't want to say anything in case it got back to her old man but she's left me with no choice. She's scared of him, you see. Reckons he's emotionally and physically abusive.'

'The same Mr Roberts who is a specialist at Fitzwilliam Hospital?'

124

'Just because he's a rich and successful surgeon it doesn't make him any less of a liar than someone like me.' Dino complains.

DI Banks shrugs his shoulders as if to say *point taken*.

'She came on to me, I swear. You have to believe me,' Dino pleads. 'I've just lost my wife and if I go to prison, I could lose my kids too.'

Banks glances away as if he might actually believe Dino. This is Dino's only chance.

'Caroline is doing this to get back at me for turning her down. I can't think of any other reason why she'd falsely accuse me.' He screws up the paper cup in his hand and tosses it to the floor. It's a bad move. They'll now suspect him of being violent as well.

'Okay, Dino. There's no need to get wound up.'

'You seriously think there's no need for me to get wound up when all this crap keeps happening to me!' Dino raises his voice without realising it. 'I can't take any more of this shit. I'm sick and tired of women thinking they can go around telling lies and getting away with it.'

CHAPTER 26: TARA

The picnic

'What's up, Tara? You've been in a bad mood since we got here.' Dino asks for the third time, sighing into baby Bella's frizzy ginger hair. I watch her wriggling in his lap, knowing with a mother's instinct that she's hungry and tired. Bleary-eyed but refusing to sleep. Thirsty but not touching her juice.

She's a year old already. And into everything. Much more of a handful than Fabio was at that age, but not in a bad way. I adore both of my kids but they're growing up far too quickly. I want to keep Fabio and Bella as babies forever, otherwise how else will I protect them from the world? But Fabio, *my little soldier*, is already three and a mini-Dino.

'Nothing,' I respond more sharply than I intended, popping open a bag of cheese and onion crisps and munching on a handful. Dino, I know, doesn't believe me, and will keep on at me until I either cave in and admit what's wrong or retreat into one of my silent sulks. I could put him out of his misery right now and tell him it'll be the latter, but I don't because I'm angry with him even though this isn't really his fault. It's not like he deliberately set out to upset me. He has no idea what he's done wrong but I'm not about to let on.

'If there's nothing wrong, why are you being so snappy?'

'Snappy as a crocodile,' I laugh, tickling Fabio under the chin. He giggles and holds up one of his toy soldiers for me to admire. I grimace at Dino and narrow my eyes, mouthing 'What are you doing?' We don't usually quarrel in front of the kids but he's put out that the surprise he planned for us hasn't worked out so he's making an exception.

'I've told you before I don't like surprises.' I hand Fabio half of his favourite peanut butter sandwich and watch it disappear in a mouthful of pink tonsils.

'Not even nice ones, like this?' Dino gestures to the picnic blanket spread out on the patchy green grass and the cold box filled with sandwiches, boiled eggs, snacks, and drinks, all lovingly prepared by Dino. He's even remembered to bring me a flask of black coffee, something I can't live without even on a sweltering day. To his credit, he's also found the only space next to the wooden play area that is on level ground. All of the other families are having to put up with bumpy terrain for their picnics.

The sun beats down fiercely on our heads, leaving us all tired and irritable. I've forgotten my sunglasses so I'm having to squint at everything, especially earlier when the children were playing on the wonky wooden bridge which I kept on insisting they were too young for, but Dino overruled me which didn't help improve my mood. Admittedly, he was holding Bella and closely supervising Fabio, so there had been no real danger of either of them falling, but it still made me nervous.

'You've got to let them be kids. We can't mollycoddle them all the time,' he'd urged.

'By we, I suppose you mean me,' I'd muttered through gritted teeth, hands on both hips, barely able to see because of the yolky yellow sun. 'They're still only babies,' I had insisted, before returning, alone, to the blanket, turning my back on my family so I wouldn't have to watch Fabio and Bella on the rickety structure. My anxiety wouldn't allow it.

'I thought a day out with the kids at Ferry Meadows would make you happy. You're always saying we never go out as a family enough, just the four of us,' Dino complains, cutting through my thoughts.

'Why can't you just drop it? I'm here, aren't I?'

'Except you're not.' Dino peels Bella's sticky hands from his unruly curls, places her on the blanket, stands up and aggressively starts packing away the food. When Fabio senses the day out is over before it's properly started, he leaps to his feet and begins punching his dad in the leg.

'Not going. Want to stay.'

'Tell that to your mum,' Dino snaps before stomping off with the picnic basket, leaving me stranded with both children.

'Sit down and finish your sandwich, Fabio,' I tell him gently, patting the blanket. At the same time, I reach out for Bella and pull her towards me, so she can sit between my legs. When I offer her the juice in her favourite training cup, she drinks from it straightaway. I can tell she's about to nod off by the way she's twirling her hair in one hand and leaning into me.

The truth is, of course, that Dino has no idea this so-called beauty spot is where I was raped.

I'm afraid to tell him. He'd be furious with me for keeping it from him all these years. Lies seem to get between us all the time these days, as if one of us were cheating on the other, but we aren't. Besides, I'm the liar. Not Dino. I love my husband and value his qualities but on an emotional level, he can't keep things from me as I do him. It's not in his make-up.

But I can't bear to be so close to the wobbly bridge where I'd hung out with Sean and his gang before one of them attacked me on the unlit bark-lined trail, which is visible from here. It snakes its way from the Fox Play area where we're sitting to Badgers, winding through woodland and grass, the large lake peering through the trees like a giant watery eye. Now it feels like my children's lives have become tainted by my fifteen-year-old self's disturbing memories, which is the last thing I wanted.

Families eat, drink, and laugh around us. Some have dogs with them, kept on leads. Older children play on the climbing frames or run around in the woods, which are only safe during the day, but they don't know that. Worn-out parents remain glued to their phones, oblivious to what is going on around them.

A trip to Ferry Meadows and a relaxing tramp around its varied landscape which stretches for miles is good for some people's mental health and wellbeing, but for me it's torture. Instead of inhaling the aroma of freshly cut grass, I smell rank vodka breath and a cocktail of tobacco and weed. And dog piss. I'll never forget the dog piss or the wet patch. I see moonlight and a hooded face rather than the hundred-year-old elm and poplar trees that tower above us. And the beautiful birdsong all around us is blocked out by the dreaded sound of crunching footsteps and a muffled voice that came with a wet, searching mouth, 'You'll like it. All girls do.'

I'd fled that night. From the boy's greedy hands. And from my problems. But most of all from myself. I've been running ever since. I may as well still be wearing the dark hoody I wore to hide my teenage face from the world. Avoidance is my thing. 'A Tara thing,' Dino calls it. It's what I'm known for. Everyone says so. Everybody except Babbo, that is, who seems to understand me in a way that my husband does not. He wouldn't have brought me here, to this place, without asking me if it was something I wanted to do. Dino, on the other hand, had decided that I'd enjoy it because he would, and that it would be a fun thing for him and the kids to do.

Putting others before myself has become more than just a habit. It's a way of life. I'm constantly taken advantage of. At work. At home. By Dino's mother. Even by Dino at times, because aren't I the perfect wife and mother who does everything around the house, and for the kids, while he goes to the gym and hangs out with his mates, me not minding. Shit, I even make his packed lunch every day when he's perfectly capable of doing it himself. I always promised myself that I would never become a mother to my husband but that's exactly what I've done.

It doesn't stop there. I'm also the colleague who listens. The employee who works late. The unpaid childminder other people leave their children with because they need adult time, which usually involves alcohol. But I've never needed space from my children. Having given one baby away, I appreciate what I have. Being a mum is more important to me than anything.

When I gaze down to see Bella sucking on the beak of the cup, despite being asleep, my heart shifts, like a giant piece of furniture being moved from one room to another. They're so precious at this age. It's not healthy for me to be having such unsettling thoughts while I'm holding an innocent child in my arms.

But what about my other child, born as a result of that night and no less innocent than my daughter? Ryan will be thirteen this summer. A teenager. Not much younger than me when I gave birth to him at fifteen. I long to see him. To know he's safe. He could be any one of the older kids running around in the woods but even if he were, I wouldn't know him. It kills me to know that I wouldn't recognise my own son if I saw him.

CHAPTER 27: DINO

'You're free to go, Dino,' DI Banks says, with a hint of a cool-dude smirk, as he comes back into the interview room.

'Seriously?' Dino can't believe his luck. He hopes to God Banks isn't messing with him. 'Just like that?

'Just like that.' DI Banks flops into the chair opposite Dino and clasps his hands together as if to say *job done*. 'Caroline Roberts has withdrawn her statement.'

'I told you, didn't I? That I was telling the truth. Did she confess? Is that what happened?' Dino pounds the table in a congratulatory gesture. He's over the moon. Kind of.

'No. She's sticking to her story, but she said she didn't know that your wife had recently died and, in the circumstances . . .' Banks lets the implication of what was said hang in the air.

'Oh, come on, not the pity vote,' Dino objects. 'Let me get this right, she's making out she feels sorry for me when she was the one who lied in the first place.' Dino gets to his feet and angrily paces the room, conscious that the detective's gaze never leaves him.

'Be grateful she dropped the charges,' Banks warns.

'Yeah, right. What about the truth?'

'What about it?'

Dino sits back down and looks DI Banks in the eyes, man to man. 'She could have destroyed me with one word, one lie.'

'Go home, Dino.' Banks leans away from Dino, glancing again at his fancy watch.

'You do believe me, don't you?' Dino asks. It's important to him that the detective doesn't think badly of him.

'I believe both of you.'

'What's that supposed to mean?' Dino is both insulted and intrigued. Banks is quite a character. He's having a tough time figuring him out.

'The truth doesn't always matter. It's what we do with it that counts.'

'Bullshit,' Dino chuckles, something he hadn't expected to do today. 'You made that up.'

'You got me, Dino.' Banks grins.

'And you wouldn't say that if *your* wife had been killed.'

'No, you're right.' DI Banks sits up straight in his chair and does up a button on his jacket, appearing suitably chastised.

'Is there any more news on the hit and run?' Dino asks. Now that the charges against him have been dropped, he's immediately back to wanting to find out what happened to Tara.

Banks sighs and shakes his head as if he really cares. 'Sorry.'

'I have another theory about the Grants if you're interested,' Dino offers, deciding to jump in headfirst.

'I don't want to hear it, Dino,' Banks warns. 'Stay away from them. They've done nothing wrong.'

'You don't know that for sure.'

'I could say the same about you when you ask me to believe you.'

Dino sighs and hunches his shoulders. He's exhausted and feels like he could fall asleep in this chair right now. He would have stayed in bed, hiding under the duvet, had he known what awaited him when he woke up this morning. Like he and Tara did once when the bailiffs knocked on the door. It was either that or give up their new state-of-the-art TV. And there was no way that was going to happen.

Dino had waived his right to a phone call when they brought him in which means his parents will be worried sick by now, wondering where he is. They might even have rung the station themselves, thinking he'd gone missing or that he'd been involved in an accident. Dino could imagine how a call from him in a police cell would have gone down with his papà: 'Sorry, I might not make it home after all. Ever, in fact. Because some bird is claiming I sexually molested her.' If anyone was going to be on his side it was going to be his mamma. She'd believe him no matter what, whereas his papà always thought the worst of him.

'So, I can go?' Dino wants to know.

'Whenever you're ready.' DI Banks gestures to the door with his hand. 'But you know, Mrs Roberts might be right about one thing.'

'What's that?' Dino answers tetchily.

'That the stress is getting to you.'

'I think it's safe to say that my life couldn't get any worse right now,' Dino admits. 'After my wife died, I found out she'd been lying to me for most of our married life and that she'd had another kid with somebody else. I also believe she was having an affair and no one but me seems interested in finding out who with so we can catch her killer, and on top of all of that, I've got to bring up two small kids by myself.'

DI Banks gives him a sympathetic look. 'Is that why you're in no hurry to go home, Dino?'

CHAPTER 28: TARA

A ghost

It's a day like any other. I get up at 5.30 a.m. and drink two cups of black coffee before showering and dressing for work. I don't have to be inventive because I wear the same outfit every day more or less. In winter, a checked flannel shirt and a company fleece with thermals underneath, dark denim jeans and CAT boots. In summer, safety trainers, a fleece, and jeans. It's always cold in the packhouse regardless of the season.

I then wake the kids up. They hate having to get up this early, so it's always a chore. For them and for me. Dino wakes up even earlier than me as he starts work at the ridiculous hour of 3.30 a.m., which means he gets home before me as well. Usually, he'll call in at the gym first. He loves to work out but isn't over-muscular, thank goodness.

Fabio started at Old Fletton Primary School three months ago, in reception class, but I don't have the luxury of dropping him off at school like the other mums do since I have to clock on at 7 a.m. This means I have to take them to Dino's mum's first and she's the one gets to take them to school. She looks after Bella full-time and has done since I went back to work after my maternity leave ended. It isn't an ideal situation but we can't afford to send her to a childminder. Things will be better once they're both in full-time education, but I don't want to wish my kids' childhoods away.

I'd love to be a stay-at-home mum. Dino and I both work hard but we've little to show for it. I'm on minimum wage and he isn't much better off. I've thought about going to college part-time, or in the evenings to gain some qualifications so I can get a better-paying job, but even that costs money. My teachers always said I was a bright student so I reckon, if given the chance, I could make something of myself. Even a job here in the office would be a step up . . . except I can't stand Jo in finance who has a thing for my Dino. She'd better watch out, that one.

Instead, I spend eight hours a day packing organic fruit and vegetables into recyclable cardboard boxes, that then get delivered to customers by drivers like Dino. He's good at his job and consistently receives complimentary reviews on the company's Facebook page. The customers love him. Too much sometimes, I think. But I suppose that's the price you pay for having a good-looking husband.

I'm one of a hundred employees who work at Nene Organic Vegetables in a 35,000 square metre building on a working farm in the middle of the countryside just outside Peterborough, which is a fifteen-minute drive from my house. Of that number, I know of at least five women who regularly look out for Dino when he returns to site after finishing his delivery round. They brazenly call out compliments to him from the production line they're working on even though they know he's married to me.

Luckily, I don't have to worry where he's concerned. I know he's faithful and loyal to me, but I don't let on to them. That would spoil their fun. I don't have a best friend at work, but I'm popular with most of my co-workers. Mainly because I work hard, keep my head down and refuse to gossip. It's the simple things that earn you respect here. I work with all kinds of people too, which keeps the job interesting. Old and young. Black and white. Male and Female. Many of them are from the European Union. Poland, Lithuania, Latvia, and Romania are all represented. Put it this way, there are more of them than there are us Brits, but diversity is a good thing. Dino doesn't agree, even though he's Italian.

It's the run-up to Christmas so it's our busiest time of the year, which means the days are longer and more stressful. Those who can't consistently grade out damaged or rotting fruit and vegetables will be moved off the line and given other jobs to do, like sweeping and cleaning, as quality is everything to our customers. When that happens it's a real walk of shame. I'm good at my job and have an eye for quality so there's no danger of it happening to me. I've been working here since I was eighteen so I know everything there is to know about fruit and vegetable grading.

While we wait for the fridge guys to bring out fresh carrots, I make myself useful by tidying up under the roller belt line, retrieving a lost apple and a squidgy rotting clementine that my finger sinks into. When I look up, I see that a new worker has joined the line opposite. They're easy to spot because they wear a different coloured high visibility vest to the rest of us, with "I'm new" printed on the back. Ours are yellow. He's wearing blue.

Although it's been eighteen years since I last saw him, I recognise him immediately.

SEAN.

The druggie.

The potential father of the child I gave up.

The boy, now a man, who may or may not have raped me.

CHAPTER 29: DINO

Dino had complained to DI Banks that his life couldn't get any worse, but he had to retract that statement the very next day when he turned up for work and was sent home again. They had marched him out of the building as if he were a criminal, explaining that he was being suspended on full pay while they investigated Mrs Roberts' allegations. That was three days ago. He's back again now because they've summoned him to the office for a disciplinary hearing.

He hasn't slept a wink all night and has had the shits all morning because he's so nervous. He can't afford to lose his job, so he's hoping they'll be lenient. Since Tara died, Nene Organic Vegetables have been nothing but supportive but he fears his luck may have run out. When he was originally told he had to leave the building he pleaded his case, arguing that the police were not pressing charges and that Caroline's statement had been withdrawn. However, they were insistent on completing their own investigation because she was a customer and had reported the complaint to them as well as to the police. Even if she asked them not to take it further, they would persist with the grievance, Dino had been told.

He's been waiting in reception for a full twenty minutes. The wait only heightens his anxiety. Sweat oozes from every pore on his body and his hands tremble. Whenever a co-worker enters through the main door and acknowledges him, Dino hangs his head in shame, in case they know what he's here for. Rumours spread like wildfire in this place.

He'd put on a shirt and tie for the meeting. Aftershave too, so he'd smell nice. As it stands, he's more likely to stink the room out with sweat. His mamma had cried upon seeing him and wished him good luck before he left the house but his papà had glared at him coldly, saying nothing. Dino could have done with his advice but didn't dare ask.

He wonders which member of the people team he'll see. He hopes it's Helen. She's always pleasant and can deliver any message, no matter how difficult, in a gentle way. If it's fat, near retirement age Terry, Dino is screwed. The guy hates him. When Dino objected to being called a cocky git by him, he quickly claimed it was a joke. But everyone knows the guy has no sense of humour. When Helen arrives, Dino feels his shoulders relax. Her smile offers him a much-needed confidence boost. If it were bad news she wouldn't be smiling.

'You can come through now, Dino.'

'Thanks,' Dino says gratefully, following her through the main office maze. He's known around here as the Italian Stallion which could go against him today, so, for once, he's careful not to watch the arse of the woman he's trailing. He's determined to keep his nose clean and be the perfect employee from now on. As they make their way through the myriad desks and different departments he keeps his eyes straight ahead, never looking to the side, because he knows the office workers' eyes will be on him. Even though he can't see them he can feel their interrogating stares. He wonders if Jo from finance is among them.

Dino's heart sinks as he's ushered into the meeting room. He's to face both of them then. Helen *and* Terry, who is already sitting at the table going through a pile of incriminating paperwork. Helen slides into position next to him and has her laptop open in no time at all, fingers poised.

'Sit down, Dino,' Terry instructs in a no-nonsense voice.

Dino folds himself into the chair that has been purposefully pulled out for him, facing the two members of the people team. He notices that Terry is wearing glasses and wonders if he put them on to make him look more authoritative.

'Thank you for coming in today,' Terry tells him, glancing through his notes once again. 'I'm leading the disciplinary meeting today and Helen has kindly agreed to take notes.'

Dino can't help but notice how self-important Terry sounds. He must be loving this.

'Can you confirm that you have received a copy of Mrs Roberts's statement as well as a letter advising you that the allegations made against you are considered gross misconduct?'

'I can.' Dino coughs nervously into his hand. His voice is no more than a squeak.

'Can you also confirm that you understand the outcome of this meeting may result in summary dismissal as advised in the letter?'

'I can. I mean, I do.' Dino coughs again and nods to indicate he's fully aware, but what he really wants to do is to yank Terry out of his chair, knock off his glasses and ram him into a wall. The prick is acting like he's a prosecution lawyer in a major courtroom trial.

'You've worked here for five years, I understand,' Terry comments.

'Yes, and I've never been in trouble before.'

'Until now,' Terry interjects harshly.

'Anyone will tell you that I've got a solid track record,' Dino protests weakly.

'That's not strictly true, is it, Dino?'

Dino looks at Helen, hoping to see a supportive expression on her face but she refuses to meet his eye. Her head is bowed as she types furiously. Dino knows it's all over when he returns his gaze to Terry and realises the dickhead is grinning at him in a sick twisted way.

CHAPTER 30: TARA

My rapist

The TV in the living room is on so loud that it drowns out the radio in the kitchen. Dino has been into the living room twice already to *politely* ask Fabio to turn it down, but each time he has been ignored. Dino is now seated at the kitchen table, reading a newspaper, feeling that he's done his best and is deserving of a cold beer for his efforts. I want to storm into the living room and unplug the TV, but I know if I do that Dino will think I'm undermining him. Then I'll have two grumpy boys on my hands.

I don't have time for that so I concentrate on getting tea ready. Because it's Wednesday we're having jacket potato, cheese, and beans. Dino mocks me for sticking to the same meal plan week after week, but I'm savvy and planning saves time and money. The kids never complain. They like the predictability that comes with my routine. Sausage and mash on a Monday. Fish fingers, chips, and peas on Tuesdays. Wednesday, it's jackets. Thursday, soup and a roll. Saturday, homemade pasta and on Sunday we have a traditional roast.

I check the potatoes but they need another five minutes so I grate cheese and warm up the beans while shuffling around the tiled floor in my slippers. Although it's only five o'clock in the afternoon I'm already in my PJs. Dino takes the piss out of me for changing as soon as I get in from work but I prefer to be comfy in my own home. The kids are the same. Some Sundays we don't change out of our PJs at all.

The draughty kitchen is a shambles as usual. Boxes of cereal and tinned tomatoes purchased last week still need to be put away. That is not going to happen tonight. I have a hundred other things to get done first. After I wash up tonight's and this morning's dishes there's three lots of packed lunches to make. And then there are the kids to bathe and put to bed. Don't even get me started on the ironing. Although I'm tired enough to sleep standing up, I won't make it to bed before ten. If Dino thinks he's getting lucky tonight, he can think again.

'You'll never guess what,' Dino suddenly exclaims.

'What?' I ask without any real interest as I go on stirring the beans. I'm used to Dino having his nose buried in *The Peterborough Evening Telegraph* and reading out bits of local news to me. Train strikes. Break-ins. Lottery wins. I tell him to get with the times and read the paper online instead of buying it from the corner shop every night but he refuses.

'A kid I went to school with has killed himself.'

'Oh, no. How awful. So close to Christmas too.'

I go to stand behind Dino and lightly place my hands on his shoulders, a small comforting gesture from a worn-out wife. Anyone who commits or is contemplating suicide has my sympathy. I came dangerously close to it myself once. *It could have been me.* But when I peer over Dino's shoulder to look at the article, I feel as if I've stepped off a cliff edge.

SEAN.

The potential father of the child I gave up.

The boy, now a man, who may or may not have raped me.

Dino does not glance up from his newspaper so he doesn't notice the horrified expression on my face as he says, 'I can't believe he was the same age as me. He looks so much older.'

Looking at Sean's unflattering photo, I find myself agreeing with Dino but I don't say so. I remember thinking the same thing when I saw Sean at work. He was only thirty-five years old, but he looked like he was in his late forties. My blood runs cold just thinking about Dino being friends with such a man. I can't stand the fact that they knew each other. Since Sean only just started working at the same company as us, and Dino doesn't return to the site until late in the day, he can't have spotted him. Otherwise, he'd have said so. It suits me not to let on, so I say instead—

'I've never heard you mention him before.' I prompt subtly.

'Why would I? It's not as if we were friends,' Dino scoffs. 'He was a drug dealer. Somebody I knew from school, that's all.'

When I hear this my heart settles back in my chest. I don't remind Dino that he too was a rebel in his youth, and that, while he hadn't been a druggie exactly, he'd smoked weed. But it's not fair of me to compare my wonderful husband to a monster like Sean. But did he deserve to die? And am I glad he's dead? If I weren't the one responsible for his suicide the answer would be a resounding yes. Nobody can ever know that his death is on my hands. This is another secret I'll have to take with me to the grave.

'I heard he did time in prison, more than once.' Dino is intrigued by the article but, I for one, can't stand hearing him talk about it, so I turn away, pretending I'm no longer interested, and lay the table forcing him to abandon and put away his newspaper. Later tonight, when Dino's snoring beside me in bed I'll sneak downstairs and read it.

* * *

In the end, I waited until Dino left for work at 3.30 a.m. before going downstairs, scared he'd creep down in the middle of the night and discover me reading the article. He'd think that was strange after I appeared not to be interested, which would have prompted him to interrogate me. He was never one to let things go. I always said he should have been a policeman.

I had to retrieve the newspaper from the bin. The pages were damp and stained with tea leaves, the ink blacking my fingertips, but the picture of Sean was undamaged and the words still visible if a little blurred. I felt dirty reading about this man at the kitchen table that hugs my family during the day. There are keepsakes of them all over it. Colouring books and crayons. Toy soldiers. A homework book with Fabio's name written on it in large childlike capitals. Dino's mug is still warm from when he left it there.

The write-up is hard for me to stomach and not what I was expecting. I didn't want to feel any pity for him after what he did to me. *You'll like it. All girls do.* But according to the *Peterborough Evening Telegraph*'s chief reporter, Debbie Davis, Sean had been in rehab and had finally kicked his drug addiction, which, she said made his suicide all the more tragic. She went on to report that this had come about after Sean became a father for the first time.

'Not the first time, Debbie-know-it-all-Davis,' I grumbled through clenched teeth.

His six-month-old daughter was named Georgia. *Another half-sibling for Ryan. They were stacking up.* The devastated girlfriend and mother of his child, Vicky Hull, was quoted as saying, 'He'd managed to turn everything around at last and had gotten a job and everything, but he came home from work depressed one day and took his own life.'

I didn't want to read about how he'd done it, but the bold headline screamed at the top of its lungs to be heard, LOCAL MAN, SEAN HUNTER, FOUND DEAD IN THE BATHTUB BY HIS GIRLFRIEND WHO HAD HER BABY IN HER ARMS AT THE TIME.

This is all my fault. Oh, my God, I've killed a man. Taken him away from his family and now that child will grow up without a father as Ryan did.

It never occurred to me that something like this could happen as a result of my actions, but now that it has, I realise just how much my hatred for this man, and others like him, has taken over my life and turned me into a toxic and revengeful individual. When I think back to last Tuesday when my efforts to destroy Sean had been realised, I feel physically sick.

CHAPTER 31: DINO

Dino had not gone home after being sacked. He knew he was being selfish by not telling his mamma the news straight away when she was beside herself with worry, but he couldn't face her. Instead, he's at the gym working off his anger, doing weights that cause his biceps to bulge and his veins to explode. Dino's a long-standing member of Definition. It's cheap and up the road from his house so it suits his purposes. It's also not one of those fancy places with a pool and Zumba classes. Or women. It's full of testosterone, sweat, men and machinery.

No matter how much weight he adds to the barbell for his back squats he can't erase the image of Terry's fat, bespectacled face from his mind.

'Regardless of who is telling the truth, you or Caroline, any kind of sexual "banter" as you call it, is inappropriate and we cannot tolerate it in the workplace.'

'That's insane,' Dino had argued. 'No one's allowed to be a human being anymore or make a mistake. I don't even work in an office. I'm a driver.'

'I'm sorry, Dino, but our decision is final.'

'You don't seem very sorry,' Dino had growled.

'This isn't personal.'

'To you, maybe.' Dino had taken a breather to wipe sweat from his forehead. His mind was racing from the shock. Nerves caused his stomach to cramp. *What the fuck.*

'Under the circumstances,' Terry lowered his voice an octave as if overcome with compassion, 'we'll pay you a week's notice, even though we're not obliged to.'

'A week's notice! What am I supposed to do with that?' Dino had gotten to his feet. He couldn't remain within these four hostile walls for much longer. Not with Terry's condescending face in front of him. The magnitude of Dino's situation had him bent over double, his head in his hands, groaning aloud. 'What am I going to do if I don't have a job?'

'Drivers are usually in high demand, so I'm sure you'll find something soon.'

'You are, are you?' Dino barked sarcastically. He'd been tempted to flip the table upside down and chuck it out of the window, preferably with Terry following it.

'And when you do, we'll be able to provide a reference for your new employer. It will not go into detail about your dismissal or mention what you did,' Terry informs him.

'But I didn't do anything,' Dino had shouted, powerless to stop himself.

Terry and Helen had stood up then, sharing anxious glances. 'I believe we should terminate the meeting at this point. You have five days to file an appeal if you wish, Dino, and as mentioned before, we'll get a letter out to you in the post today with all the details in it.'

Dino is in a dark place as a result of what they put him through today. His head is still pounding. *Jab. Jab. Jab.* Like an axe attacking a log pile. He'd come close to begging for another chance but pride had held him back. He's glad of that now because it wouldn't have made any difference. They'd already made up their minds about him. At least Terry had. The fat fucker had never liked him.

What is he supposed to do now? And what will his mamma and papà say? He can't wrap his head around what's happened. A few months ago, he had a good life. A wife he adored. A job he loved. His self-respect. He thinks he must be suffering from PTSD. Is he meant to just suck this up and add it to the battleground that his life has become?

He suddenly feels nostalgic for his childhood, when he had no responsibilities. Deep down, he's still a boy, like most men are. A boy who wants his mamma. No other female is really necessary in life. Not Tara. And certainly not Caroline Roberts. Dino knows this is just his anger talking but no woman, not even his wife, should have such power over a man that she can break him so easily, just like that. No, strike that, he's being sexist, which is what got him into this mess in the first place. No other *person* should have that power over another, he corrects himself. After all he's been through recently is it any wonder that he's gone off women altogether and believes they're all lying bitches.

To think he'd felt sorry for Caroline when she'd confided over their weekly cuppa that her husband was a narcissistic bully, an emotional and physical abuser, and indicated through her body language that she had developed feelings for Dino. She'd never said it openly, but he was a man who could read between the lines. That didn't mean he had to act on it. And he hadn't. He would never have cheated on Tara, no matter what anyone else thought.

When a shadow falls over Dino, he looks up to see a figure standing motionless in front of him, watching him. Dino blinks in astonishment and slowly lowers the weights to the floor, straightening up and snapping his neck muscles. His skin crawls with heat as the man's fierce, angry, and persistent gaze consumes Dino like a forest fire.

'What are you doing here, Papà?' Dino asks, his heart freezing over in fear in case something has happened to his mamma. Or worse still, his children.

CHAPTER 32: TARA

Karma

I waited until most of the office staff had gone to collect their lunches from the canteen before entering the code I wasn't supposed to know by heart. The one that opened the confidential filing cabinet. I'd seen members of the people team stabbing in the code in passing, and as I've said before, I'm good at maths so I never forget a number. I didn't know Sean's last name at the time but I soon found him under new starters. That's when I noticed the surname, Hunter.

'You couldn't make it up,' I seethed, thinking back to that night when my attacker—the predator—had hunted me, the prey, down, waiting until I was alone to make his move.

I didn't have much time before the others returned to their desks with their plates of food, so I skim-read the document until I found what I was looking for, the disclosure at the bottom of the job application. Sean had ticked the box claiming he had no unspent convictions. This was a lie: I knew he would never have got a job here if they knew about his past.

Back when I knew him, he was a known druggie who was always in trouble with the police. I felt a smug rush of adrenaline when I Googled his name on my phone and the results popped up instantly to condemn him. Sean Hunter had served time in prison on three separate occasions, racking up an ugly criminal resume of theft, robbery, and drug dealing. The last time he'd been inside was six years ago when he served four years. *Bingo. Got him.*

It was Dino who'd told me that you had to disclose any unspent criminal convictions to an employer if they asked you, especially if you had been in prison within the last four years, otherwise you could be dismissed if they later found out you'd lied. Dino had looked the subject up before applying for a job here. He'd been arrested for stealing a car as a teenager years before and was terrified it might come back to haunt him. He wasn't sure if he needed to notify his employer or not. It turned out he didn't. But that wasn't the case with Sean.

I wasn't entirely sure what I was going to do with this information until I ran into Sean in the canteen. When I first saw him, he was sitting alone, tucking into a plate of freshly prepared organic food cooked by our team of chefs. Although our canteen is heavily subsidised, Dino and I still can't afford to eat here and have to make do with a packed lunch. It annoys me that our hardworking, clean-living little family is worse off than him.

I continued to observe him out of the corner of my eye as I poured myself a strong black coffee. He didn't pay any attention to me or anyone else, so I assumed he didn't know who I was. Good. I was glad about that. It gave me the chance to study him without fear of him approaching me. My heart felt like it was being ripped out of my body when I saw his locked gaze staring straight ahead. His intense eyes, which are so similar to Ryan's and are forever imprinted in my memory, are enough to convince me that Sean is the father of my child and therefore my rapist, just as I'd always suspected. And because I hadn't seen my baby since giving him up when he was only a few hours old, this was the closest I'd get to seeing my son. Will Ryan grow to be extremely thin like this man? Did he have the same dark wavy hair and hazel eyes? I was more than curious about Sean. I was obsessed.

I hoped Ryan wouldn't grow up to be so haggard looking, but in Sean's case, I suppose this was down to the drugs and cigarettes. He stank of smoke. The smell had almost made me gag when I walked past him as I entered the canteen, reminding me once again of that night in the park. He sported stud earrings in his nose and ear and I glimpsed faded tattoos on his bony arms. His complexion was greyish and acne ridden. He wasn't particularly ugly, but he was someone you'd avoid standing next to at the bus stop. I seem to recall that girls thought he was good looking when he was younger but he has changed dramatically since then.

I must have taken my gaze away from Sean for a brief moment because the next thing I know I sense his presence beside me. The stink of stale cigarettes gives him away, and I recoil, spilling chocolate-coloured coffee — the same colour as Dino's eyes — everywhere. When I look up, Sean is staring at me, one eye on the spillage, the other on my spoon, which is spinning around in my cup quicker than a washing machine on a fast spin thanks to my trembling fingers. His being so close to me causes me to panic. *Am I safe? Does he mean to hurt me again?*

'Excuse me. It's my first day and I'm new here . . .' He pauses as if expecting me to acknowledge him in some way but that is never going to happen.

'And I'm dying for a fag,' he says, dangling an emaciated rollup in his fingers. 'Could you point me in the direction of the smoking area?'

I'm incapable of doing anything except stare wide-eyed at him. The shock of his approaching me has thrown me off my stride. I'm unable to formulate a response, so without saying anything I point to the fire door which leads to the smoking area. It's now his turn to widen his eyes. He's staring at me as if I'm an idiot. *Special needs*, he'll be thinking, but his glance is kind. He then grins, exposing two black gaps in the centre of his top row of teeth. I wish I'd have been the one to knock out his missing teeth.

'Thanks,' he appears grateful, although all I've done is eyeball him and point rudely. I'm surprised by how humble he appears, as though he genuinely wants to fit in and be accepted by his new co-workers. But how can that be true of someone like him? The Sean I know is a criminal who preys on women and robs old ladies. A monster who rapes underage girls. But there's a fragility about him that I hadn't expected. After what he did to me, I'll be damned if I'll feel sorry for him. *You'll like it. All girls do.*

He nods and walks towards the fire entrance and my eyes rotate in a 360-degree turn to watch him. A slight limp is the first thing I notice and I wonder where his cocky strut has gone. I forget about my cup of coffee as soon as his scrawny stooping shoulders vanish around the corner and I immediately make a point of paying Terry in the people team a visit.

Because Terry can't stand my husband, don't ask me why, he's particularly nice to me. Not in a creepy sense, but I get that he'd do anything to spite Dino. I choose him over Helen because he's ruthless and capable of making swift decisions. I've seen him in action so I know exactly what he's capable of. Those who don't better watch out.

'That new guy, Sean,' I whisper, so he knows this is private and just between him and me.

'Hunter?' Terry questions.

'Some of the workers are asking how he managed to get a job here?'

'Why?' Terry instantly goes on the defensive.

'There's a rumour he's done time in prison,' I reply, ignoring his question and rolling my eyes as if this were all news to me.

'It's not like you to gossip, Tara,' Terry pulls a disappointed face.

'That's why they wanted me to come and speak to you. They said you'd be more inclined to believe me.'

Terry's cold blue eyes narrow, but I can tell he's taken my comment on board because it smacks of the truth. I am respected. And I don't gossip as a rule.

'He passed all the usual checks,' Terry tells me, guiltily, rustling papers on his desk as if dying to look into it further, but only after I've left the office. Nothing makes Terry happier than a sacking. The power fix will set him up for days, if not weeks. 'And it's all hearsay without evidence,' he continues pompously.

'I thought you might say that.' I shove my phone with Sean Hunter's search results into Terry's chubby face and watch his brows rise as high as a three-storey building.

'Anyone can lie on an application form,' Terry stutters, looking sheepishly around the office at his co-workers, as if afraid of being held personally accountable for this cock up. 'We don't have the time or resources to check everything.'

'Are we meant to take criminals, drug dealers and thieves at their word or should we be doing proper checks? I ask innocently, my head held to one side in what I hope is an engaging way. 'Who knows what our trade union rep will say when he finds out? Nobody is safe around this Hunter guy. He might rob our bags in the changing rooms to pay for his drugs.'

I knew that going public with this was the last thing the people team would want, so what I was doing amounted to blackmail but I would have done and said anything to get rid of Sean. He'd caused enough turmoil in my life and I wasn't going to allow him to spoil my peace at work as well. One of us had to go, and it wasn't going to be me.

This happened on Tuesday and on Wednesday Sean didn't show up for work — not that anybody but me noticed — so I had to assume he'd been let go of and that Terry had done his HR magic. You can always trust the people team to impose their will on the workforce. As a result, I would never have to see Sean's face again, which was something to be celebrated. Or at least that's how I felt at the time. Until I came across the article a few nights later in Dino's newspaper. What a shock that was. How could I have known that Sean would kill himself.

The revenge I'd dreamt of for years had finally been realised and my rapist was dead, but I couldn't be less happy about it. I've heard it said that karma is a bitch but I'd argue that karma is an abused woman. I'd robbed Sean of his last chance. His life. There's no point in crying over the fact that he'd done the same to me because it just didn't cut it anymore. Sean had lost his job because of me. This must have been the last straw for him. Other people have been hurt because of what I did. Now I must quit playing Tara the victim.

What about Sean's girlfriend and their six-month-old daughter? What of his son, Ryan? What was I meant to say to my boy if he came looking for us, only to be told his mum was responsible for his dad's death? On the other hand, how would I ever explain to him that he had been born as the result of a violent rape? No child wants to know that.

CHAPTER 33: DINO

They're sitting side by side at opposite ends of a pigeon shit-stained bench in Fletton Avenue Park that overlooks the older-style graves in the cemetery next door. A woman in a burqa supervises two small children on swings in the playground. The squeak of the metal chains is all Dino can hear because his papà hasn't said a word to him since they left the gym.

Dino had thought the worst when he first saw his papà but thankfully, he'd been lucid enough for Dino to wring it out of him that all was well at home before they drove here.

'Is Mamma okay? The kids?' Dino had demanded.

'She's in bed with a migraine brought on by stress because of you,' his papà had torn him off a strip. 'So, I walked around to your place to see Tara and the kids,' he'd added, his face lighting up. His papà had even chuckled at the false memory before returning to his usual harsh demeanour. 'I promised Fabio I would take him to the swings. Is he here?'

His papà's Alzheimer's is getting worse and he's clearly confused. That's why Dino had thought it best to bring him here, to the park, rather than straight home. If his mamma saw him like this, she'd insist on another visit to the doctor. Not that it would do him any good.

Dino shuffles his feet among a windswept pile of rotting leaves and rubs his arms. He has on a leather jacket and a scarf to keep out the cold but his papà is in a short sleeve shirt. On impulse, Dino removes his jacket and slips it around his papà's thin shoulders. Then he winds his knitted scarf, another so-called charity-purchased item, around the older man's neck.

His gesture causes his papà to stir at last. Dino watches his eyes widen with puzzlement as if he's not sure where he is and then he sighs deeply as if accepting his fate. His sagging shoulders, which cut Dino up no end, seem so frail all of a sudden. When did his papà get so old? Dino still thinks of him as being around forty and in his prime. A grafter. A good man. Sometimes angry. Often impulsive. But always dependable.

'I know what you did, Dino,' his papà says gently, his gaze fixed on the leaves.

'What did I do, Papà?' Dino asks just as gently.

'I'm not sure where I went wrong with you, but you were a bad son.' His papà shakes his head, as if at a bad memory that won't go away.

Dino's eyes immediately fill with tears but he tries not to get angry. It's the illness talking. He doesn't know what he's saying. Or does he? Dino has to know.

'What did I ever do that was so bad you couldn't forgive me?' He questions softly. Nothing too harsh, that would set his papà off.

'I followed you, son.'

His papà's gaze is now on Dino, but not in a critical way, which is what he'd grown accustomed to as a child, just as he'd come to assume that his mamma would always be there for him in the background. He couldn't have had two more dissimilar parents.

'One night,' his Papà continues, 'I wanted to know what you were up to, so, as I said, I followed you.'

Dino is surprised but unconcerned. He can't think of anything his papà could have seen that he wasn't previously aware of, but he has to ask, 'You mean when I was a kid?'

155

His papà nods and self-consciously blinks a tear away from his eye. 'I saw what you did, Dino. I watched you.' Then, unable to meet his son's gaze any longer, he rips his watery age-spotted eyes away and looks down at the limp grass and trodden-in leaves.

Dino stalls. He's shocked and has no idea what his papà is talking about. When it comes to his rebellious, weed-smoking, teenage years there are plenty of blank spaces in his head. Places he doesn't want to revisit. What could his papà have seen? Them drinking. Smoking. Fooling around with girls. Isn't that what most groups of lads get up to behind their parents' backs when they're growing up? Surely, his papà must know this. Or was it that they'd been disrespectful to their elders in this very park? It's possible he might have sworn at one of his papà's friends causing embarrassment. But that's not enough to hold a grudge against your son for the rest of his life . . .

Wait. He has it now. He recalls that one time when a girl he hardly knew gave him a blowjob behind one of the gravestones. They'd thought it was hilarious at the time but Dino shudders at the memory now. He'd be gutted if any of the local kids did that to Tara's grave. Is that what this is all about? If so, it feels weird and cringeworthy at the same time. The thought of his papà spying on him while he was being sucked off makes him feel ashamed.

'You know, Papà, that was a long time ago. And boys will be boys.' Dino goes easy on his papà even though his temper and sense of injustice is escalating. He keeps reminding himself that his papà is unwell. It's not his fault.

'I should have handed you into the police myself.' His papà plucks at Dino's vintage leather jacket, marking it.

'The police!' Dino is more confused than ever. Since when did getting a blowjob as a seventeen-year-old become a crime?

His papà heaves a regretful sigh. 'But your mamma would never have forgiven me if you'd ended up behind bars because of me. Besides, you are my only son and I love you, no matter what you might think.'

Can this be true? Dino can hardly believe it. He'd spent his entire adult life trying, and failing, to earn his papà's love, attention, and respect. Is he saying that it was there all along? Hidden in the cold introverted heart of a misunderstood man?

'You've never said so before, Papà, not once. Not ever.'

'Well, I'm saying it now,' his papà responds gruffly before pulling Dino into his arms.

Dino freezes, not knowing what to do, because this is unknown territory for him. But when he relaxes against his papà's unfamiliar body it feels natural to reciprocate by wrapping his arms around him. It's not long before he's sobbing like a child into his papà's loose-skinned neck.

CHAPTER 34: TARA

Brianna

It's pouring with rain and I'm sitting on a damp plastic chair in my faux fur-lined hooded purple jacket at the hand car wash on London Road, the one next to Kwik Fit and opposite KFC, watching a bunch of Polish men vacuum and polish my scruffy Ford Kuga. In hindsight, this wasn't such a clever idea because I'm sodden, but, because my seen-better-days car hasn't been washed in months, it's filthy and I'm ashamed to be seen in it.

There's that word again. *Shame.* Secrets breed shame faster than vermin and it's something that has been eating me up for months since Sean's death, but I'm trying to move forward because that's all I can do. Unlike Sean, I am alive and I have a family to raise and a husband to care for, so life has to go on. And life has a way of defining itself as a list of ordinary chores like grocery shopping, tick, housework, tick, piles of ironing, tick, and getting the car washed, tick.

It's a cold day and luckily for me I'd thought to put on my warmest coat and scarf, which Dino believes I got at one of the charity shops in town that I've never once set foot in. He'd be horrified to learn that I lied and that most, if not all, of our clothes, are brand new and come from shops like Next and M&S. Bought with Babbo's money. He slips me cash whenever he can but never under the watchful eye of anybody else, not even the kids, in case they accidentally gave him away. Dino and his mamma would be annoyed if they found out. Babbo has been so good to us and I wish I could tell Dino this, but I'm on strict orders not to do so.

It's not that my in-laws are loaded, but Babbo claims Dino's mamma has been frugal with money all their lives and that he now wants to spend some of it spoiling his daughter-in-law and grandchildren. According to him, he receives a generous pension from the London Brickyard Company, where he worked as a labourer in the late 1970s and early 1980s, after emigrating from Italy to the UK. Like most of their generation, they own their own home on Oakdale Avenue in Stanground and the mortgage is paid off. I know he says all of this to ease my guilt and I thank him for all he does for us by helping him with his English.

We've been meeting up for lessons most Saturday afternoons at the Coffee Hive in Fletton Avenue for almost a year now. As a result, his spoken and written English have improved no end. Dino, who isn't the most perceptive of sons, hasn't noticed, but his mamma has. She doesn't like it. It bothers her because up until now she's been the voice of the family wielding complete authority and control. I fear that's what she loves the most, even more than her grandchildren. I might be being unfair and cruel but I've never really taken to her and the feeling is mutual.

This car wash is the cheapest in town and they do a decent job but a tenner is still a lot of money for a job Dino could easily have done. I'd asked him several times but he kept forgetting. Babbo would have gladly done it for me if I had asked but he hasn't been quite himself lately and has even forgotten to meet me for coffee a couple of times, which is unlike him. Dino reckons his papà is becoming more and more forgetful and he has a point. If he was unwell, I didn't want to trouble him or make Dino's mamma cross by giving him too much work to do when I'm perfectly capable of washing the car myself. Or, in my case, paying somebody else to do it.

Because on top of everything else, I have more than enough to do with the house, the kids, the job, and the bills. I love my husband but he isn't the provider I had hoped for. This is why his papà gives him such a hard time and why his mamma is always coming to his rescue. It's not that I blame Dino, because he's one of the nicest, most generous people I've ever met and is perfect just the way he is, but — and there's always a but isn't there — he's had several different jobs in the last ten years, and there have been periods when he's been out of work for months at a time, which has meant we've had to survive on my wages alone.

There are worse things than being poor, so I try to be grateful for what I do have: counting my blessings because Dino is a great dad and a fantastic husband and, thankfully, he seems settled at Nene Organic Vegetables. Of course, I'd helped get him the job, and warned him that he'd better not fuck up this time, no matter what, otherwise it would look bad on me. So far, touch wood, it's worked out and I'm pleased for him.

The women at work are jealous of me for good reason because not only is my husband gorgeous but he's also loving and kind, treating me like the princess that I am not. But he's next to useless when it comes to helping with the kids and the housework so, like the good wife I am, I urge him to go to the gym instead, where his mistakes don't matter. If I left my children to Dino, they would not be fed, washed, or put to bed and would stay up all night watching child-inappropriate TV. When he *is* present, he brings magic to all our lives. He just doesn't have staying power. I admire his optimism that everything will turn out wonderful in the end and that one day we'll have a big fancy house of our own and live like millionaires but our reality is far from that.

A dreamer, Babbo calls him, unfairly, I think, whereas he sees me as the doer. He has no idea that I am the biggest dreamer of all. Or that I spend too much of my time thinking about the long-lost son I gave up rather than the children I do have.

The workers are waving me over which means my car is ready and I'm about to dash across the forecourt and hand over my tenner to the guy in the high-vis vest when a smart grey freshly washed and valeted Volvo appears out of nowhere to cut me off. The driver, who doesn't even acknowledge me, then dares to hoot his horn as if the near miss was my fault. *How rude*, I think, wondering if I should go over and give him a piece of my mind. I'm too late, the car is already pulling onto London Road. But it isn't too late for me to notice, and instantly recognise, the woman in the passenger seat.

Brianna.

CHAPTER 35: DINO

Dino opens the front door to find two strangers on his doorstep. A man and a woman, both dressed unflatteringly and wearing chunky black boots. The woman wears her mousey brown hair in a severe bun and holds a small black book in her palms, open to a specific page. The man holds a plain black umbrella over her head because it's bucketing it down.

'Good morning,' the woman says, dodging a puddle that has formed on the path.

'Well, it's definitely morning,' Dino mutters.

Eyes heavy from sleep, or lack of it, Dino peers out at the gloomy black clouds and lashings of rain. Looking up, he notices where the large puddle is coming from; a leaking downpipe that he'd meant to fix last week but hadn't gotten around to.

'We're sorry for interrupting you so early.'

'What time is it?' Dino cuts in, worried that it's later than he thinks and that he's supposed to be somewhere.

Was he meant to be picking the kids up from his parents? He doesn't think the children are at home because the house remained quiet when he awoke to the persistent knocking on the door, but he could be wrong. He honestly has no idea what day of the week it is. The only thing he is sure of is that he doesn't need to show up for work anymore.

'Just after eight,' the man says, glancing at his watch.

'That is early,' Dino rubs his stubbly chin. He's still in his PJs, which for him means a pair of crusty boxer shorts and a shrunken-in-the-wash T-shirt with tomato ketchup down it. He's unwashed and barefoot with exposed toenails that are in desperate need of cutting. Let's face it, he's a fucking disaster.

'How can I help you?' Dino asks, not smiling, because what's there to smile about?'

'We're here to tell you that God loves you and wants you to do something special with your life.' The woman announces in an animated hallelujah voice.

'I think you've got the wrong house,' Dino groans, berating himself for not immediately recognising the fact that they're Jehovah Witnesses.

'No,' the man disagrees meekly. 'We are here specifically for you. God sent us, after hearing of your plight.'

'Oh, he did, did he?' Dino is instinctively sceptical, but also curious.

'May we come in and talk to you about how God's kingdom can bring you peace.' The woman again, in the same passionate tone.

Dino wonders if he should invite them in. He could do with some spiritual guidance right now and promises of peace are tempting, but, he decides against it when he remembers the house is a shambles, with empty beer cans and leftover takeaway boxes strewn about the living room like guests who won't leave. Besides, his mamma would kill him. Knowing these "fake prophets", as she refers to them, were in the house would be enough for her to accuse him of converting to another faith, which would be a massive betrayal in her eyes and a major pain in the arse he doesn't need.

Then, he notices how the woman is looking at him, in an odd, almost pitying way and realises what a state he must look.

Worse than the living room! Things must be bad if religious doorknockers, who have a harder time than most, are feeling sorry for him.

'Another time,' Dino mutters, slightly closing the door, a signal for them to back off.

'But we have a secret that we want to let you in on right now, brother,' the man implores, as if he can't believe Dino is about to shut the door on him, despite the fact that it must happen frequently to him.

'I've just about had it up to here,' Dino raises a palm high above his head, 'with secrets. And I don't have a brother. I've heard they're shit.'

Dino slumps against the door as soon as it closes. *How could Tara lie to him?* Easily. It's something everyone does. Caroline Roberts. The Fountain brothers. What's worse is that it seems like every door is being closed on Dino. The investigation into Tara's death. The Grant woman's involvement. His job. The fabricated accusations of sexual assault against him.

The only good news he's had lately is that his papà loves him, but even that has come too late because he soon won't know who Dino is. His mamma told him only the other day that Papà asked her who the new people were next door when they'd had the same neighbours for seventeen years. These days he lives more in the past than the present and talks constantly of Tara as if she were still alive. When that happens, his mamma darts worried eyes at Dino, as though they're not supposed to mention his late wife. He's had words with her since, explaining that it's important that they do, for the kids' sake if nothing else.

'She'll always be their mother,' he'd told her, ignoring her wounded expression.

He hopes to be able to forgive Tara and love her again one day but that day is yet to come. As it is, he's not ready. And won't be until he finds out what happened to her and whoever is responsible for her death is punished. The only person who can help him figure it out is Banks.

CHAPTER 36: TARA

Holywell House

It's ten years since I last saw Brianna when she showed up at the hotel where my wedding reception was held. As soon as I recognised her, I knew there was no point in flagging down their car or making myself known to her, even if I could have done because she'd have ignored me like she had the last time. But that didn't stop me from following her. As soon as I realised who it was, I leapt in my car and trailed the Volvo all the way here to Holywell House on Cherry Orton Road. I'd always likened Brianna to a princess and I see she has the house to match.

My beat-up car is parked a few houses down out of sight. In Brianna's Disney-like world where every neighbour has a prestige BMW, Mercedes, or Alfa Romeo it stands out as an eyesore. I'm standing outside the gates looking in, feeling like I've been doing same with my life up until this point. Brianna is one of the missing pieces from my past, as is my son, and now that I've finally located her, it's as if I'm a step closer to Ryan.

This is what my life was meant to look like, I tell myself, gazing at the impressive three-storey building beyond the gates. A successful husband. A beautiful mansion. A child I wasn't made to give up. Brianna really does have it all and I hope it makes her happy. I'm glad that one of us has made it. If it couldn't be me, I'd want it to be her. And what of her daughter, Dana? Is she inside even now with Brianna and her husband? I'd love to see her. Meet her even.

She'd be eighteen now, like my Ryan. *Except he's not mine, is he?* Their joint birthdays were three weeks ago. I'd foolishly thought he might be in touch on that day or shortly after, and that he'd be eager to meet his biological mother. But the weeks came and went without anything happening.

On my son's eagerly anticipated coming-of-age birthday, I'd taken the day off work without telling Dino and spent it at home, because I was convinced there would be a knock at the door at some point and that when I opened it, Ryan would be standing on my doorstep. I suppose his being eighteen tipped me over the edge for a while because, in reality, it was far more likely he'd hate me for being the type of mother who gave her baby away. Or worst still, feel indifferent towards me.

Making up my mind that if I can't see my son the next best thing would be to see Dana, I try the gates but they won't budge. From my car, I'd watched at a distance as Brianna and her husband drove into their affluent driveway and my eyes shot out on stalks when I saw the electric gates opening for them. I figured they probably have cameras everywhere which means my entering their grounds for a snoop around is not a good idea. Not today anyway. The best thing for me to do is to come back another time when the husband is not around. Brianna is more likely to be at ease when he's not there and she might even admit to having lied before about not knowing me.

And if that doesn't work, I'll return the next day, and the next, until I eventually force Brianna to face me and own her truth. I'm desperate to find out why she's lying, or more accurately, what she's hiding. Why is she claiming that she doesn't have a daughter called Dana? Maybe something happened to her that Brianna is unable or willing to discuss? If this is the case, then she has all my sympathy but why lie about not knowing me as well. It doesn't make sense.

I can feel my old obsession with Brianna stirring within me and I warn myself not to let it take over my life, as it threatened to do after she betrayed me. The girl I knew back then was neither cruel nor a liar, far from it, nevertheless, through no fault of her own she may have become both. For some unknown reason she has denied ever having given birth to her baby and I feel protective of Dana whose life is being denied, possibly because I had no choice but to give mine up when I was just a teenager.

Can it be true that this woman who has everything that I don't, such as beauty, brains, an affluent lifestyle and a multi-million-pound property, lacks the one thing I have in abundance: healthy, happy, gorgeous children? Have our lives been so flipped that the girl who got to keep her baby is now childless, whereas I, the one who was forced to give up hers for adoption, have a family of my own?

If it were true that Brianna had somehow lost her baby all those years ago, perhaps due to natural causes or later as an older child, say to cancer or another similar childhood disease, that would be heartbreaking and I would grieve her loss, but I have my doubts.

My intuition tells me that Brianna is lying about Dana's whereabouts for a more sinister reason and I intend to find out what it is.

CHAPTER 37: DINO

When Dino was trying to figure out where Peterborough police were most likely to hang out for drinks after work, a gym buddy of his, who happened to be a retired police officer, gave him a heads up that this culture was dying out in the modern-day police force. But he nudged Dino in the direction of the Woodman on Thorpe Road anyway, saying, 'You might find a handful of five-O in there early on a Friday night if you're looking.'

Dino is looking. That isn't to say he isn't nervous about what he's doing because even if he is lucky enough to come across DI Banks on his first attempt, it's unlikely the detective will want to be seen with somebody who had recently been arrested for sexual assault. He might even be pissed off that Dino had gone in there looking for him. *Might as well find out*, Dino thinks, as he pushes open the pub door.

'Just don't tell anyone I sent you,' his mate had cautioned. Dino didn't need telling twice. Not when the mate in question was built like a wall of muscle and weighed sixteen stone.

It's surprisingly busy for six o'clock. And nicer than he expected. A bar with a glossy oak counter runs the length of the room. Sparkling glasses are lined up behind it. As is a bald barman with a friendly smile and bone-white teeth. There's a fire in the grate and a pair of silver grey dogs sit stiff tailed at the bar with their owner, eating crisps out of his hand. Couples huddle over tables in the dining area, chatting and stealing scraps from each other's plates. Dino's impressed with the place. He'd like to come here again. Bring his mamma and papà. The kids too. They could do with cheering up.

The food smells good too, so Dino grabs a menu from the bar, orders a coke and a packet of peanuts and takes them over to a soft corner seat by the window. He's decided to abstain from alcohol this evening as he could have a long wait on his hands. That's not the only reason. Just this morning he'd promised his mamma that he'd lay off the drink for a while and start looking for another job. So far, he's done nothing except mope about the house feeling sorry for himself. His mamma, meanwhile, has already started emailing him links to jobs in the *Peterborough Evening Telegraph* and printing out online job applications for him to find. He has another reason for not drinking tonight, the reasons keep stacking up, he wants to stay sharp in case he bumps into Banks. But he might as well eat while he's here. The fish and chips sound delicious. He'll put his order in soon.

Dino is tucked out of the way, but from where he's sitting, he can see both entrance doors, so nobody can enter or leave the pub without his knowledge. He awards himself points for choosing a surveillance point that would make any police officer, including Banks, proud. To blend in, as if he were one of the beer stains on the carpet, Dino pretends to swipe through his phone. When he next checks out the bar, he's relieved to see that nobody is paying him the slightest bit of attention. This means that if Banks does show up, he's less likely to notice Dino, who hopes to observe him first before approaching him. He wants to speak with him away from the police station, preferably after a drink or two, when he's more relaxed.

The background music — a mix of modern dance hits — isn't loud enough to drown out all of the typical pub sounds like laughter, the clinking of glasses, sport on a giant screen and the man with the dogs who insists on bringing up the subject of Donald Trump with the barman. Dino munches on peanuts while listening in on the debate, which quickly gets heated and political, and winces when an unhealed cut on his finger sinks into the salty nuts. He fidgets because he's bored and it doesn't take long for him to begin obsessing over the beer he can see being pulled at the bar. A cold Guinness with a lovely foamy top would go down well right now. He can almost taste it. Feel it slide down the back of his throat, chasing the salt.

Then Dino shrinks in his seat as DI Banks comes into the pub from the side entrance furthest away from him. He's accompanied by two other suited and booted men. Cops too, most probably. All three are tall, slender, and good looking. Regular adverts for Tinder dating. The kind women don't swipe by but actually read their profiles. DI Banks would have no trouble scoring with women, Dino concludes. Because of that, the guy goes up in his estimation. Dino has never been a player. He's too much of a romantic for that and prone to becoming smitten over a girl too soon but, all the same, he'd had his share of women back in the day.

Dino doesn't like to appear conceited, even though he suspects he is, but when he was younger, long before he married Tara, the girls couldn't get enough of him. He's always been a one-woman guy though and never understood why some of his mates cheated on their other halves. Mind you, some of the girls he'd hung out with during his cocky, Dino-the-stud days weren't the kind he'd take home to meet his mamma. They were slags. Not girlfriend material at all. Tara had told him off for calling girls names like that and he knew she was right but he still felt some of them deserved it . . .

Like the girl who gave him a blowjob in the graveyard next to the park. He can't remember her name now although she'd grown up only two streets away from him. But he can remember his papà's shocked, disappointed expression when he told Dino he'd followed him and then spied on him that night. Fuck. Didn't his papà realise what that kind of knowledge can do to a grown man? Dino feels shit about it. Talk about humiliating.

Dino doesn't like to dwell too much on how many boyfriends Tara might have had. Now that he knows she lied about being a virgin, which had been a huge blow to his male pride, he doesn't necessarily accept her claims that he was her first in every way, as she'd stated in her letter. Once a liar, always a liar. It strikes him then, like a gym weight falling on his big toe: he has no idea what sex her baby was. Does it matter? Not really. Even though it would have been a half-brother or sister to his own children. But if he'd been able to obtain Tara's medical records, he'd have felt like he'd accomplished something. If he's being honest, he's more interested in learning who her child's father was. But whenever he thinks about it, he gets depressed so it's best he doesn't dwell on it. That's what his mamma would advise him to do.

Throughout their marriage Tara had repeatedly accused him of being a "mamma's boy" but Dino refused to bite, instead reeling off names of famous and successful men who'd all been so-called "mamma's boys" — Elvis Presley, Dwayne "The Rock" Johnson and Justin Timberlake, to name a few. Tara would shake her head and glare at him as if he were insane, before calling him some other name, like "big baby", or "namby-pamby", to see if she could get a rise out of him. She never could. Dino could be stubborn, even pig-headed when he wanted to be. He wasn't always the pushover Tara took him for and he knew she respected him for it, even if she didn't say so. She had no idea she was more like his mamma than she realised. Of course, he'd never dare say such a thing. He'd have been lynched.

They were both strong women who liked to dominate and control. If there had ever been a fight between them, and by that he means a proper scrap, he believes his firework of a wife would have come out on top. Tara had set boundaries with his mamma that she objected strongly to and wasn't

afraid to say so, but Tara had stuck to them, never once budg-
ing an inch. She was much more resilient than Dino was and
he admired her for it but he also felt sorry for his poor mamma.

He loved them both but he knew it was his job as a
husband to side with his wife. Tara wouldn't have had it any
other way. So, like the weak husband and son he was, he'd let
his mamma believe that any unpopular decisions they made
as a couple came out of Tara's mouth. That didn't improve
his mamma's opinion of Tara, nor did it help the two women
unite. Dino knew it was cowardly of him but he just wanted
an easy life. That's all he's ever wanted if he's honest.

'Dino, my man,' said a familiar voice. 'What are you
doing here? You on a blind date?'

Dino jumps and looks up at DI Banks standing over
him. 'She'd have to be to go out with me,' he chuckles nervously, wondering how he'd let Banks creep up on him unnoticed like that. He'd been so wrapped up in his thoughts he'd
lost sight of why he was here. So much for being stealth-like.
He'd make a rubbish private investigator.

DI Banks laughs too loudly and for too long at Dino's
joke. He's already had too much to drink, Dino observes, and
it's not yet seven o'clock. They must have been to another
pub before this one. Perhaps they're on a pub crawl. Dino
remembers those days.

'Sorry, that was probably the wrong thing to say when
you've not long lost your wife,' Banks sobers up momentarily. 'What a wanker I am.'

This is a different Banks to the one Dino is used to. Less
sharp. More blokey. More open. More friendly. More . . .
everything. It must be the drink talking.

'Can I get you a drink?' Banks asks as if Dino is already
one of the guys.

Dino is sorely tempted to take him up on his offer, but
he remembers his promise to his mamma and shakes his
head. 'Nah, I've got to get back soon.'

'Go on. It's on me. Least I can do after all you've been
through.' Banks pauses to glance back at the bar where his

two mates are doing shots, laughing loudly, and shaking paws with the two grey dogs.

'Just one, then,' Dino caves, telling himself he'll stop drinking as of tomorrow.

'That's my man,' Banks slaps Dino's arm in a celebratory gesture. 'Just promise me one thing, Dino.'

'What's that?' Dino asks patiently, getting to his feet.

'No more jokes with the ladies. They only get you in trouble.'

'Not even banter?' Dino chips in surlily, which is lost on Banks because his face breaks into a comical grin.

'Not even banter.'

CHAPTER 38: TARA

Watching

I watch her all the time. I think about her all the time. But she doesn't know I exist. I've lost count of the number of times I've stood outside Holywell House hoping to catch a glimpse of Brianna or Dana. Normally, the grey Volvo with the personalised number plate is in the driveway but this afternoon it's missing. This makes me wonder if they've gone out somewhere as a couple, or as a family. It's Saturday afternoon. They could have gone shopping.

I'd like to bet Brianna shops at Waitrose. No Lidl or Aldi for her, which is where I spend half my time searching the aisles for bargains. The rest of my free time is spent here, outside the imposing metal gates in Cherry Orton Road, gazing in on Brianna's privileged world, when I should be concentrating on my own house and family. Poor Babbo has been stood up more times for coffee in the last month than he's had hot dinners. The good thing is he doesn't remember afterwards that I was meant to be meeting him, so he isn't any the wiser. The poor bugger. What he's going through, in terms of memory loss and confusion is awful and I do feel for him, but not enough to give up my Saturdays peering in at Brianna's life.

Dino's mamma has the kids most Saturdays, despite caring for them throughout the week after school. She'd have them all weekend every weekend if we let her, and even though I'm absent from the house for hours at a time, nobody thinks to ask me where I've been. To be fair, Dino has his own Saturday routine and this usually involves the gym and a few pints at the pub afterwards with his mates. It never occurs to him not to trust me so I simply tell him what I believe is necessary, like *I've been shopping in town again*, and nothing more.

If anyone were to put Dino on the spot and ask him outright if his wife ever lied to him, his answer would be an unequivocal *no*. This thought destroys me. I don't want to be a bad wife but Brianna is like a drug to me and I'm addicted to watching her house and waiting for her to make an appearance. I'd spend all day and night camped on her doorstep if I could, making me one fucked up human being. I glance down at my scuffed CAT boots and faded skinny jeans knowing I don't belong here — in the enviably exclusive Cherry Orton Road or in Brianna's life. But I can't help myself.

Holywell House is the last mansion in the lane and because it's the largest it's situated far enough back from Brianna's neighbours, that they don't notice the stranger in their midst—standing at the end of the street and staring in at its gates. Even if they did, I've already planned out what I will do. Pretend to be on the phone with someone, complaining about how I went to the wrong address and am now on my way back. If the Neighbourhood Watch committee questions me, I'll tell them I'm a replacement agency cleaner for Brianna and that the old one has gone off sick. In a high-end residential area like this where everyone has a housekeeper, gardener, and nanny, no one will challenge that.

I train my eyes on each of Brianna's windows, hoping for a glimpse of a face with long black hair. There are sixteen of them at the front of the property, yet I've never seen a single person in any of them. Not once in the four weeks I've been spying on the house. Sometimes, I imagine nobody lives here at all. Just Brianna's ghost . . .

So when the real Brianna finally appears, storming down the drive towards me, she takes me completely by surprise.

She's dressed entirely in cream with flashes of gold at her ears, neck, and wrists. Her oversized fur boots pad, rather than stomp, making her approach freakily silent. Her long black hair, blunt at the edges, swings with each stride and her nude pencilled-in mouth is set in a firm grimace. My heart stops as I see the way she is glaring at me, as if she could kill me.

'You! I warned you once before to stay away from me. Get away from my house.'

She's only a few steps away from me now, fiercely stabbing a manicured finger in my direction but I stand my ground, even though I tremble all the way down to my toes.

'I haven't waited this long to see you, Brianna, to walk away now.'

'I told you before, you crazy bitch, that my name isn't Brianna.'

We're standing face to face, inches apart and nose to nose. The only thing separating us is the metal bars of the electric gates. It's as if we are cellmates squaring up to each other in prison. She's taller and bigger boned than me, but I have truth on my side, so I reckon I could take her.

'You're a liar and I'm not going anywhere until you tell me the truth.'

Brianna's heavily lashed eyes widen in surprise and she bites down on her bottom lip in irritation, leaving a crease in her otherwise flawlessly sculptured mouth. Did she have me down as weak? Someone she could easily frighten or manipulate. But then it occurs to me that she's the one who is scared. Terrified even. But of what? Me?

'What are you afraid of, Brianna?' I soften my voice. 'Why won't you talk to me?

'I'm not afraid of anything,' Brianna juts out her chin. 'Least of all a little thing like you.'

176

'You don't scare me and you're not going to get rid of me either. I'll stay here for as long as it takes. I'll come back every day if I have to. And if you won't talk to me, I'll speak to your husband instead.' I cross my arms, steely in my resolve. 'Is that what you want?'

I'm shocked when Brianna punches the wall, worried she might have broken her fingers or bruised her knuckles, but then I realise she must have hit a button on the wall next to the gate which has deactivated the smaller pedestrian side gate.

'Get inside before you're seen,' she hisses, as the gate opens.

CHAPTER 39: DINO

Four pints and six shots later, Dino stubs out his cigarette in an overflowing ashtray on a table outside and, dodging the sudden downpour of rain, heads back inside the pub where it's warm and welcoming. He's not exactly sober, but he's also not drunk. What he is, is shattered. It's gone ten o'clock and, like an old man, he's ready for bed. Shivering with cold, and feeling damp around his neck and shoulders, he approaches the bar, blowing on his hands to warm them up, and is surprised to find DI Banks alone. The other two coppers must have hit the road, leaving by the other door, when Dino nipped outside for a smoke.

'Good riddance,' Dino mumbles to himself as he slides onto the stool next to Banks. If he were being honest, he'd felt intimidated by them. They'd looked him up and down like he was something on the bottom of their fancy designer brogues and made it clear they didn't want him hanging around with them. They didn't think he was good enough.

Tossers. Who did they think they were?

'So, you're the guy whose wife got killed in the hit and run?' The one with shiny shoes had asked in the same casual manner that Dino would ask a stranger for directions.

Dino's eyes furrowed at the man's tone but he nodded anyway because he didn't want to piss Banks off by being arsy with his mates.

'Didn't you get arrested once for stealing a car?' Shiny shoes had frowned into his Jagermeister, alerting Dino to the fact that Banks must have run a full police report on him when he was accused of sexual assault.

'You sound like my dad,' Dino had sniggered but not as loudly as Banks, who had clapped Dino on the shoulder as if he'd come out with something truly hilarious and ended up spilling beer down himself. Everyone but Banks noticed yet nobody said a word. Dino guessed by this that Banks was the higher-ranking policeman of the three. The other guy, who was missing a tip from one ear, making him appear very Spock-like, never said a word to Dino all night. Just stood there giving him daggers.

Despite being pissed off by the other two's attitude towards him, Dino could not have wished for a better outcome when he entered the pub. Not only had he run into Banks on his first attempt but the guy was more than friendly outside of work, thanks to a few drinks which had warmed him up beforehand. Now that Dino has Banks to himself, he'll be able to quiz him about Tara's case. Find out if the Grant woman, *bitch*, can drive. But the detective, who started drinking much earlier in the evening than Dino, is by now pissed as a fart. Dino's not sure if he's capable of talking any sense at all. Still, it's worth a shot.

'Dino, join me for one last shot.' DI Banks lifts his sagging head out of his empty glass and slides weary, bloodshot eyes in Dino's direction.

'You've been saying it's the last one all night.' Dino cracks a grin and shakes his head in pretend admiration.

'Two more shots, barman.' Banks orders amicably.

'A half a lager for me.' Dino chips in, not wanting any more of the hard stuff to muddle his thoughts. He never did get around to ordering fish and chips which means he's drinking on an empty stomach and he wants to be able to interrogate Banks with a clear head so he'll remember their conversation in the cold light of day.

'Don't be a pussy. We're doing shots,' Banks insists, flashing his Apple watch at the card reader the barman is holding out for him. 'On me.'

Dino groans loudly, for Banks's benefit, and lets out a long sigh. He's on a hiding to nothing. Banks simply will not take no for an answer. He reminds Dino of someone. *Himself*, he realises with sudden insight. Dino can also be tenacious when it comes to getting what he wants. He has more in common with the detective than he thought.

'I may not be able to get you your job back, but the least I can do is buy you a drink,' Banks slurs.

'You heard about that?' Dino grimaces. His shame and pain still very acute.

'I make it my business to know everything about you.' Banks screws up his face, hamster-like.

Dino doesn't knock his shot back as Banks does. He takes his time and sips it. He's determined this will be his last drink of the night. Otherwise, he's screwed.

'Is that why you ran a police report on me?'

'You're brighter than you look.' Banks observes dryly, appraising Dino in the way he does sometimes like he's searching for something. A missing clue. A character flaw. *Who knows?*

'I suppose you haven't heard any more about the hit and run driver?'

'Mate, I'm sorry.' Banks gives Dino a brotherly pat on the arm.

'I hope they burn in hell.' Dino's eyes blaze with flames but his anger is short lived. It dies down, just as the fire in the grate is about to go out. 'I felt like I owed it to Tara to make things right but I couldn't even do that,' Dino admits, overcome with emotion. It was the pat on the arm that did it.

'I know exactly how you feel,' Banks agrees, his eyes mysteriously going off someplace else for the count of three before returning. 'I promise you, if it's the last thing I do, we'll catch the fucker who left Tara for dead,' Banks grinds out, sounding like he means it.

'I don't suppose you know if Mrs Grant drives, do you?' Dino drops in ever so casually.

'Shit, man, we're not back to that, are we?'

Banks is not as inebriated as Dino imagined. He's no fool either. *Dammit.*

'I've told you already. They're good people. They're not the ones we're looking for. I guarantee it.' Banks pulls rank.

'You do?'

'Trust me on this, Dino.'

The alcohol must be making Dino soft because for now, he does believe Banks and he tells him so. Hell, he's even tempted to give him a manly hug but thinks better of it, just in time. That would be going a step too far.

'So where are you from, originally?' Dino changes the subject. A homage to Banks to demonstrate that he trusts him.

'Me?' Banks appears momentarily baffled, then proudly juts out his chin. 'I'm Peterborough born and bred.'

'No. Never. You're kidding me, right?'

'I grew up in Eye and attended Park Crescent Campus. How about you?'

'Lived in Stanground all my life. And I went to Stanground Academy.'

'You and I are probably around the same age,' Banks points out.

'I was under the impression you knew everything there was to know about me,' Dino grins.

'On paper,' Banks concedes bluntly. 'You want me to get my notebook out here?'

Dino backs down because it sounds like a half-threat. 'Thirty-five,' he tells him.

'Same.' Banks slams his empty glass down on the bar and gestures for the barman to fill it. Dino swiftly raises his glass to indicate to the barman that it's full. Fortunately, Banks doesn't notice or Dino would be forced to knock back another. *Phew.* Dino must be getting old. He can't drink like he used to and he definitely can't keep up with his new drinking buddy.

'We're practically brothers,' Dino chuckles, almost wishing it were true. He'd have given anything to have had a sibling when he was little. Somebody to show him the way. An older, wiser brother who would have taken away some of his papà's intense scrutiny from him.

He's still reeling from the notion that his papà witnessed him being given a blow job. The thought makes him feel dirty. It's not only twisted and sick, but it also feels abusive. If he's having difficulty coming to terms with something as insignificant as his papà spying on him, like some dirty pervert, how the fuck was it for Tara with three brothers looking over her shoulder the whole time?

'So, tell me one thing, bro,' Banks tosses a cheeky grin at Dino and leans in closer. 'What really happened between you and Caroline Roberts, you old dog? I mean she was hot, right?'

When Dino feels his phone vibrate loudly in his pocket, sending shockwaves up his thigh, he is saved from answering. It's getting late. Nobody calls him at this hour of the night. He becomes even more panicked when he pulls out his phone and sees his mamma's number flash up on the screen.

'I've got to take this,' he says as he holds the phone to his ear.

'Dino. Where are you, son?' Her voice is filled with terror, as well as disbelief. Dino's heart rate spikes. *Don't let it be the children. God, please, let them be safe.*

'What is it, Mamma? What's wrong?'

'You need to come home.' On the other end of the phone, his mamma is sobbing. 'It's your papà.'

CHAPTER 40: TARA

A glossy world

At a large glossy kitchen island, I'm seated on a vintage retro stool with a plush velvet seat, staring at a walled display of prints of zebras, thoroughbred horses, and cows. The horse prints are yellow and gold, the zebras are orange, and the cows are red, which seems like an odd mix to me, but who am I to judge? Brianna has her back to me and is making coffee using one of those fancy contraptions that I'm sure cost more than my car.

Is it anger that makes Brianna's shoulders tremble, or is it fear? I'm not sure. I raise my eyes to stare at her as she slams the coffee cups on the island in front of me.

'Sit down, Brianna,' I tell her.

She obeys grudgingly, sliding gracefully onto a matching stool, but pulls a face. The kind that has the potential to kill. I'm struck once again by her beauty as I watch her curl her hands around a shiny orange mug. Everything about her and her house is perfect. Her hair, her satin blouse, her painted fingernails, the kitchen island and even the orange mug are all glossy. Like a glamorous celebrity article in an upmarket magazine.

'So, what exactly do you want to know?' Brianna sighs and slumps at the same time.

Can she have given up quite so easily, I ask myself? This doesn't seem like the girl I once knew. Or is she acting?

'Why you lied to me for starters,' I say, as I take a sip of my velvety coffee. It's delicious.

Brianna snorts. 'How long have you got?'

'Forever.' My eyes burn into hers.

I can tell my intensity makes her uneasy as she physically backs off from me. As usual, I'm too much too soon. She barely knows me but I feel as if I've known her my entire life. But what if I don't know her at all? Only the image I've created of her in my mind. For all I know, the real Brianna is a ruthless bitch who doesn't give a shit about anyone including her daughter.

'I'm sorry if I treated you badly at your wedding.'

'If?' I scoff, recollecting just how much of a bitch she had been, but her apology still takes me by surprise.

'I had to pretend I didn't know you. That we'd never met. I was terrified you'd blurt out something about the baby and me being an underage mum in front of everyone.'

'Ditto. I was terrified of the same thing.'

'Yet you came looking for me,' Brianna states simply.

'I couldn't not. I'd thought about you for years on and off. And when I saw you—'

'My husband, Edward, is not Dana's father,' Brianna interrupts as though it's vital that I know this. I'm not sure I do at this stage. We can talk about the paternity of her baby later. I'd rather hear about Brianna and her daughter first.

'I gathered that, he's far too old, but tell me first, is Dana all right?'

'Dana is more than all right.' Brianna smiles for the first time, making her appear even more beautiful, which I hadn't imagined was possible. 'She's at college studying art. Takes after her mum, that one.'

The penny drops as I watch Brianna's coffee-coloured eyes slide across to the paintings on the wall.

'Oh, my goodness. Did you do them? Are you an artist?'

'Yes, to both. I have my own online gallery, and believe it or not, it's me, not Edward, who makes the money around here.'

I understand why she needs to tell me this, it signifies that she has made it all by herself. I'd underestimated her. She did not marry into wealth as I wrongly assumed. I'm happy for her and jealous at the same time.

'Wow, Brianna. That's amazing. I always knew you were clever. And what about Dana? Does she live with you?'

'Yes, although we don't see as much of her as we'd like. You know how it is with teenagers,' Brianna replies conversationally, as if to a stranger at a supermarket checkout, but I sense a wariness in her eyes whenever I mention her daughter.

'I wouldn't know. I don't have a teenager at home,' I point out churlishly.

I can't see the rush of blood to Brianna's face but I can tell she's embarrassed, and rightly so. It was a stupid thing to say when she knows I had to give up my baby all those years ago.

'I'm sorry, Tara. I didn't mean anything by it. It was thoughtless of me.'

'You sound like the old Brianna now,' I reply, warming to her.

'I am the old Brianna, but in a new body,' she jokes.

'And what a body.' I pause to admire her all over again. 'I knew you'd grow up to be beautiful.'

'As are you, Tara. I wanted to tell you how amazing you looked on your wedding day, but I couldn't.'

'I remember thinking at the time that you seemed scared of your husband.'

'Of Edward?' Brianna's neatly threaded eyebrows rise, not producing a single crease on her smooth forehead. Botox, I'm guessing. 'He's a pussycat. Always has been. No, it wasn't him I was scared of.'

'Who then? Surely not me?' I reach out for Brianna's hand, hoping to erase the flash of terror that I see ignited in her eyes, but she pulls it away after a brief pause. A battle seems to be raging inside her head, judging by how her face crawls with uncertainty before finally hardening.

The awkwardness has returned and neither of us can think of anything to say without offending the other, so I take a look around the minimalistic room, admiring all its fancy designer gadgets, quickly concluding that this kitchen alone would buy us half a house in my neighbourhood, before saying, 'You seem to have made a great life for yourself.'

'Sometimes the life you're supposed to live isn't all it's cracked out to be.' Brianna averts her eyes and bites her lower lip.

'It looks pretty good to me,' I quip, casting my eyes over the kitchen again.

'Things aren't always what they seem, Tara.' Brianna sighs. 'You see, Edward thinks he's Dana's dad.'

'You mean, like a stepdad?'

'No, I mean like a real dad. Her biological father,' Brianna lowers her voice as if afraid of being overheard in her own spookily silent house.

'I don't understand why he'd think that. You were fifteen when you had Dana and he must be at least ten years older than you.'

'He's fifteen years older.' Brianna admits bluntly as if it's something she should be ashamed of.

'My point exactly. So, there's no way he could be—'

I catch her glancing away from me again, her eyes deliberately avoiding mine, and I know in that split second why she's ashamed and what she's struggling to tell me.

'But you were only fifteen at the time and he must have been . . . thirty.'

'Yes, but it wasn't like that. It isn't how it looks.'

'It's always how it looks, Brianna,' I react angrily.

'Edward is not a child molester.' Brianna's eyes blaze with indignation.

'He was a man and you were a child. Not only does that make him a paedophile in my book but also in the eyes of the law.'

'We were, and still are, in love.'

'That doesn't excuse what he did.' I raise my voice. *These men. How dare they do this to us? When will children ever be safe from the likes of her husband? Not to mention scumbags like Sean Hunter.*

When I see the fire in Brianna's eyes fade and her shoulders fall in defeat, I feel sad for her, but I can't help but be disappointed in her for defending her husband who'd had sex with her when she was still only a child. How can that be considered love? She must have been manipulated into thinking so. I hope I never meet this Edward Grant. There's no telling what I might say to him.

'Wait, but I thought you said he *wasn't* Dana's father,' I say, waving an imaginary white flag.

Brianna is on the brink of tears. 'He isn't. But I let him think he was.'

'There was someone else then? A boy your own age?' I ask hopefully.

Brianna violently shakes her head. A big no goes unsaid.

'I was raped.'

CHAPTER 41: DINO

Dino feels angry at himself for not having the willpower to give up alcohol, even for one night. If he'd stuck to his guns and refused DI Banks' offer of *just one drink*, and then *another*, and then *one more for the road*, he could have driven his car to fetch his papà, instead of having to call a taxi and being told there'd be a thirty-minute wait as it was Friday night and pub emptying time. He's also annoyed with his mamma for leaving it so late to call him.

'You should have called me as soon as you knew,' he'd fired at her as soon as he walked through the door of their ageing, old-fashioned brown-throughout house where he'd grown up, and which hadn't altered since the day he left to marry Tara. His former bedroom has the same curtains, duvet cover and wallpaper it had ten years ago. His mamma still has hopes of him returning home one day. She'd love nothing more than to have him and the kids living under her roof so she could take care of them.

'I didn't want to worry you, Dino.' She'd sobbed and buried her runny nose in a tea towel. Day or night his mamma always wears an apron and usually has a tea towel or a cotton hankie tucked in a pocket somewhere. She is a caricature of a 1950's housewife, but with attitude.

'Worry me? Jesus, Mamma, he's my papà, it's my job to be worried, especially when he's got Alzheimer's and has been spotted wandering about the city centre on his own at night, lost, for hours.'

'I kept hoping he'd be back any minute so I wouldn't have to tell you. Then the police called to say they'd picked him up, so I had no choice. I didn't want to burden you with it if I could help it. You've been through a lot lately, son.'

'As has papà.' Dino mumbles to himself, knowing full well that his mamma can still hear him. She may be older and frailer than she used to be but there's nothing wrong with her hearing. Shrugging off his jacket in a jerky, irritated manner, he's ready to march over to the door that leads into the hallway when she tugs at his arm.

'Where are you going, Dino?'

'To check on the kids and then I'm going to get papà.'

'Have you been drinking?' His mamma eyes him suspiciously.

'You know I have. You must be able to smell it on me.' Dino sighs impatiently.

'You said you wouldn't. You promised, Dino.'

Dino's mamma is scowling at him and his heart melts when he observes how fragile she looks. Her once plump attractive face has grown gaunt and her grey hair has badger-like white streaks running through it. She appears to have aged ten years in the last few months, and he blames himself for that. He should be looking after his parents, not the other way around, and he should never have let them take on the responsibility of caring for the kids. Or him. Tara would have accused him of being selfish and she'd be right.

'I think we have more important things to worry about right now.' Dino places a hand gently on her cheek, capturing her sunken cheekbone in his palm, and she crushes his fingers in hers, bringing them to her lips.

'I'm worried about your papà, Dino.'

'I know you are but you mustn't be. Things are going to be okay.' He tries to reassure her but his heart isn't in it. He's not convinced they *are* going to be okay. How could they be? What with Tara and now his papà.

'This isn't the first time he's got lost,' she blurts out.

'What do you mean, Mamma?' Dino's heart twists in his chest.

'It happened last week too. I know I should have told you—' she holds up a stalling hand, 'but, I didn't want to admit, even to myself, how bad things have got. He keeps saying he's going off to meet Tara for coffee and when I try to stop him, he barges past me. I thought he'd eventually find his way back like he did last time, but when he didn't . . .'

'I'm going to look after you and papà, no matter how bad things get and I promise I won't let you down again. Okay?'

She nods tearfully and Dino suspects that she doesn't entirely believe him. He doesn't blame her for being distrustful, but he means it this time and intends to prove it. It's time for him to step up as a son and a father.

'I love you, Mamma.' His eyes well up as he says this because he thinks the world of his mamma and is deeply grateful for all that she has done for him, but it has to stop. Then, just like his papà would have done, Dino walks abruptly away, masking his feelings. By mirroring his papà, Dino senses, on a level he's not used to, that he's finally growing into the man his papà wanted him to be. But is it too late?

* * *

Fabio has dozed off with one leg in and one leg out of the bed. He sleeps with his face down, lost in the pillow. Tara used to stress out every time she caught him like this, scared that he'd be suffocated to death, but they couldn't get him to break the habit.

An army of toy soldiers stands guard at his son's head, rifles raised, ready to shoot. Fabio spends all day every day wanting to kill things, which also used to concern Tara until it became evident that their boy had the softest of hearts since he would rescue all kinds of animals from harm, even spiders. Tara would typically have shown no mercy to any eight-legged creature who dared to venture into her domain until Fabio ordered that she stop hoovering them up or stomping on them until they were nothing more than stains on the floor.

Dino and Tara would spend hours watching their first-born sleeping. Neither of them said anything during those nightly vigils but their love for their son brought them closer together. It went unsaid that either one of them would have given up their lives, and each other's, to protect him.

Dino moves the plastic soldiers away from Fabio's cheek, so he doesn't scratch himself in the middle of the night. As Dino tucks him in, wrapping him up in an Action Man quilt cover, he notices that there is no whiff of ammonia or any sign of damp spots on the sheets tonight. Fabio has been wetting the bed, on and off, since losing his mum, which isn't surprising given how deeply her death has affected him. *A boy like that needs his dad around more*, Dino reminds himself.

He strokes his son's forehead and it feels warm to the touch. Dino hopes he's not coming down with anything. Heaving a sigh, because he feels such a bad dad for leaving, he moves on to his daughter's bed. Bella's emerald eyes, so like Tara's, are looking for him. She must have been patiently waiting for Dino to come over to her side of the room.

'Hey, angel.' Dino feels a familiar choking sensation in his throat, as if he's swallowed his tongue. This has been happening a lot lately whenever he looks at her.

'Hey, Papà.' She grins, showing off freckled cheeks, a mop of ginger hair and a wriggly raspberry tongue.

She smells like minty toothpaste, talcum powder and something else he's never been able to place. But whatever it is, her mum had it too. Tara used to comment that she and Bella had their own special scent and didn't need expensive perfume. It breaks Dino's heart to inhale it now. He feels closer to Tara than at any other time when he is alone with Bella.

'Still awake?' Dino asks.

Bella nods. 'I'll sleep now, Papà, now that you're here.'

'You will? How come?'

'Mummy always used to say we were safe from monsters when you were around.'

Dino can't handle this. His heart is overflowing. For Tara and his beautiful children, who deserve so much better than this. His bones are weary. His head pounds. Guilt and shame wash over him like a dirty flannel as he realises what a waste of space he's been, focusing on himself and his suffering when he should have been putting his family first.

Even when Tara was alive, he'd let her do the lion's share of raising their kids and keeping house. He now regrets it. What kind of man allows his wife to work her fingers to the bone like that?

Feeling like a gigantic failure, Dino bends to kiss his daughter goodnight, wishing he could reassure her that there weren't any monsters in the world. But that would be a lie.

CHAPTER 42: TARA

A shared secret

At the kitchen island, we perch on our stools staring into our cold coffees. Brianna sniffles into a tissue, leaving behind traces of neutral lip gloss. She has stopped wiping her tears away and instead lets them fall. They land, like puddles, on her cream satin blouse, darkening it to the colour of quicksand. Her eyes never leave me. I can tell she's been saving her story up for years and fears drowning in her own emotions if she doesn't unburden herself. I understand how this feels but I won't admit it. Not yet.

'Tell me more,' I say tightly, unsure whether I want to hear a blow-by-blow account of the sordid details because it can't be healthy for me. But I'm committed now. More's the pity. This isn't exactly turning out to be the reunion I had hoped for.

'I was out with a group of friends one night and I somehow got cut off from them. We were laughing and joking one minute and then I was alone the next. I stopped to tie the laces on my trainers and when I looked up, they'd moved on. It was dark and I couldn't hear them. I kept looking for them, using my phone as a flashlight, but I seemed to get further away. The next thing I knew, there was a boy. He must have followed me.'

The kitchen, with Brianna in it, drifts away until she appears to be at the opposite end of the room when she is still in fact seated in front of me. My insides churn. My skin burns with hatred. Fury replaces the blood in my veins causing my heart to spike. I'm tempted to make a bolt for it as the girl I once was would have done. Brianna has taken me back to that night eighteen years ago in an instant. I can feel hands tugging at my jeans. The cold air on my exposed skin. The smell of sweat. Sperm. Grass. Cigarettes. Alcohol. Weed. Dog piss.

'Where?' I muster the word from the depths of my being. 'Where did this happen?'

Brianna glances at me, puzzled, as if the crime scene is unimportant. Sensing she's going to ignore my question and continue to tell me about the attack, I pound my fist on the glossy island top making her jump.

'Where?' I demand.

'Ferry Meadows if you must know.' Brianna relays with some alarm. 'We used to hang out there sometimes . . .'

I only hear the first two words and none of what follows. I jerk to my feet and run my hands down my jeans as if trying to erase the touch of my rapist's hands. Sean Hunter's tobacco-stained fingers have left a permanent imprint on my body, like a disgusting watermark of ownership. I recall how his wet mouth sloshed against mine. His words. His laughter.

'Toilet?' I bark.

'Through the cloakroom on your right.' Brianna points to one of the doors going off the kitchen. She seems offended that I'm going to abandon her in the middle of her emotional outburst, but that's not my immediate concern. I need to vomit. As I dash from the room, I feel her eyes suspiciously burning into my back and I wonder if she thinks I might steal something of value as I pass through her immaculate, white-walled mansion.

* * *

194

I return to the kitchen a few minutes later, having thrown up a shot glass measure of bile and one solitary kernel of sweetcorn from last night's dinner, of which I only ate a few mouthfuls. As I shakily retake my seat at the island, Brianna's eyes are waiting for me, as I knew they would be, but she's not going to get an explanation from me any time soon. Once I've sat down, I notice that the coffee mugs have disappeared, replaced with two huge glasses of white wine. One for myself and one for Brianna.

'I don't drink,' I grumble, well aware of how rude I must appear.

'Fine,' she snaps, snatching back the glass and moving it over to her side of the island. Holding my gaze, she rebelliously takes one long gulp from the glass that had been meant for me and another from her own.

'It's the middle of the morning,' I remind her disapprovingly.

'It's the middle of the night somewhere in the world,' Brianna quips childishly.

'Go on. Tell me the rest,' I instruct her, crossing my arms across my small chest, adding an extra layer of protection to my shattered heart. But first, Brianna downs another large mouthful of wine. I suspect it's a tongue loosener. Despite her anxiety, she remains perfectly poised, sitting straight-backed on the stool, chest proud as if she were a model on a photo shoot. I wonder what she'd make of my impoverished, sometimes-foodbank-fed family who slurp, kick each other beneath the table, spill drinks and talk with their mouths full. Dinner at our house can be messy.

Brianna makes me feel inadequate without even meaning to. She isn't good for my self-esteem. 'Well?' I prompt as if I haven't got all day.

'Well,' she repeats, as she pulls out a packet of cigarettes and lights one. I find I'm easily shocked. You'd think she'd want to take care of her beautiful, glossy skin. Everyone knows that smoking causes wrinkles and makes you look older. Even as I think this, an image of Sean Hunter's haggard, fag-smoking features flashes through my head to torment me.

'Aren't you going to tell me how bad they are for me?' Brianna wants to know, but there's a smirk at the corner of her mouth that tells me she doesn't give a flying fuck what I think.

'I never had you down as a goody two shoes,' she adds dryly, inhaling deeply on her cigarette.

Since she knows I'm less than perfect, having gotten myself pregnant at fifteen, even if she doesn't yet know the circumstances around how it happened, I choose not to respond to her taunt.

'What were you doing in the park that night?' I ask instead. 'I'm curious.'

The truth is I'm more than curious. Everyone knew the park was frequented by vandals and druggies and wasn't considered safe at night. I had a reason to be there on the night I was attacked since I was one of the bad and broken kids, therefore I belonged. But Brianna couldn't have had any possible excuse to be there. She came from a good home. Her family loved her. She was protected in a way that I wasn't.

'Mum had just been diagnosed with cancer and everything was so depressing. Normally, our home would be filled with family and friends, music, and cooking smells so when she was at the hospital the house was unbearably quiet. Mum usually had a huge pot of Jamaican curry chicken on the stove and fed anybody who came in, hungry or not.' Brianna, lost in a world of memories, takes a moment to smile.

'She sounds amazing. I'd have loved a mum like that.'

'I was lucky,' Brianna admits.

'Is she still alive?' I ask gently.

'No,' Brianna answers, her head slicing down like a guillotine. 'She died when Dana was a year old.'

'I'm sorry.'

'She was the best mum and grandma, always cuddling us. Everyone adored her and she was a devout Christian as well. She'd have been ashamed of me had she known I was out drinking at the park that night, having got in with the wrong crowd, so when I found out I was pregnant I made out I'd slept with a boy on my school trip to France. Anything was better than the truth.'

'What about Edward? Did she know about him?

'God, no,' Brianna shakes her head. 'She'd have killed him. Literally. I was her only child. Her baby. And he'd have gone to prison.'

'How did you meet?' I ask grudgingly, knowing that I don't want to hear about him, *the predator*, but anything was preferable to having to confront the fact that she and I had most likely been attacked by the same person around the same time, in the same park. *What the fuck. You couldn't make up something like that. Two fifteen-year-old schoolgirls. Both raped. Both pregnant. We gave birth on the same day in the same hospital for Christ's sake. God really fucked up that day.*

'I was never interested in teenage boys. They all seemed juvenile, rude, and disrespectful. From an incredibly young age, I was attracted to older men and knew what I wanted. Someone who would respect me.'

I don't respond with the obvious sarcastic comment, *since when did respect equate to sexual abuse of an underage child*, because that is what it was, whether or not it was consensual. Instead, I pretend to be super interested in a man who deserves to have his balls cut off.

'Every day on my way home from school he would cycle past me.'

I groan at the prospect of her being stalked and groomed by a paedophile while wearing her school uniform. I'm sure he couldn't keep his pervy eyes off her. I say nothing again but seethe silently.

'Then one day, these two lads followed me home and made sexual remarks to me. Horrible, nasty things that made me cry. It was so embarrassing. When Edward saw what they were up to he chased them away. We then sat for a minute or two on a bench talking. He was incredibly sweet and wouldn't leave me until he was sure I was okay.'

I'm sure he wouldn't, I think, shuffling in my seat and clutching my waist, anything to help me bite my tongue.

'He offered to take me home and explain to my mum what had happened but I wouldn't let him. After that, it became natural for us to stop and chat for a few minutes every day, and eventually, I began to go out of my way to look for him. He wasn't like anybody else I knew.'

Brianna's eyes have softened and become dreamy, making me want to shake her by the neck until they roll around in her head. *That's because he was a paedophile*, I want to scream at her.

'He was interested in art and history, as well as classical music and opera and it awoke something inside me. I'd never been introduced to art and culture before. I asked if I could go to his home one day to see his paintings. He was unsure at first but I convinced him to let me. I'm embarrassed to admit that I did all of the chasing. I'd already decided that I was going to marry this man and nothing was going to stop me.'

Now she sounds like the Brianna I remember, I become more interested and I lean in closer, propping my chin up with my hands.

'He had this really nice flat in the city centre, with a balcony overlooking the River Nene, where we could feed the swans. I couldn't stop staring at the Andy Warhol-style prints he had on the walls but it was him I was really obsessed with. And it was me who seduced him not the other way around. He wanted to wait until I was eighteen, saying we had all the time in the world for that sort of thing, but I wasn't having it. The rest as they say is history.' Brianna gulps uncomfortably, as though afraid of my response.

'How do you know he's not Dana's dad if you were sleeping with him around the time you were attacked?' I ask, not wanting to say the word *rape* aloud in case it triggers her.

'He knew how bad it would look if he got me pregnant so he was extra careful. The plan was that I would introduce him to my family when I turned eighteen. We agreed to knock a few years off his age and make out he was twenty-five

198

so it didn't sound like such a big age gap. And in the mean-time, we would keep our relationship a secret.' Brianna comes to a halt abruptly, and her hands fly to her stricken face, as if terrible memories were gouging out her eyes.

'But it didn't work out like that?' I suggest knowingly. I'm dreading hearing the harrowing details of her rape but I know it's unavoidable. Brianna has made up her mind to trust me and I cannot let her down.

'No,' she squeaks, her face peering out from under her hands, in a macabre game of hide and seek. 'My attacker must have followed me. Because one minute I was walking, trying to find my friends, and the next I was on the ground with a stranger on top of me, laughing as if we were just fooling around. Acting as if I wanted it as much as he did. And, Tara, do you know what he said to me?' She demands angrily, her eyes swirling around as much as the glass of wine in her hand.

'You'll like it. All girls do,' I finish for her, startling her.

CHAPTER 43: DINO

Dino's back at Thorpe Wood Police Station under the critical eye of its authoritative blue light. Except this time, he's not banged up in a windowless interview room being grilled by DI Banks. He's free to go whenever he wants.

It's pointless pretending he's not still bitter about Caroline Roberts's phoney sexual assault charges. Jesus. Imagine if the case had gone to court and he'd been found guilty. He'd have been labelled a monster. They wouldn't have allowed him to see his kids except under supervision. Fabio and Bella mean everything to Dino but he's only just starting to realise it. Has it really taken the loss of Tara to make him appreciate what he has?

It's almost midnight, and Dino is exhausted and hungover, but his mind is on high alert, in case God decides to throw another of life's challenges his way tonight. He feels like he's been tested to the limit over the last few months.

While he waits, his fingers drum impatiently on the enquiry desk. He's already read most of the signs on the wall, which promote diversity, anti-racism, advice on drugs, and a warning not to drink and drive. Dino can't see that without seeing red. The mist of it is never far away. He'd love to get his hands on the hit-and-run driver who killed his wife. *The cowardly bastard.* Rage might as well be Dino's middle name at the moment because it consumes him night and day. Fury at the police for not catching his wife's killer. Anger at the brothers for the way they treated their sister. And on a lesser scale, annoyance at losing his job and indignation at being accused of being a sex pest by a woman he'd considered a friend.

Dino agitatedly swipes a hand across his face which crawls with tomorrow morning's stubble. He believes that the world has gone mad. Here he is, jobless and broke, while a taxi that he can't afford is waiting outside so he can take his papà home — from the nick, of all places. From the enquiry desk he can hear the purring of its engine outside and imagines he can also see the taximeter flashing a piss-taking electronic red as it calculates the waiting time and converts it to pound signs.

'Sorry to keep you.'

The familiar accent causes Dino's head to bounce up exaggeratedly. As he stares at the close-to-retirement-age uniformed officer standing in front of him, Dino feels his anger slide away from him, as if he were shaking off no more than an averagely bad day.

'I'm here to collect my dad,' Dino says to the man he remembers from eighteen years ago. How could he forget the cop who saved him from being prosecuted for car theft because he was Italian, friendly with his papà and believed in second chances? Dino was still a teenager back then and it was his first offence, *as far as the police knew*, so it was likely he'd have gotten off with it anyway, but he still has a lot to thank this man for. He wonders if the officer remembers him as well but he's afraid to ask.

'He has—' Dino lowers his voice even though they are the only two people in the enquiry office, 'Alzheimer's, and I understand he was found wandering around lost.'

'As has my wife,' the officer's jowly face softens, 'so I know how it feels.'

'I just want to get him home in the warm where it's safe. Could you fetch him for me please?'

Dino can't face the thought of his papà cooped up in one of the dreary, windowless interview rooms with only a paper cup of cold tea to keep him company. What if they've put him in a cell while they waited for him to be picked up, thinking he'd be safer there? His papà would hate being confined behind bars, like a criminal. Dino has inherited his papà's claustrophobia and it brings him out in a cold sweat just thinking about it.

'I'm afraid it's not as simple as that, son,' sighs the police officer.

'Why not?' Dino is stumped.

'He wasn't lost exactly.'

'What do you mean? I understood he was picked up in a police car and brought to the station for his own safety after being found wandering the streets lost and confused.'

'You understood wrong. Your old man knew exactly where he was and what he was doing.'

'What *was* he doing?' Dino's starting to think that God isn't done with him yet. He feels like he should duck his head just in case.

'He was caught on CCTV trying to set fire to a building.'

'Jesus Christ! Where? No, that can't be right. My father wouldn't do such a thing. He's never been issued with so much as a parking fine, let alone done something like that. He just wouldn't.'

'I can show you the footage if you like,' the officer patiently offers.

'Go on then. But I'm sure there's been some sort of mistake.'

The police officer pulls his phone from his pocket and scrolls through it until he finds what he's looking for. Maximising the screen and turning it on its side, he holds it out for Dino to see.

It's his papà all right. Fucking hell. Crouched over furtively, as if trying to evade detection, he's setting fire to a substantial commercial building. Although the images are grimy, jerky, and grey, due to being taken at night, his papà, who is

202

spookily white eyed on camera, is caught swinging a fuel can in one hand as petrol spills out of its spout. Dino realises it's the same one he has at home for the lawnmower, the idiot. He'd know the rusty, battered old thing anywhere. When the flames start to dwindle, his papà flicks one lit match after another at them. Fortunately, the damage is minimal because it's raining hard. When his papà lifts his head to glare at a huge business sign dominating one side of a corrugated wall, Dino strains to see it too. The policeman helps him out by zooming in on it.

'Oh, my fucking God.' Dino gasps aloud, unable to peel his eyes away from the signage:

FOUNTAIN BROTHERS WAREHOUSING AND LOGISTICS.

CHAPTER 44: TARA

A confession

Brianna strikes a match and with trembling fingers lights a third cigarette. 'How in the world could you have known that?' she exclaims.

'Because we were raped by the same boy,' I inform her, glancing away from the incredulity in her eyes. She's right. I must sound bonkers.

'What? Do you mean you were raped as well? When? How old were you?' Brianna trips over her words, desperate to get them out.

'Slow down,' I tell her wearily. 'I was fifteen, the same age as you were and it happened in Ferry Meadows as well. It was just as you described.' I close my eyes, not wanting to go back there, to that night.

'Shit, Tara.'

'I know. It's fucking mental.'

'I wished I'd known,' she exhales cigarette smoke while wafting it away from my face. I want to tell her not to bother since I'm already dead inside but it would be unnecessarily dramatic. Not like me at all.

'What could you possibly have done? We were in the same boat. I'm guessing he's the father of your child?'

'Don't ever call him that,' she snaps. 'Edward is Dana's father in every sense of the word.'

I nod and smile sadly at her, indicating that I understand where she's coming from. I feel the same and would give anything for Ryan to have had a different father. I used to wish it often enough when I was pregnant with him, convincing myself that if that had been the case, I would have battled to keep him. But that wasn't strictly true. I would have kept my baby boy and loved him anyway had I been allowed to raise him.

'Did he impregnate you too?' she questions, carefully selecting her words and avoiding the term *father*.

'Sure did,' I answer casually, but I don't feel it.

'Was that the reason you didn't keep your baby?'

'No.' I won't go into any more depth than that because I've already dissected that subject to death in my head.

'Don't beat yourself up,' she says kindly, lightly touching my hand with her ringed fingers that sparkle all the colours of the rainbow under the kitchen spotlights, 'giving birth doesn't make you a mother, as you well know, and giving up a child for adoption doesn't make you less of one.'

'Thank you, Brianna,' I respond, feeling moved.

'So, our babies, Dana and Ryan—' Brianna's eyes bulge like marbles when she realises the magnitude of what she's about to say.

'Are half-siblings,' I finish for her.

'Fuck.' That is all she can think of to say.

'Did you see his face? The rapist? Did you recognise him?' I ask earnestly.

I don't ask her if she reported her attack to the police. We wouldn't be sitting here discussing it if that were the case. One of us would have been spared a violent rape if the other had gone to the police. I don't know which of us Sean raped first, or whether the attacks occurred days or weeks apart, but if either of us had been brave enough to tell someone about it, he'd have been behind bars and out of harm's way, keeping the other safe. One of our lives would have been very different.

'Just a glimpse. It was dark and I'd been drinking,' she admits slowly.

Victims of rapists always blame themselves no matter what. She'll have convinced herself, as I did, that she asked for it. It had something to do with what she'd said or done. Wearing too little clothes. Or in her case, it was because she'd been drinking. These thoughts are as sick and twisted as our attackers and they deserve burying for good, along with them.

'I know who he was,' I break my silence, desperate to get this off my chest.

'What?' She sits bolt upright and stubs out her cigarette. 'You can't do.'

'Why can't I?' I ask in some confusion but she doesn't answer, so I continue, 'his name is, or *was*, I should say, Sean Hunter and you'll be relieved to know he's dead.'

There is no reaction from her. Nothing. I half expected her to respond with a huge sigh of relief, but she's staring at me as if she's never seen me before. Like when we met at my wedding ten years ago.

'What are you doing, Tara?' she asks warily, rising to her feet and stepping away from me as if she can't stand to be near me. As if I'm suddenly a threat.

'What do you mean? I thought you'd be pleased to know who raped you and that he was dead.'

'Sean Hunter did not rape me,' she says flatly.

'He bloody well did!' I argue.

'That's not possible.'

'Why? Did you know him or something?'

She shakes her head at me as if at a ridiculous idea but her mouth tightens as if she's afraid of saying something she'll regret. There's something she's not telling me. It takes a liar to know one. She knew our rapist and was friends with him. Why else would she protect somebody like Hunter who was a scumbag?

'Are you protecting someone?' I ask quietly.

'Are you?' she counters.

'No.'

'You're lying,' she accuses.

'Lying? Why would I do that?' I'm on my feet now and I match her cold and detached attitude with burning anger.

'I'm not sure. That's what concerns me.'

'Well, if Sean Hunter didn't rape you, who the hell did?' I yell.

'That's none of your business,' she insists snottily.

'I disagree.'

'It doesn't matter. I'd like you to leave now.'

With that, she sways model-like over to the door that leads into the spacious hallway, which is bigger than the whole downstairs of my house. When I first entered her home, I was taken aback by the grand piano and the curved spiral staircase that seemed to go on for miles, climbing all three stories. But it was the elaborate chandelier that hung from the ceiling that took my breath away. Just as Brianna is doing now.

'You can't be serious. Why?' I stumble on both my words and my feet yet I trudge after her anyway. It's her house. It would be rude not to do as she asks. But I don't want to leave. I need to understand why she's reacting like this. Treating me like I'm her enemy all of a sudden. What's changed?

'I'm nobody's fool, Tara,' she sneers over her shoulder. 'I know what you're doing.'

'All I'm doing is being honest with you,' I protest, fighting back the tears because I don't want Brianna to see me crying. That'd be the final straw.

'And to think I was beginning to trust you.'

'You can trust me, Brianna.' I plead a touch too desperately. Then despite my promise to myself, I start crying.

We've arrived at the front door and she throws it open with no sign of thawing or changing her mind. I know it's over then. We're done.

'I told you this before, and I'll say it again now, but with a warning this time.' Her eyes blaze at me until I start to feel frightened. 'I don't know you. My name is not Brianna. I don't have a daughter called Dana. And you'll live to regret it if you ever come to my house or I ever clap eyes on you again.'

CHAPTER 45: DINO

They're seated in the rear seat of the taxi on their way home. On the radio *That's Life* by Frank Sinatra plays ironically. The driver is the type who prefers not to interact which suits Dino. Every so often, he checks out the taximeter, £15.03 and counting. They still have a ten-minute trip ahead of them and as yet his papà hasn't responded to any of Dino's questions.

He doesn't want to start a fight here, in front of the driver, but this can't wait until they get home. His mamma can't find out. It would kill her.

'You've got to promise me, Papà, that you won't do anything stupid like this again,' Dino says it quietly, but with a trace of menace.

Again, he receives no response and no promise to comply either. His papà remains uncommunicative and hunched in one corner.

'Well, can you at least agree not to mention this to Mamma? She would go mental.'

Like a sulking teenager, his papà grunts but refuses to make eye contact. Dino is reminded of the night his papà rescued him from the police station, back when he was a teenager, and bundled him into the car with a stern look, afterwards hitting him repeatedly around the head. How their roles are reversed. His papà is now the criminal. Dino would return the favour of a slap or two if he thought it would knock some sense into the stubborn old git.

'What on earth were you thinking, Papà?' Dino enquires more subtly.

'I couldn't let it go,' His papà mumbles without looking at Dino.

'What couldn't you let go?' Dino believes he already knows the answer to this question but he has to ask it anyway.

'It's not right. What they did to Tara. Making her give away her baby and doing her out of her inheritance.' With that his papà begins to sob loudly, prompting the driver to turn up the volume on the radio.

Dino's head slumps on his chest. This is the last thing he needs. His papà has always been strong. The quiet, unemotional type. He was a man you could count on. Who would never let you down. His papà did not cry. Never. Ever. Ever. It breaks Dino's heart to see him do so now. It also brings home to him the fact that he is now the head of the family. It's his turn to be the strong one. But can he ever be everything his papà was? Is he capable of inner strength and self-sacrifice? Dino's opinion of himself is worse than his papà's skewed assessment of him.

'I thought you wanted me to put that shit behind us.'

'Watch your language,' his papà says on autopilot.

The way his papà shrugged off Tara's allegations of emotional abuse and bullying had angered Dino at the time but now he understands that his papà doesn't always express how he really feels. He'd have acted that way to prevent Dino from doing something stupid that could have gotten him in a whole lot of trouble. And now it's his papà's turn. The police had advised Dino that Tara's brothers weren't going to press charges given the circumstances since there was minimal damage done. But if it should happen again — Jesus Christ it doesn't bear thinking about. The *what-ifs* keep coming.

What if his papà *does* do it again? What then? And what if his mamma finds out? She would worry herself into an early grave. His sense of responsibility for his family intensifies. What was he going to do with them? They couldn't keep an eye on his papà all the time. He could easily sneak out again. What if someone gets hurt the next time? And his mamma isn't coping. *Family life at its finest*, Dino observes bitterly.

'I began to think about what Tara wrote in the letter and the more I thought about it the more it made sense,' his papà reminisces aloud.

'I'm glad it made sense to one of us,' Dino grimaces, as though he's been kicked in the groin on the football pitch by one of his own team.

'I watched her over the years and how she was with her brothers.'

Dino is mute, unsure of what to say. Every single thing his papà says feels like a direct jab at him. He was Tara's husband. Her lover. Her best friend. Despite this, he had not seen any of what his papà had. Did that make him a bad husband? Lover? Best friend? You bet it did.

'She was like a scared kid around them. If anyone needed protecting it was your wife,' his papà accuses.

Dino, stunned, bites down on his lip and any retort. His feels his Adam's apple bounce nervously up and down and his eyes well up with tears that he can't bring himself to wipe away.

'You're right as always, Papà.' Dino's voice is not his own. It feels like it belongs to one of the bastards who hurt Tara. The brothers. Her mother, to some extent. Her killer. He's no better than they are. His papà certainly knows how to knock down his only son and make him feel like shit.

'I loved Tara. I looked out for her,' his papà admits as he searches his pocket for the cotton handkerchief that he knows his wife will have put there for him.

'I know you did, Papà.' Dino gently rests a hand on the back of his papà's loose-skinned, age-spotted hand, but is brushed off cruelly.

His papà darts him a look that is meant to make Dino burn in hell. 'One of us had to.'

CHAPTER 46: TARA

The detective

I found out something that changed everything when Brianna kicked me out of her home a month ago. She has a bigger secret than I do! Since then, I've been on a mission to figure out what she's not telling me. I know she's lying to protect someone. Sean Hunter, most likely. Did she end up having a relationship with Sean after he raped her when she was still seeing Edward? It's a possibility. She had already been in one abusive relationship with an adult male, so it wouldn't be too far-fetched to assume she could have become attached to another abuser.

Then I remind myself that Hunter is dead, so why would she continue to cover for him even if she had cheated on Edward with him? Knowing she might have had sex with that pig voluntarily makes me want to puke. Strangely, she and Edward haven't had any more children since Dana. I'm curious if he's sterile. That would explain a lot. I'm determined to solve the mystery because only then will I learn the truth about my attack.

I reject the nagging suspicion that Brianna made up the rape claim to keep Edward from being arrested for having sex with an underage girl and that she may be lying about him not being the father because her description of the attack was identical to mine. No. She was definitely raped. And it was done by the same boy who raped me. Those are the only two certainties.

The real mystery is why she didn't tell Edward about the rape, knowing he'd be supportive, instead of letting him believe the baby was his, which seems cruel to me. So my brain can only come up with one explanation: Brianna became involved with Sean Hunter after he raped her. Was he blackmailing her because he found out she was having sex with an older man? Edward could have gone to prison for that. Or was she a secret drug addict back then and Sean her supplier?

The theories are endless and I start to wonder whether I've missed my calling and should have been a ballsy female detective solving crimes and kicking ass on Peterborough's streets. But a smart detective doesn't jump to conclusions, and while I can't ignore Brianna's claim that Sean Hunter wasn't her rapist, if that were true it would also mean he hadn't raped me. There is no doubt in my mind whatsoever that we were raped by the same person. Both attacks were identical. He thought we were up for it as much as him. And I was certain it was Sean because my baby had the same intense eyes. I'd noticed the resemblance when I saw him in the canteen that day. Could I have been wrong about him all along? I hope to God not, because that would imply that I was guilty of ruining an innocent man's life.

But how can Brianna be certain Sean didn't rape her unless she knows more than she admits? She confessed to catching a glimpse of her attacker that night, which is more than I did, but could she have secretly identified him as well and kept quiet about it all these years? Why would she do such a thing? Did Brianna know who he was? Was that the problem? If what she alleges turns out to be true then Brianna knows who *was* responsible for both of our rapes and I'd like to know his identity. Name. Address. Date of birth. Everything. I'm entitled to the truth.

In the last week, I've returned to Brianna's house twice. It's become like a second home, albeit a hostile one, into which I'm not permitted to enter. My thoughts are scattered and I go there to escape, hoping to see her. I have a lot of unanswered questions that I suspect only she can answer. The confusion she has unleashed is causing havoc in the De Rosa household. I've been late for work three times in a row this week, earning myself a letter of concern, and I've picked fights with Dino over petty stuff causing him to stay longer at the gym and come home late.

If I'm being honest this suits me. The Brianna situation has made me anxious and unhappy and I've unfairly been taking my mood swings out on Dino. The atmosphere at home is affecting the kids too, especially Fabio, who responds by acting aggressively towards his sister. I need to get on top of this but I'm struggling to be the mum I used to be. The idea that Brianna could be protecting the man who raped me is bringing me down. I love my husband but, at the end of the day, he's still someone who enjoys frequent sex. He seems to want to be on my body all the time. He's frustrated because I won't let him near me in bed and it's turning him into a pest. Thank God for the gym, that's all I can say. He can sweat off his testosterone there.

I waited outside Holywell House's electric gates on both visits, wondering if Brianna was watching me as much as I was watching her. And I had my response when one of the CCTV cameras on the wall made a whirring noise and clunkily swung around in a half circle to track my movements. Because there was no Volvo in the driveway, I knew she was alone. I didn't mouth anything or raise my hand to greet her since I knew it would irritate her.

She knew I was there but refused to come out. She never called the cops, as far as I know, to report me for stalking her. This confirmed my suspicions. Brianna was hiding a secret she didn't want anyone, including her husband, to know about. Otherwise, she would have had me picked up and driven away in a marked police car without hesitation.

* * *

And now I'm at Thorpe Wood Police Station anyway, questioning whether it's too late to report my rape. They'd force Brianna to tell the truth. She'd have to reveal our attacker's identity then. I need confirmation that it was Sean because of what happened to him, and my part in it. How can I live with myself if I sent an innocent man to his grave? I might not have been directly responsible for his death but I played a big part in it. Losing that job had been the final straw for him. It occurs to me then that I might get laughed out of the station. Eighteen years is a long time to wait to report a crime. And what if they find out I got Sean sacked and it became public knowledge? What would my colleagues think of me then?

As I consider what the reaction would be to me going inside and reporting a crime carried out by a dead man almost two decades ago, I realise that the last time I stood outside this building was on the night of the attack, or more accurately the early hours of the morning following it.

As I did then, I stand at the bottom of the concrete steps staring up at the enquiry office doors trying to drum up the courage to go inside. Dino need never find out about my visit. I'd make it clear to the police that no one else must know. When I hear boisterous laughter, my gaze shifts to three men smoking outside. They're tall and attractive and each of them is dressed in a designer jacket and shiny shoes which scream plain clothes copper to me. They are the type of men I would avoid at all costs. They're also the type of men who would pass me up for not being obvious enough. Glamorous enough. Blonde enough. And for not having balloon-like breasts.

I'm slumped against one of the blue metal railings, my hands in my jeans pockets, judging their penis competition, which is evident to me as they each try to outdo the other, when one of them pulls an ape-like face and makes a gesture with his hands which makes my spine spike. I've seen it done before. He's drawing a pair of giant boobs.

'Oh man, she was so hot I practically walked out of the interview room on three legs,' I overhear him boast.

I rage as I watch them guffaw. *Men are dogs that need to be put down.* There's no way I'm going inside the station now. Not if it means encountering more of the same sexist cops. It's no surprise that women don't report sexual crimes as frequently as they occur. Not when chauvinists like this interrogate and then cross-examine them in court. How can I expect the police to treat me with respect if this is how they behave outside of work? It's disgusting really. If Fabio grew up to be disrespectful of women and acted like this, I'd kill him.

Just then, one of them glances over, sensing he is being watched, and we make eye contact. He frowns at first as if he's trying to identify me but then his face relaxes in what appears to be recognition and he offers me a twitch of a smile. Growing uncomfortable under his gaze, I decide to leave. I can come back another day if I change my mind, which isn't likely.

'Hey.'

Running steps and a voice behind me.

I swivel around, angry eyes and defensive shoulders at the ready, to confront the person who has crept up on me, which is the worst thing you can do to a woman who's been raped.

'Sorry, I didn't mean to scare you,' he claims, backing off, but only by a little.

'You didn't. You couldn't.' I'm brash. My days of being scared of men are over. I won't allow anyone to diminish me because I'm a woman.

'I can see that.' He gives an almost approving grin.

'What do you want?' I get to the point, not liking the way his police-blue eyes roam over my hair and freckles.

'I think I know you from somewhere.'

'That's not possible,' I tell him, thinking I sound just like Brianna.

'Why not?' He asks, seeming surprised. But at the same time, his cheek lifts into a lively smile.

Don't ask me why, but I have a feeling he's trying to charm me. Some men find a woman's anger to be an aphrodisiac. Men like that are dangerous.

'I have to go,' I say, half turning and half enjoying the sense of power it gives me to leave a man hanging, the way his type normally does to girls like me for not being tall enough, pretty enough, or feminine enough.

'Aren't you Tara Fountain?'

I swing around. Who is he? Not another blast from the past, surely . . .

'How do you know my name?' I demand.

'I remember you from when we were teenagers.'

He says it as though I should know who he is. That's how men like him, who are arrogant and self-important, think. I wonder if he's telling the truth or simply trying it on with me, as a way of showing off in front of his mates. I scour my memory for clues, for boys whose looks match the grown version standing in front of me but come up with zilch.

'I don't remember you.'

'I'm wounded,' he tells me, placing a playful hand on his heart as if I'd pierced it.

And he's scratching his brain, as I am, trying to recall something. This gives me a chance to observe him more closely. His hair is very black, yet not dyed and he has softly curved eyebrows, like a woman's, which undoubtedly make him appear more trustworthy than he deserves to be thought. His teeth are a bleachy-white, indicating that he's concerned with his appearance, which is another personality trait that turns me off. Memory is a funny thing yet no matter how hard I try to place him, he remains a stranger to me.

'I've got it. That's where I know you from.' He comes out with this as if it must be obvious to me too, and then he slaps his thigh. 'Ferry Meadows.'

CHAPTER 47: DINO

Dino can't believe how much his life has changed in the last eight months. If someone had told him immediately after Tara died that things would improve over time, he'd have wanted to deck them. But it turns out to be true. He's not saying it hasn't been difficult, and he's suffered a lot of set-backs and bad luck along the way, but he feels his worst days are behind him. He's keeping his fingers crossed.

Having persuaded his mamma to spend some of their life savings, which they had planned to leave Dino in their will, on appointing a private consultant for his papà, he is now receiving the specialist care he needs for his Alzheimer's disease. He's had brain scans, seen a neurologist, and been prescribed donepezil, the most effective treatment for suffer-ers. Unfortunately, there's no cure, but there has been some improvement to his papà's short- and long-term memory loss. He never forgets Tara no matter how confused he becomes. He can recall conversations with her from ten years ago. *His golden girl*, is how his papà refers to her, as if he were the wid-ower rather than his son, much to his mamma's annoyance.

But on the whole, his mamma seems happier. She adores having Dino and the kids around so often and is in her ele-ment caring for them. Although she doesn't say so, she's determined to find Dino an Italian Catholic wife the next time around and is constantly name-dropping. So far, there's been Angelina, Mia, Lucia, and Gabriella. It doesn't seem to matter how old, fat, or ugly they are as long as they are Catholic and attend church regularly. Dino has other ideas. He knows what he likes.

Losing his job at Nene Organic Vegetables turned out to be a blessing in disguise because, after a few attempts at starting dead-end driving jobs and hating them because they didn't fit in with the kid's school hours, he decided to start his own business. Tara's death-in-service payout had arrived by then totalling £50k — which was more than he was expecting due to an accumulation of overtime, so after repaying the £9k he owed his parents to cover her funeral, he decided to invest in his future and *It's Dino Time* window cleaning service was born.

Fabio came up with the name, saying that all the customers had to do when their windows needed washing was call him up and say, 'It's Dino time.' Dino had laughed at the suggestion but it had stuck with him. He can thank another family member, this time Bella, for designing the logo on his van — a cartoon drawing of Dino, grinning comically, and wearing a baseball hat with a "D" on it, giving the thumbs up with one hand and holding a telescopic squidgy pole in the other. He had to make the unpopular decision to let Tara's old Kuga run-around go when he purchased the new van. He now has his own website and over two hundred customers, resulting in a daily income of £100. Not bad for a company that has only been in operation for a short time, but Dino has even bigger plans for it.

Now that he's his own boss he can finally be a proper dad to his kids. His mamma was upset when he broke the news that he would be picking them up from school from now on and that they would not be going back to her house. But since she's realised how much she's needed at home and how exhausting small children can be, she's reverted nicely back into her doting nonna role, whereas Dino has become his children's primary carer.

He's loving his role as a full-time dad. This has taken him by surprise as it is far more rewarding than he could have imagined. He wishes he had insisted on being more involved with Fabio and Bella while they were younger and when Tara was still alive so he could have taken some of the responsibility from her. He's even learned to cook and can roll his own pasta, thanks to his mamma's patience as a teacher, but he sticks religiously to Tara's meal plan because the kids have come to expect it. Dino wisely chooses his battles with them.

Glancing at the clock on his computer screen he realises that it will soon be his favourite time of day when he picks his children up from school. First Bella, who attends pre-school, and then Fabio. He never takes the van, preferring to walk hand in hand with them so he can hear about their day without the distraction of driving.

For now, though, he has to concentrate on his accounts. Invoicing is the least pleasant aspect of being a sole trader. He was never good at maths. That was Tara's domain. If he allows himself to think about it, he realises how sad he is that she did not get to see him become somebody. She was always accusing him of not having any ambition. But not everything is about Tara anymore.

It's summer and extremely warm, which means he's already got a tan, since he spends his working days bare-chested outside, *a treat for the ladies,* and he's in great shape too, having finally quit the booze. Just the odd one socially is his new rule. No drinking to excess or drinking alone. Those days are well and truly gone. No more blackouts either or waking up in a heightened state of anxiety, worried about what he might have done the night before while drinking. As a result, he's much happier. And he's appreciative of the smaller things, like when his papà remembers his name, or when he sees Fabio helping his sister with something and, lastly, when his mamma can go off to one of her church meetings without having to worry about whether Dino will be okay.

He's still reminded of Tara whenever one of her favourite songs comes on the radio or if he passes a woman in the street wearing a fur-lined hooded jacket or CAT boots, but it no longer kills him. If she's not quite as dominant in his life as she used to be it's because time has been kind to him and he's also busy with the kids, the business, and his mamma and papà. Besides, his wife is never that far away. Little Bella is a carbon copy of her. She even has the same expressions. When she frowns at Dino, if he should ever dare to displease her, Tara comes alive on her face.

He now recognises that he wasn't the husband Tara deserved. Had he been she would have felt like she could have confided in him. Where Dino once blamed Tara for not telling him about the pregnancy he now blames himself. Self-reflection doesn't come naturally to Dino, but six weeks of intensive therapy has changed his world. He's embarrassed to recall how dismissive he was of his former employer's attempts to include him in discussions about his wellbeing. They called it reaching out. But it had the opposite effect on Dino, making him want to run. He'd often chastised his papà for being emotionally unavailable, but Dino never imagined he had some of the same traits.

He can now openly discuss subjects he once avoided and he's been given the skills to manage conflict without resorting to aggression. This is reflected in his healthier new outlook on life, making him future fit for quality parenting. He doesn't want history to repeat itself, which is why he's determined not to let Bella down, as her mother had been, when she becomes a young woman. He wants her to feel comfortable discussing anything with her papà, no matter how embarrassing. Periods. Sex. Boys. Babies, God forbid.

Dino isn't pretending that everything has been easy. He has to continually work at being a better version of himself, listening to and modifying his critical inner voice, replacing it with a more positive narrative. He's been encouraged to think of it as the child within. Being a grown man doesn't get rid of it either. He's found that out the hard way. Change is never easy. Didn't Albert Einstein once say, "The measure of intelligence is the ability to change," or something like that?

Therapy helped him understand that the overwhelming anger he was experiencing was not anger at all, but rather unresolved trauma. To help him recover he's had to forgive Tara and has even allowed himself to fall back in love with her, if only to say a proper goodbye. Every Sunday afternoon he takes the children to visit her grave. Bella insists on bringing shop-bought flowers despite Tara's dislike of them in general.

This reminds him not to forget to pick up a bunch of flowers for his date tonight. He hasn't told anyone about Claire yet, not even his mamma. He's worried people will say it's too soon. He fears they could be right. Claire is not Italian or Catholic, which is something he'll have to break to his mamma when the time's right. That's a long way off yet as this is only their first date but because they've Facetimed and chatted so much in the past few weeks, having met on the Plenty of Fish dating app, he feels like he knows her already.

She's never been married and has no children but he can tell by the way she talks about them that she'd be up for having some of her own. Dino couldn't be happier as he'd love more. Another two would be perfect. Claire is twenty-six, nine years younger than him, and works at a betting shop where men come onto her all the time. She's funny and smart, just like Tara, but without the potty mouth. To be fair to his late wife, she'd binned that side of her soon after having the kids, claiming she didn't want Fabio or Bella effing and blinding at school and her getting the blame for it.

It's not as if Dino's desperate to move anyone in or marry again but being at home with the kids most of the time makes him crave adult company and not of the parental kind. It's not even the lack of sex that's driving his need for a companion. He's lonely. Which is why he's feeling excited about meeting Claire in person. He wonders what he should wear tonight. His black jeans and white shirt? Or will that make him look like a waiter? Should he put on a tie? No. Not a good move. Much too formal. What about jeans and a T-shirt with a smart jacket over the top? Perfect.

When he recalls his and Tara's first date, which was a ride around the Speedway track on his motorbike, the smile slides off his face and he is overcome with guilt. Wasn't she meant to be his lifelong love? Hadn't he vowed to stay true to her for all eternity? He knows Tara wouldn't want him to be on his own forever but would she consider it a betrayal if he started dating someone now when she hasn't even been gone a year yet?

She'd want to be remembered and for her children to be raised in a way that she'd approve of, which is what Dino strives for every day, but she'd also want him to be happy. Wouldn't she? Or is he merely convincing himself of this for his own benefit? He had no idea what Tara wanted when she was alive, so how can he guess what she'd want for her family now?

CHAPTER 48: TARA

Christian

I want him to go away. To stop talking. Cease breathing. Would it be too much for him to just disappear back up the steps where he came from?

'The name's Christian,' he announces, oblivious to the fact that I'm trapped in time and unable to speak or move. 'Christian Banks.'

'I have to go,' I stammer, spinning around and marching away, terrified that he'll stop me, put his hands on me and say, *you'll like it, all girls do.* I don't glance over my shoulder until I reach the bottom of the next flight of steps. When I eventually peer back at him, he's standing at the top, staring down at me with a bewildered expression on his face. He reminds me of a little boy who has done something wrong and doesn't know how to fix it.

I think I've made it. That I've managed to escape him, when—

'Tara, wait up.'

And then I freeze.

'Please don't run away,' he jogs down the steps and comes to stand beside me, his sapphire eyes clashing with my emerald ones until I'm reminded of Brianna's rainbow-coloured rings. 'Anyone would think I'd done you a wrong in a previous life.'

I could slap him for saying that. Only my attacker knows how much I've been wronged in the past. Does he know something I don't? Does he really know me or is he saying that to lure me somewhere so he can hurt me? He could be a serial killer, and not a policeman, for all I know. I don't know anything about him. Only that he has a loan shark smile and is aware of how attractive he is and the effect he has on women, although it doesn't and never could work on me.

'Do you make it a habit to chase after women?' I demand.

'Only ones I know.' He obviously thinks this is a joke.

'You're persistent, I'll give you that.' I jut out my chin to prove how equally obstinate I can be.

'Thank you,' he play bows.

'It wasn't a compliment,' I cut him down, and I find I'm almost enjoying myself.

'Same old sense of humour, I see. It must be eighteen years since we last met, but I'd have known you anywhere. That red hair and those freckles.'

'I believe you have me mixed up with someone else.'

'There's only one Tara Fountain,' he objects good-naturedly.

'I've told you already that I don't know who you are.' God, I sound more like Brianna every moment.

'Sure, you do. A group of us used to hang out sometimes. You must remember.'

'We did?'

I screw up my eyes so I can think. He seems certain that he knows me but there is nothing familiar about him. I had no trouble recognising Brianna after eighteen years, so why can't I remember him?

'I was really shy back then,' he feigns modestly, 'hardly said a word.'

I'm about to reply with something sarcastic like, *you certainly don't have that problem now*, when something in my memory stirs, *hardly said a word*, and then it's screaming at me, warning me to run, to get away. Quick, before the past drags me back, with its rapist's hands, to that night—

Sean Hunter was one of three boys present in the park the night I was attacked. The other two never said a word to me. They barely looked my way. Could Christian be one of them? And if Brianna was right about Sean not being our rapist, could this man be our attacker instead? I know there must have been other boys in the park that night but I was followed and attacked minutes after walking away from Sean's gang. It had to be one of them.

Am I looking into the eyes of my rapist? I wonder.

'You do remember, I can tell. You had me worried there for a minute.'

'Christian, you say?' I manage to get out, even though my throat is as dry as the cardboard Peterborough's homeless sleep on in shop doorways.

'Seeing you brings back memories of the good old days. I shouldn't say this now I'm a police officer but I can still remember us getting up to all kinds of things we shouldn't.'

'Us?' I blurt out dumbfounded. But I really want to scream. *Prick. Dumb arsehole. Insensitive idiot. Knobhead.*

When I'm away from the house, Dino, and the kids I slip back into teenage-hoody-Tara. The potty-mouthed fifteen-year-old tragic girl of my past. The one this man claims to have known. Hung out with, even.

'Nothing too terrible,' he backtracks, sensing he's offended me.

I get the impression he wants to be thought of as a good guy. Everyone's hero. To go with his police badge. Yet I can see straight through him. Because I'm not stupid I don't fall for it.

He then lowers his voice as if confessing to a vulnerability he doesn't possess. 'A joint or two and a swig from a bottle, that's all.'

'I don't drink or smoke. I never have,' I point out bluntly.

'Everyone has a weakness, Tara. What's yours?' He chuckles. It's a surprisingly pleasant sound. I can imagine some women wanting to wake up to it. Not me though.

'Murder,' I say without a smile, thinking of my role in Sean Hunter's death, causing my stalker's grin to disappear. Then he's laughing again, as if everything I say is amusing. This causes me to groan aloud.

'Were you one of Sean Hunter's friends?'

'I wouldn't go that far.' He shrugs off the acquaintance as if it were nothing, as if I'm certain he does with women he's finished using. I'm not sure why I have such a negative opinion of him since I don't know him. But when it comes to men, I've learned to trust my instinct and I'm rarely wrong.

'Do you want to go for a drink?' he asks unexpectedly, his eyes flicking down to my mouth as if he were thinking of kissing it. He'd better not.

I scowl. 'It's the middle of the afternoon.'

'No better time. No queues at the bar.'

'I told you already, I don't drink.'

'A lemonade then,' he suggests amicably.

'I'm not a child,' I grumble.

'Jesus, Tara. You're hard work.' He runs his fingers, *no wedding ring I notice but that doesn't mean shit*, through his glossy black hair.

'I didn't know I was meant to be easy.'

'That's not what I meant.' His eyes sparkle with the promise of fun, the kind you have in a hotel room, and he breaks into an easy grin. It's then that I see the boy he was, although I still don't recognise the man.

I surprise him by grinning back. 'Okay.' I have to know more about this man.

'Okay what?' He appears baffled.

'Okay I'll go for a drink with you.'

CHAPTER 49: DINO

They meet in the city centre at the Turtle Bay restaurant known for its Jamaican food, vibrant colours, reggae music on repeat, Bob Marley canvases on the walls and the smell of jerk chicken and spices. Claire is just as pretty and sweet in person as she was over WhatsApp and Facetime and Dino is instantly smitten. She's as unlike Tara as he could've asked for. Blonde. Doll-like features. Perfect manners. Feminine. Taller. Heavier. She laughs a lot too, exposing teeth that aren't shy of being seen, and she maintains lots of eye contact with Dino, which he likes.

Dino ordered fried chicken and fries, not wanting any-thing too spicy in case he's in with a chance of a kiss this evening. It might feel right. It might not. Dino will wait and see what happens. He's in no rush. Claire is a vegetarian so she had the avocado and poached eggs on toast, making him try some when he admitted to never having had avocado before. He isn't a fan but doesn't let on. During their meal she matched him drink for drink, which is new to Dino, but neither drank to excess nor stressed about a refill when their glasses were empty, so that was a good sign.

Claire has a habit of running her hands through her hair and touching her face. He wonders if she does this on purpose to draw attention to her peaches and cream skin and curious blue eyes. They are an unusual colour. Faded denim. She has a mild Devon accent because she grew up there, moving to Peterborough with her parents when she was eleven and has two sisters but no brothers, which Dino is secretly pleased about. She's had two long-term relationships and was engaged once to a man called Vince, whom Dino dislikes already.

'So, Claire, what do you think of Turtle Bay?' Dino asks, splaying his hands as if he was the restaurant owner after a five-star review.

'I love it,' Claire gushes in a way Dino has quickly become used to. She is enthusiastic about almost everything. It's refreshing.

'How about you?'

Another thing he appreciates about Claire is that she always follows up with a question of her own which shows she's interested in him.

Dino chuckles. 'I like it better tonight than on my previous visits.'

'How come?' she asks like she's unaware he is flirting with her.

'Because you're in it, of course.'

'How many times have you been here?' She raises one teasing eyebrow.

'Not on dates, I'll have you know,' Dino protests playfully.

Claire smiles, satisfied, and then pulls out her phone, holding it in front of Dino's face, saying, 'My dog.'

'So, this is the famous Truman?'

'All forty kilos of him.'

Dino flinches, aware of the age difference for the first time. He thinks in pounds. She thinks in kilos. He wonders what else they'll have to negotiate.

'He's a white German Shepherd. I got him as a rescue dog.' Her face glows as she talks about her pet.

'I've always wanted a dog.'

'Really? You could come for a walk with us if you like. We go to Ferry Meadows most weekends.' Claire offers shyly.

'I'd like that, Claire,' he tells her.

'We could go tomorrow if you're free. It's my day off,' she ventures.

'I have the children tomorrow.'

'Oh.'

Dino feels her shrinking. She'll be wishing she hadn't asked now. Feeling embarrassed. Thinking it was too much too soon. He can't have that, so—

'Unless Truman can handle being chased around the park by a five- and three-year-old?'

Claire's eyes sparkle. 'Oh yes, he loves children. I have two nieces and he adores them.'

Dino reaches out for Claire's hand. She catches the movement out of the corner of her eye, interprets it quickly, seems to think about it for a nanosecond and then her hand naturally settles into his. There's no song and dance about it. No pretence. It feels like they're a couple already, which is just as well, because Dino has broken his promise to himself to take things slowly. He hadn't planned to introduce his children to her so soon, but it feels like the right thing to do. He wonders what his mamma will say when she finds out. People don't change deep down, he realises, despite all the therapy and hard work, he's still an impulsive romantic.

They've stopped talking and are staring into each other's eyes, playing face Cluedo, which amounts to a lot of guesswork going on between them, when Bob Marley's, *Could You Be Loved*, begins playing in the background.

'You do realise,' Dino breaks into a cheeky grin and leans in closer, 'that this is going to be our song from now on. We don't have a choice.'

Claire's instantaneous laughter is cut off by a voice Dino recognises.

'Sorry to interrupt.'

And when he glances up, to discover it's not the waiter with a dessert menu or someone bringing them another two Mojitos, but DI Banks, he feels a cocktail of blood and adrenaline rush to every part of his body.

'I drew the short straw, I'm afraid,' Banks apologises, seeming genuinely mortified to find himself here. He also notices their clasped hands on the table right away which causes Dino's face to burn. He's certain it must be bright red. Not a good look for a first date.

'What is it, Banks?' Dino bristles, keen to get rid of him so he can hit a button and reset his evening with Claire.

'Do you want to talk outside?' Banks enquires, darting a furtive glance at Claire, whose peachy complexion has paled to white.

'I've got nothing to hide, detective. There's nothing you can throw at me that the world can't know,' Dino boasts, not wanting to appear diminished in front of Claire. But has he spoken too soon? He doesn't like the way Banks is looking at him, as if observing him with pity. What has Dino done wrong this time? Surely not another bogus sexual assault complaint? That wouldn't go down too well on any date.

'Is it about Tara?' Dino suddenly exclaims. 'Have you found her killer?'

The very thought of his wife tricks Dino into believing he's still married. Feeling like he's been caught cheating on Tara, he drops Claire's hand as if it belonged to the devil.

'No, sorry, Dino. It's about another matter. I didn't mean to give you false hope.' Banks takes a long pause before returning his eyes to Claire. Dino recognises Banks's cautious expression.

'How about no hope?' Dino responds flatly, realising that his date with Claire is over before it ever began.

He thought he was getting better, but the return of Banks, who has no doubt brought more unwelcome news, has hurled him, kicking, and screaming, back to a place in his past where fear, anger and pain were his only company. Dino looks at the girl in front of him, the one he hoped would be his future companion and admits to himself that he isn't ready. Claire is aware of what happened to his wife but she doesn't need it shoved in her face. He cannot subject her to the ordeal of being with him. It wouldn't be right. Maybe she'll understand and maybe she won't.

'There's been a development,' Banks says, at last, realising that Dino isn't going to take this outside.

'I thought you said this wasn't about Tara's case.'

'It isn't,' Banks stresses. 'Edward Grant has gone missing.'

CHAPTER 50: TARA

The Woodman

I'm installed on a soft corner seat near the window, watching Christian talking to the bald barman while he pours our drinks. Judging by the banter going on between them, I'd say Christian is a regular. He was right about the pub being quiet at this time of the day though and he doesn't have to queue for our drinks, which is a shame because I would have liked to have observed him for a while longer, subtly of course. He pauses on his way back from the bar to allow an elderly gentleman to pass.

'After you, sir.' He drops his head respectfully as if at an old soldier but I notice he looks at me rather than the man as if he wants to demonstrate how considerate he is. He seems desperate to impress. I haven't yet figured out why unless it's to get me into bed. He'd be better off not wasting his time, because that's never going to happen. Christian returns to the table and places a tonic water with ice and lemon in front of me as well as what I suspect is a double gin and tonic for him. As he sits next to me our knees accidentally collide and it takes all my effort not to shift away.

'So, Tara, how come I never see you around town?' he inquires casually.

'More of a home person, I suppose.'

'You don't give much away,' he observes candidly, adding, 'Have you always been such a private person?'

I ignore him and take a sip of my drink, feeling rather spoilt to be sitting in a pub in the middle of the day. No kids or Dino to worry about. No more fretting over Brianna either while I'm trying to figure out if the man sitting next to me is the same boy who raped me all those years ago.

'You don't look like a Christian to me,' I observe bluntly.

Christian splutters into his drink, appearing to choke while laughing. 'Say what's on your mind, why don't you?'

I don't say what's on my mind since I'm thinking there is nothing remotely Jesus-like about him and there's no godliness behind his dark-blue, investigative eyes either. Instead, I just remark, 'Churchgoer my eye.'

Laughing good-naturedly, he leans back in his padded seat and appraises me with what seems to be open and honest eyes, but I'm not buying it. 'You have me all wrong, Tara.'

'Do I? That remains to be seen.'

'What name do you go by these days?'

'De Rosa,' I admit grudgingly, not wanting to share details of my private life with him.

'Unusual.'

'Not really. Wasn't Banks the surname of the children's dad in *Mary Poppins*?'

His eyes light up with interest. 'It was.'

'With a name like Christian Banks, your parents must have been hoping for something special when you were born.'

Have I gone too far? Maybe I'm being rude for the sake of it when he hasn't done anything to deserve it, except invite me out for a friendly drink.

'Ouch,' he replies, pulling a pained expression that doesn't diminish his good looks. He really is the stereotypical tall, dark, handsome stranger that drives some women crazy. I'm glad I'm not one of them.

'Did you hear about what happened to your friend, Sean?' I ask covertly as if it wasn't the main reason for my being here.

'As I said before, he wasn't really my friend. Just some-one I used to hang out with sometimes as a kid,' he responds a touch defensively. 'But yes, I did hear about it. Very sad.'

'Was it?' I surprise myself by asking aloud what I thought was a subconscious thought. 'I mean, wasn't he a druggie and a thief?'

'And more,' Christian says quietly, 'but he was also a really nice guy who'd been through an awful lot in life.'

'I doubt it,' I snort, unable to keep the scorn out of my voice.

'How come?'

'He hardly gave back to society, did he?' I'm not sure where I'm going with this as I know nothing of Hunter's private life and feel like I'm digging myself a grave-sized hole.

'Not true. He worked as a volunteer helping other drug addicts, kids mostly. That was after he'd kicked the habit of course.'

'I didn't know that,' I sigh despondently, not wanting to know that the man I helped send to his death might not have been my rapist after all and that he was also considered a saint.

'He was found in a bath of blood, apparently, after cut-ting his own wrists,' Christian informs me, this time with his policeman's professional tell-them-the-bad-news-in-per-son hat on.

An image of Sean's grey, haggard face tilted to one side facing a grubby tiled bathroom wall flashes through my mind. Unseeing dead eyes. A pallid, needle-holed, wasted body with faded, tattooed skin. The sound of warm blood dripping methodically into cooling bathwater. His final thoughts on his girlfriend and baby. Losing the job that was his last chance.

'What are you thinking about, Tara Fountain?'

I look up to see Christian staring at me. He is now openly flirting with me. The way he says my name has an effect on me I don't understand.

'It's De Rosa,' I insist, sliding my eyes away from him, feeling uncomfortable under his gaze. I sense that he's the type who is always on the lookout for an adrenaline rush. The kind you get from having sex with a stranger somewhere public. The dirtier the better. Before I can examine how that makes me feel, I sum him up in an instant. Married with kids, probably. Outwardly, the perfect husband and parent. Charming. Loving. Generous. A great son-in-law. But secretly goes his own way. Cheating on his wife as often as he can. No regrets and no remorse. I don't know if any of this is deserved or not, but I'd sooner he be a demon than not.

'How long have you been married?' he asks inquisitively. 'And don't say too long.'

'I wasn't going to,' I reply with raised hackles, before asking, 'Are you married?'

'Seven years. Two kids. A boy and a girl. You?'

'Snap.'

'Any pictures?'

I shake my head. There's no way I'd want his woman-ising gaze falling on Fabio's and Bella's angelic little faces. It doesn't stop him from pulling a photograph out of his wallet and dangling it under my nose.

'That's my beautiful wife.' He points to a sad looking but stunningly pretty woman with dark blonde hair but then moves on almost too quickly to his children. 'This is Nathan and Poppy. The pickled onions we call them.'

'Cute,' I comment, thinking his children look just like him. But just a bit too perfect for my liking with their matching all-white toothy smiles and glossy black hair. I imagine their house to be furnished in complementary monochrome too. Only the wife, with her tight mouth, thinning hair and fading looks, stands out as different.

'He's four.' Christian points to the boy who has the same eyes as him.

It slices through me then, like the cold serrated blade of the knife that had been held to Sean Hunter's wrists, that if Christian *is* my rapist, I could be looking at Ryan's half brother and sister. I'm about to lean in for a closer look at the boy when the photo is whipped away from under my nose.

'And she's five going on fifteen.'

He seems inordinately proud of his kids, just like any other doting father. Like Dino, really. *Dino. What would he think if he knew I was having a drink with a man in a pub in the middle of the day?*

'What we wouldn't give to be fifteen again, huh?' he reminisces.

'Not me.' I fix my burning gaze on him, wondering if he's trying to provoke me. I was raped when I was fifteen, and the only way he can know that is if he's the one who committed the crime. My attacker always thought I was as game as he was. Is that why Christian Banks is bringing it up now so we can talk about how much fun we had? It makes my blood boil.

He's good, I think, realising his talk of his wife and kids almost swayed my opinion of him. Very crafty, I'll give him that. Knowing this guy is much smarter than I originally thought him, I remind myself that I must always stay one step ahead.

'Did you used to know a girl called Brianna?' I blurt out.

'Brianna? Not sure I did.' He shakes his head, acting suddenly bored and uninterested in where this conversation is going. 'What did she look like?'

'You wouldn't forget her if you'd met her. She's gorgeous.'

'As are you, Tara. Everyone fancied you back in the day.'

'They did not,' I say, reddening.

'Me included.'

Sweat. Semen. Grass. Cigarettes. Alcohol. Weed. Dog piss. *You'll like it. All girls do.*

'I have to go. I shouldn't be here,' I frantically search for the nearest exit. Suddenly I can't breathe. My chest feels tight. I'd rather be anywhere but here but I also don't want to be anywhere else. Christian is awakening all kinds of bad and confusing thoughts in me. Guilt prods me into action and I scramble to my feet. But Christian, panicking at my reaction, stands up too, preventing me from leaving.

'You're not leaving already, are you?'

'If you don't move out of my way in the next five seconds, I'm going to knee you in the balls,' I bark out like an irate sergeant major.

His eyes become searchlights, dulled by confusion. 'You've got me all wrong, Tara. I'm a good guy. I wasn't coming on to you. I'm sorry if you thought that.'

'Five . . . four,' I begin the countdown, ignoring what appears to be a genuine response from him because I know it's a trick. A lie. Men like him can't be trusted. Correction. No man is to be trusted.

He moves. Not as fast as I'd like. He does, however, move. And I'm finally able to storm past him, heading towards the door and the clean air on the other side of it. His protests stab me in the back as I go.

'What sort of man do you take me for?'

CHAPTER 51: DINO

'What sort of man does that?' Dino complains from the back seat of Banks's black Audio.

'Are you really telling me you can't think of any reason why Edward Grant, the man you accused of having an affair with your wife, might have vanished into thin air after parking his car in your driveway?' DI Banks marvels.

'Maybe the multi-storey car park was full. Who knows? Am I being arrested again?' Dino responds tetchily, staring at the back of the detective's neck which has turned crimson.

'It's just an informal chat for now, Dino,' Banks exclaims, sounding unusually stressed.

'Yeah, I know your chats,' Dino grumbles, 'they usually take place in a locked interrogation room.'

'You've got to admit something doesn't add up. I mean, what was he doing at your house? Do you really have no idea?'

'I'd rather not say anything till we get to the station. That way, I'll only have to answer your questions once.' Dino curls forward, his head in his hands. It's as if a bomb has been detonated in his skull. He has no idea what he's being accused of exactly. Murder? Kidnap? He believed he'd seen the last of Thorpe Wood Police Station, and good riddance, but he was mistaken. Story of his life. He can't seem to move on no matter what he does. He thought he had it all figured out. The kids. His parents. The business. Claire. All of that changed the moment a stranger pulled into his driveway, left the engine running with the keys inside before disappearing, alerting the neighbours to the fact that something was wrong, who then contacted the police.

After paying the bill and saying goodbye to Claire at the restaurant, Dino had gone outside with Banks to discuss Edward Grant's disappearance. He didn't feel he was in a position to decline Banks's invitation to accompany him to the police station. He's still unsure whether it was a request or an order. He'll find out soon, no doubt. He's been told that Grant's wife and daughter are also at the station giving statements. Dino isn't looking forward to running into that stuck-up bitch again after the way she treated him.

Blurred images of Peterborough's streets flash by. An electrifying mix of red and blue illuminated bar signs, youths smoking in shop doorways, young girls with barely any clothes on falling drunkenly out of wine bars, and a homeless person pushing an old shopping trolley containing all their worldly goods. Black cabs scurry, like ants, along Bourges Boulevard, impatient to be somewhere. On his left, a fast train to London whizzes by.

'You okay in the back?' Banks asks.

Dino shifts his gaze away from the window and manages a sharp nod.

'Once I heard about Grant, I did a bit more digging, thinking you could have been right all along.'

'How do you mean?' Dino asks, puzzled.

'About his having an affair with Tara. And him keeping quiet about it.'

'But you said he wasn't even in the country at the time.' Dino's chest constricts at the prospect of having Tara's life and subsequent death investigated all over again. Not that the case has ever been closed.

'He wasn't. I double-checked. Then, I double-checked again and I couldn't find a shred of evidence to support your theory.'

'So why did he show up at my house then?' Dino asks, relieved, for once, that Banks had failed to pin anything on the Grants. He doesn't think he could handle having to go over the whole, was Tara cheating on him or wasn't she scenario again? He's not up to it.

'You tell me. The wife doesn't know why either.'

'He must have wanted to talk to me, but I wasn't there and so he left.' Dino contemplates aloud.

'Without his car?' Banks expresses doubt.

'Maybe he planned on coming back later.'

'He's been gone over four hours,' Banks replies.

'I thought you had to wait twenty-four hours before reporting a missing person to the police,' Dino observes, finding Banks' gaze waiting for him in the rearview mirror.

'That's a US detective series myth right there. We could hardly ignore the fact he left his car running in your driveway with the door open, and his wallet and phone on the dash.'

'When you put it like that . . . I feel like I should turn *myself* in.' Dino grunts, conscious that his stomach is churning nervously. 'It feels like someone's trying to stitch me up for something I didn't do. Has he done anything like this before?' Dino clenches his fists in his lap.

'According to the wife and daughter, nothing unusual had occurred to make him take off like that. He wasn't depressed. Or ill. His business was thriving. He didn't owe anyone any money. Life at home was good.'

When Dino thinks back to the night he'd gone to the Grants' property, intent on accessing their garage, and he'd peered in through the kitchen window, his first thought on seeing the family all together was that it had not been a happy home. They had been rowing with their daughter and even before that, when they were quietly having dinner together, the atmosphere between the couple had been tense.

He considers telling Banks this but realises he could be charged with trespassing and decides against it. It's none of his concern. He's long since given up on the idea that Tara was fooling around with Mrs Grant. He was going through a hard patch at the time, and he's embarrassed by some of the ridiculous conspiracy ideas he'd thrown at Banks about his wife's death. He's relieved when they pull into one of the police station's secured parking places because he just wants to get this over with so he can go home and close the curtains on the world. And Edward Grant's Volvo in the driveway if it hasn't already been towed away by then.

* * *

Dino runs into them as soon as he enters the police station. *Of course, he does, given his current run of luck.* Mother and daughter are sitting on grey plastic chairs in a brightly lit corridor to the right of the enquiry office. They look like they've been dragged out of bed half asleep. For once, they're not perfectly groomed and wearing designer clothes. Mrs Grant is in a velour lounge suit while the daughter wears jogging pants with unlaced expensive trainers. When they spot Dino, they both sit up straight. Head down, eyes averted, Dino follows Banks over to the enquiry desk, where he pauses to speak briefly to the desk sergeant, leaving Dino twiddling his thumbs.

'This way, Dino.' Banks places a guiding hand on Dino's shoulder and steers him towards Mrs Grant and her daughter.

'Where are we going?' Dino demands, coming to a screeching halt. He can't believe Banks is taking him over to Mrs Grant. No way . . .

'Relax, just down the corridor to one of the interview rooms. Don't worry, I'm not going to lock it.' Banks rustles a set of keys at Dino.

Dino feels Banks's calming touch on his shoulder again, as he's steered towards a grey-walled corridor. But first, they have to pass the Grants. As Dino approaches, one head bounces up, followed by another. He'd intended to stroll straight by them without glancing at them, but Mrs Grant's anger pierces him like a bullet in the side of the head. Her eyes burn his skin. After that, he has to look. They're both staring at him with wide eyes. Something about the girl's broken countenance and traumatised eyes penetrates Dino's heart, but Mrs Grant's ugly-for-once screwed-up face appears to want to reach inside Dino's chest and yank it out of him.

In the girl's eyes, he sees nothing but pain. Because he's experienced emotional trauma himself, he can recognise it in others. Although she comes across like a wounded animal, in need of help, he reminds himself that all women have claws. He's learned his lesson when it comes to the female of the species. There'll be no more going to the rescue of damsels in distress for him. God no. He's proved right when Mrs Grant leaps out of her seat . . .

'You!' she cries. 'This is all your fault.'

'Stop it, Mum.' The daughter tugs her back into her seat and, mirroring her mother, aims an equally furious stare towards Dino that catches him off guard. He's taken aback by it. Oh well, *like mother, like daughter*, he supposes. Banks does not pause or even look at the two women. He simply pushes Dino onward till they reach a metal door.

As Dino waits for him to unlock it, he wonders what Mrs Grant meant when she screamed, *this is all your fault*, at him. Is he missing something? Were she and Tara in a relationship after all? Was his hunch right all along? Had his insistence that Banks question the Grants finally paid off? Had the other duped husband discovered their affair and came knocking on Dino's door? To learn more.

Man, Dino is exhausted from attempting to solve the mystery of his wife's secretive past. When he thinks about it, it blows his mind. Tara was a normal, everyday woman, nothing special, *in the nicest possible way*. They, the De Rosas, were an ordinary family. Struggling along like everybody else. Yet extraordinary things had happened to them. When will it all end? Dino would give anything to know.

CHAPTER 52: TARA

Dana

I'd give anything to know what Brianna knows, which is why, after escaping Christian Banks, I rushed straight back to Holywell House, determined to see her this time, ignoring her threat that I'd live to regret it if she ever clapped eyes on me again. I had to ask her if she knew who he was. I couldn't help myself. Knowing he's a police officer might make it harder for us to report the crime, if it turns out he's our attacker, but it's not impossible. And if one of their own were being accused then the police would have to investigate the claim all the more thoroughly.

But, if she *can* identify him, will she back me up? Join me in doing what we should have done eighteen years ago. She no longer has to fear putting Edward in danger of being thrown into prison for having sex with an underage schoolgirl, so what has she got to lose?

Oh, Brianna what a tangled web of deceit we spun together when we were only girls — as a way of surviving men.

I was out of breath after running all the way from Oundle Road to Brianna's house. I couldn't get the car to start and I was too impatient to walk all the way here so I caught the bus which dropped me at Orton Waterville. Since fleeing the Woodman, I've had the uneasy feeling that someone is following me, but every time I stopped to look back over my shoulder, I saw no one. At first, I feared it was Banks, but I was out of that pub as fast as a bullet leaving a gun, so there was no chance he would have seen which direction I took, let alone followed me. But even on the bus I'd felt eyes burning into my shoulders but didn't turn around to see who it might be in case it was a mental case who would cause a scene.

The grey Volvo is missing from the driveway, but when I try the side pedestrian gate, which I always do but always find locked, it swings open with a whoosh. *This day was meant to happen*, I decide, slipping through the gate like a thief on the prowl. I'm walking up the driveway, wondering if Brianna's angry eyes are watching me from one of the house's many windows when I hear the sound of the electric gates opening followed by the purr of an engine behind me, so I dive to the side, intending to hide, when—

'Hi. Can I help you?' A pleasant sing-song voice calls out.

Knowing I've been spotted and that there's no point in hiding, I straighten up and walk over to the shiny new Mini Cooper, overcome with emotion as I recognise the girl driving it.

'You must be Dana?' I'm taken aback by how stunning she is and how much she resembles Brianna. 'I'm a friend of your mum's. I've come to see her. Is she in?'

Dana chuckles. 'She's always in.'

It doesn't enter her head to challenge who I say I am. It's a symbol of smug security. She has been shielded from harm her entire life, unlike me. The high, impenetrable electric gates. The quiet, studious father. The protective mother. A life of privilege. Of safe, reliable cars with built-in airbags. Brianna has cushioned her daughter in a protective cocoon. I wish I could have done the same for my son, Ryan, but I didn't get the chance. Even after all these years, I'm still resentful about it.

'Want to hop in?' Dana motions to the passenger seat.

'Sure,' I answer as I stroll around to the opposite side of the car.

'How long have you known my mum?' Dana asks, criss-crossing her eyebrows as soon as I get inside the car.

'Oh, forever,' I respond casually, hoping she doesn't see straight through my lie.

'Really?'

Acting surprised, Dana starts up the vehicle and we drive forwards, approaching the house. She can't have been driving for very long and it shows. The car jerks like an out-of-control muscle spasm and she spends too much time checking her gears and gazing in the rearview mirror. But it's Brianna's reaction to seeing me that is making my stomach churn, not the driving. Will she throw me out again? I wonder.

'I never get to meet Mum's friends,' Dana confides as if she's known me all her life, reminding me of how Brianna was with me in the maternity ward. Best friends one minute and then not wanting to know me the next.

'You'll have to tell me what she was like when she was my age.' Dana rolls her eyes as if that were a hundred years ago and parks the car in front of a double garage with locked doors.

'And what she used to get up to,' I joke.

* * *

Brianna's expression, as I accompany Dana into the kitchen is priceless. Shock, rage, and dread swarm her face, like angry bees, but a mask quickly comes down on it, camouflaging her real feelings with a perfumed smoke screen as she kisses her daughter on the cheekbone.

'Sorry, I didn't get your name . . .' Dana laughs. 'How rude of me.'

'Tara,' I tell her. 'But it's okay, your mum doesn't need an introduction. We go back a long way, isn't that right, Brianna?'

'Absolutely,' Brianna plays along, pretending to be nice to me, but one eyebrow lifts as she adds, 'for longer than I care to remember.'

She then puts on the kettle, insisting I sit at the kitchen island as if I hadn't sat there just a few weeks earlier. From here, I watch Dana's head vanish into a massive American fridge as she scavenges for food.

'There's never any food in this house,' she complains over dramatically as most teenagers do.

'It's the same in my household.' I try to engage with Brianna, but she's glaring aggressively at me behind her daughter's back.

'Do you have children too?' Dana pokes her head out of the fridge to enquire, her mouth full of something chewy.

'Two,' I respond, with a tight smile, wanting to say *three*.

'How old?'

'Much younger than you,' I explain because it's clear she's hoping I might have a teenager or two knocking around. 'Five and three.'

'How adorable,' she squeals with delight. Then, armed with what appears to be a plate of cold leftover chicken, coleslaw, and a chunk of cheese, she makes her way to one of the doors leading off the kitchen.

'Nice meeting you, Tara, but I'd better get on. Lots of revision to do. You'll have to tell me all of mum's secrets the next time you're here.'

'Oh, I will,' I laugh, wondering how Brianna can keep a straight face and not launch herself across the island to attack me. 'And it was lovely to meet you at last, Dana,' I remark to her fast disappearing back.

'Dinner at seven, darling,' Brianna calls after her.

And then we're alone.

CHAPTER 53: DINO

It's just the two of them. In interview room four. Again. Jesus. You couldn't make this stuff up. Banks seems insistent on not believing Dino's rehashed theory about Tara and Mrs Grant but why won't he consider it? It's obvious to Dino, staring at him in the face just as much as the detective is doing, with an odd expression as if he thinks Dino has lost the plot and perhaps, he has. One minute he thinks he's finally grasped the situation and is certain of his facts only to collapse in a mountain of self-doubt the next.

'This is just routine procedure, no one is accusing you,' Banks reminds him.

'Mrs Grant is,' Dino protests.

'You know, I take back what I said earlier about Tara and Edward Grant because I don't believe they were having an affair any more than she and Mrs Grant were,' Banks concedes.

'You don't?' Dino feels misty-eyed from hearing that. He wishes Banks could have met Tara and gotten to know her in person, rather than through her death. He only knows her as words on a page. Bruises, blood, and a broken body on a colour photograph.

'What if the common denominator is you?' Banks cross-examines.

'How could that be?' Dino stammers. 'I'd never met the Grants before Tara died and I can honestly say I never wish to again.' Dino's anger is back. He thought he was done with it but it isn't done with him.

'Hmm . . .' Banks reclines in his chair, tilting it onto two legs, and places his hands behind his head.

It's a gesture Dino has come to know well. He's of the opinion that the detective does his best work in the air.

'I don't think Tara would be impressed by your accusations,' Banks observes.

'How do you know? You never met her.'

Banks' face flushes red as if he's hiding something, but Dino supposes that's what a policeman's job entails.

'By now, I feel as if I do.' Banks rotates his head full circle as if wrestling an inner conflict. 'You've told me so much about her,' he explains with sorrowful eyes, adding, 'I don't think she would have cheated on you.'

'Then what's the connection? Have you asked the Grant woman if she knows?' Dino explodes.

'Of course, but she's not exactly thinking straight at the moment. I did come across something interesting though when I was doing my digging on Grant.'

Dino leans forward in his chair. 'I'm all ears.'

'I have a theory of my own if you want to hear it,' Banks admits this while lurching forward and letting his tilted midair chair crash to the floor.

'You bet.'

'A woman, Tara, died outside their house and no matter how cold or unlikeable you think the Grants are, they had to be affected by it. They couldn't be otherwise.' Banks poses this information as a question.

'They sent flowers,' Dino admits.

'Huh?'

'To the funeral home. For Tara.'

'Exactly my point.' Banks punches a fist in the air. 'I think her death acted as a trigger.'

'You mean like PTSD?' Dino knows all about that, he's been suffering from it himself, as his therapist had explained to him.

'Apparently, and I'm telling you this off the record, his brother was killed in a car accident.'

'Now I get where you're coming from. That would make a lot of sense.'

'They were very close and he blamed himself because he was the older brother and he was meant to be watching him at the time, but he dropped his hand for a minute, and the rest as they say is. . .'

'History,' Dino finishes for him.

'So, here's my take on this. Mr Grant felt so bad about Tara dying outside his house, that it stirred up all kinds of unpleasant memories for him and he thought he might be able to fix it by talking to you. That's why he went to your house. On an impulse.'

'Except I wasn't there.'

'Except you weren't there,' Banks repeats back to Dino. 'That would explain Mrs Grant's hostility towards you. Because she was aware of the impact Tara's death would have on her husband.'

For the first time since arriving at the police station, Dino smiles. 'You know, you're actually rather good at this.'

The door is rapped sharply before it opens. A uniformed police officer motions for Banks to join him outside, his face grim. The detective follows, frowning. Dino thinks he hears hysterical screaming and weeping from down the corridor just before the door closes behind them. Mrs Grant?

When Banks returns, he appears so serious it throws Dino into a panic. He knows he's innocent, but he's starting to worry that he'll be punished for something he hasn't done. He gets to his feet as a wave of anxiety washes over him.

'What is it, Banks?'

'You'd better sit down for this, Dino.'

Dino's heart plummets as he collapses into his chair, sighing and hanging his head as Banks takes the seat opposite him. He doesn't want to hear what he fears is coming — that they're going to arrest him. He wishes he were at home with his kids. That he'd never gone out on a date in the first place. He should have spent his evening with his family. Seeing happy smiles. Toothy grins. Refereeing fights between Fabio and Bella and rolling pasta for tea. It's Saturday. They always have pasta on Saturday.

'He's dead,' Banks announces deadpan.

'Who?' Dino knows. He just doesn't want to face the truth of what Banks is trying to tell him until he knows if he is being implicated in any way.

'Edward Grant.'

'Shit! How?' Dino probes.

'He jumped off the top floor of Queensgate's multi-storey car park.'

'Fuck.' Dino doesn't know what else to say but it's easy to imagine what Edward Grant must have looked like when he hit the ground. A body torn apart. Head and limbs ripped from the torso. A disgusting, sticky, bloody mess. Dino tries not to think about Tara's broken body that had been left outside Edward Grant's house like unwanted rubbish.

'That's the first question people ask after a suicide: how?' Feeling guilt-ridden for being so predictable and morbidly curious about how a man's life ended, Dino says nothing.

'You don't find bodies at such scenes. Just body parts,' Banks confirms grimly. 'It simply goes to show that you never really know people. Edward Grant seemed to have it all. A beautiful, talented wife. A lovely daughter. A successful business. Plenty of money. A multi-million pound house. But it wasn't enough to take away his pain. It's the mother and daughter I feel sorry for.'

'If you ask me, Edward Grant is a selfish son-of-a-bitch,' Dino seethes, as a wall of hatred forms around him. Brick by brick. Trapping him inside it. He'd give anything to have his wife back. Be a family once more. Yet Edward Grant had thrown his life away, as if it were nothing, leaving his family devastated. That was something Dino couldn't forgive.

'You think?' Banks' face stretches into a sceptical frown.

'I know,' Dino scowls, slamming both palms down on the table. 'A real man would never do that to his family?' Dino, shocked by his own words, begins to think he is turning into his papà.

'Guilt can kill a man quicker than any gun,' Banks murmurs softly.

'Tell me about it,' Dino grumbles, noticing for the first time that Banks appears both sorry and tired, so he avoids complicating his job any further by asking whether he's off the hook and can go home, instead stating, 'I appreciate you letting me know.'

'It's the least I can do, Dino, after dragging you away from your date to haul you in here.' Banks stands up, hands in his trouser pockets, a contemplative expression on his face, and says, 'I won't give up looking for them, you know.'

'Who?' Dino asks vaguely.

Banks lowers his eyes. 'Whoever did this to Tara.'

CHAPTER 54: TARA

The real Brianna

'You bitch,' Brianna hisses at me now that we're on our own. Her eyes burn with anger. Her skin is aflame with hatred.

'You brought this on yourself, Brianna. I had to speak to you.' I stammer. She's standing, while I'm sitting. It gives her the upper hand.

'I want you out of my house,' she fires at me.

'All in good time,' I say, adding, 'but first I have to ask you if you know a man called Christian Banks.'

She looks at me like I've gone mad. 'No. Why?'

'He was one of Sean Hunter's friends and he might have been there the night I was raped.'

'What exactly are you saying?' Brianna's body relaxes somewhat and she reluctantly takes a seat across from me, but keeps her distance.

'That he could have been the one who raped us. Not Sean.'

'I've told you already. It wasn't Sean.' Brianna lets out a frustrated sigh. 'He might have been a druggie but he wouldn't have hurt a fly. He was kind and thoughtful. Even sensitive. Maybe misunderstood, but never violent. He helped take care of his sick mother. He was my friend.'

I'm stunned into silence. My God, what have I done? If this is true, then I'm responsible for Sean's suicide. I pushed him to do it. Made him feel like he didn't have any other choice. His blood is on my hands. This means I'm not the decent human being I thought I was. A part of me dies in Brianna's kitchen when I realise this. I'm also deeply wounded that she chose him as a friend while looking down her nose at me.

'You knew him all along and you never said anything,' I accuse. 'Why didn't you tell me this before?'

Brianna sighs and rolls her eyes. 'I thought when you sat in my kitchen that you knew who the rapist was and that you had an ulterior motive for being here.'

'It must have been the policeman then. He used to hang out in the park too with Sean. I'm sure he was there the night I was raped. One of the quiet boys. The ones who hardly said a word . . . And to think—' I come to a halt, unwilling to examine how Christian had made me feel. I can't deny that there was an attraction between us that I hadn't felt before. Even with Dino. *What does it say about me if I could fancy a man who had raped me?*

'Are you insane? What are you going on about now? What policeman?' Brianna demands to know. 'You seem desperate for it to be anyone except the person who did this. That's why I can't trust you.'

'I'm not asking you to trust me,' I stammer. 'That's not what this is about.'

'No, because it's all about you, isn't it Tara?'

I clench my teeth. 'Me and Ryan.'

'And what about Dana?'

'What about her?' I check out the door as I say this in case Dana should return.

'She can never know that she was born as a result of rape and that Edward isn't her father. I couldn't fall pregnant again after having her, despite there being nothing wrong with me, so I assumed Edward couldn't . . . that he was infertile. It would kill him to know this as he absolutely dotes on her.'

The truth at last. Hadn't I guessed all along that Edward was unable to get Brianna pregnant? So far, it's the only thing that has made sense.

'I won't let you do that to her, us,' Brianna goes on to say.

'I would never do anything to harm Dana.'

'Sure, you would if it meant getting your way,' she pauses to look me in the eyes. 'That's what you do, Tara.'

Do I? I ponder, my gaze fixed on my lap. I'm not sure what she means exactly. It's not like she even knows me. Or what I've been through. She seems insistent on taking our conversation in a different direction when I want to discuss our rapist. Nail the bastard for good this time. When I look up again, I see that Brianna has angrily risen to her feet. Her shoulders are ramrod straight and her fists are bunched at her sides.

'Everything has to revolve around you. Your rape. Your baby. Your life.'

'That's not true,' I object, my eyes welling up with tears. 'You don't even know me.'

'I know enough to know I could never be friends with you,' she sneers bitchily. 'I want you out of my life for good after today. I swear to God, if I have to see your face again, I'll do something to you.'

I lurch to my feet, determined to stand up to her, but she gets in my face. She has a primitive and dangerous aura about her. Something I've seen somewhere before. A long time ago. And then I remember. The girl who was there the night I was attacked. The one who got in my face and warned me off.

Or what? She'd demanded when I warned her friend to *watch out* after she'd thrown the burning cigarette end at me. In the dark, I couldn't make out her features but she had reeked of cheap perfume, and was chewing gum. My body tenses as I realise that she and Brianna are the same person and a firework of fury goes off in my head.

'I know who you are. You were there that night.' I go on the attack.

'What are you talking about now, you crazy bitch,' Brianna scoffs.

'It was my birthday,' I mumble, taken aback by this latest betrayal, but then again when has Brianna ever not deceived me? I should have known she was no good. Why couldn't I see it? I'd put her on a pedestal back then.

'I thought you were special, Brianna, but you were just like all the rest, no worse, a cheap slut who smoked weed and hung around with boys *and* older men. You were no virgin when you were raped, that's for sure.'

'Keep your voice down,' she warns, her eyes hardening. Her mask has well and truly fallen off now, not just slipped, and I see her for what she is.

'I left the group because of you that night. I was fifteen and if it hadn't been for you, I might not have been raped.' I jab a finger at her soft chest.

'Don't even try to pin that on me,' Brianna argues, but she retreats from me anyway. 'I was raped too. But not by Sean Hunter or your copper.'

'No. You probably opened your legs to Sean for nothing,' I say nastily.

She slaps me then. Hard. My cheek pulses from it. I can feel a trickle of blood running down my face from where one of her rings has snagged my skin. I stare at her in a daze as she clasps her hands over her face, horrified by what she's done.

'There you are,' I say quietly, 'the real Brianna at last. You were never nice, were you?'

'Who is?' she barks. Her eyes pierce into mine as if she wants me dead.

'Why did you pretend to be my friend?' I ask, unable to shake off a feeling of being tricked.

'You were clingy and intense. It put me off. That's why I never contacted you. But I didn't know it was you that night, okay.' She shrugs one shoulder. 'It was pitch black in the park and we'd all been drinking, so when I met you in the maternity ward nine months later there's no way I would have recognised you.'

'Were you ever raped? Or did you make that up as well as pretending to be someone you weren't?' The words fall out of my mouth before I can stop them. No victim wants to hear those words of doubt.

'How can you of all people say that to me when I was raped less than a week after you by the same boy?'

'How do you know that?' I gasp, reeling from this latest revelation. 'I never told you when it happened.'

'There were rumours,' she sighs. 'No one knew it was you but somebody must have blabbed. The boy who did it, probably. I didn't find out until after I was attacked, and by then it was too late for me.'

'So, I was the first then?' My mouth drops open as I point to my chest.

'There you go again, making it all about you.' Brianna's shoulders go back a notch as indignation swells in her chest. 'Do you still not know? Haven't you guessed? I can't believe you haven't twigged it yet.'

'What?' I stutter, perplexed.

'If you really want to know who our rapist is you should try looking closer to home.'

'What do you mean?'

'I mean, Tara, it's a small world. Imagine my surprise when I turned up at your wedding reception to discover that my rapist was the groom.'

I feel like I've been hit by a train. For a moment, all I can do is stare at her. 'You're lying,' I exclaim, as all of the oxygen in my body is sucked out of me. 'Dino wouldn't. He couldn't. I'd know . . .'

'I knew that's what you'd say, which is why I never told you. To think I even felt sorry for you,' Brianna expresses her disgust. 'I was horrified when I found out you and him were tying the knot and for your sake, I hoped he might have changed. I didn't know then that he had raped you too. How could I have done?'

'He hadn't. He didn't. You're lying,' I repeat.

257

My brain has gone blank. I'm unable to think. The kitchen with all its fancy gadgets falls away. I'm at home. With Dino and my children. We're watching a family movie together. Bella is asleep, half on mine and half on her daddy's lap. Fabio is playing battles with his toy soldiers. My world hasn't just exploded.

Before I'm ready, Brianna's lies bring me back to the room.

'Then I saw the way he looked at me and I knew he hadn't changed one bit. He recognised me straight away, I could tell. He was smirking, Tara.'

'Shut your filthy mouth,' I yell. 'There's no way my Dino would have raped you or anyone else. That means he can't be Dana's father either.'

'Mum.'

Brianna and I both turn our heads to look at a horrified, wide-eyed Dana. I've no idea how long she's been standing in the doorway or how much she's heard but it's time for me to make a bolt for it as teenage-hoody-Tara would have done. Run, Tara, run . . .

CHAPTER 55: DINO

Dino's legs eat up the ground as he pushes himself to run faster, harder, and for longer. He's promised himself nothing short of a five-mile run today. He's in training for Peterborough's half marathon next May to raise funds for Victim Support, who helped him when he reached out for their assistance, signposting him to all the relevant organisations and charities he could access for counselling, grief recovery and financial guidance.

It's Sunday morning and it's already a glorious day. Ferry Meadows is perfect for joggers. Lots of greenery and open spaces. He passes the wobbly bridge as he continues on the bark-lined trail, remembering the picnic he took Tara and the kids on. It was meant to be a pleasant surprise but she had hated it. He remembers that they had a fight that day and left early. The kids had cried. He had sulked. Tara had gone completely silent on him. Like she always did when he did something wrong. But on that day, he had no idea what he was meant to have done.

The kids stayed at his parents' house last night, like they do every Saturday, to give him some time alone, or in case he wants to go on a date. Dino believes that his parents need the kids more than he needs time off. But he doesn't want to deprive them of their grandchildren, so he says nothing. He still feels bad that he and Tara distanced themselves from them for a while. But that was largely his mamma's fault because she could be controlling which Tara objected to. Every mum wants to bring their kids up a certain way and his mamma should have respected that.

Dino's throwing a family barbecue this afternoon. Although it's already the middle of July, this will be their first of the summer. They'd not done one without Tara before, as it had kind of been her thing, but the kids had begged so he finally caved. Yesterday afternoon he went shopping. Steak. Sausages, burgers. Fizzy pop. Beer. Ice.

He was surprised to run into Claire and her new boyfriend in the supermarket. It had been almost a month since their ill-fated date and she wasn't the least bit embarrassed to see him, unlike Dino, and even offered up her peachy cheek for a quick peck. The boyfriend's gaze was fixed on Dino's face the entire time. Claire was dressed in a short flimsy dress that showed off her shapely, golden legs. Dino had a few regrets but he was confident he'd made the right decision when he ended things with her as it had been the wrong time.

Dino leaves the trail and goes to stand under a giant tree to grab a bit of shade from the sun. Swigging from his water bottle, he puts a hand against the tree trunk and pauses for breath, recalling the article in the paper he'd read last night. It was the smallest of write ups but the surname *Roberts* and word, *doctor*, made him sit up and take notice.

According to the *Peterborough Evening Telegraph*'s chief reporter, Debbie Davis, Dr Roberts, husband to Caroline, had been arrested on charges of domestic violence against his wife. While this vindicated Dino, he remains enraged by the false accusations she had levelled against him. He'll never recover from the humiliation of being arrested on charges of sexual assault as if he were some kind of monster.

It's been a week of shocking revelations because he also learned about what had happened to DI Banks. He'd been taken off Tara's case and transferred to Newmarket in

Suffolk. This all happened so suddenly, Dino knew there had to be more to it than that and he was correct. The retired copper, his gym buddy, filled him in on everything else. Banks, it appears, has been a bad boy, having been caught cheating on his wife with multiple other women and as they both worked for the same force, he had to go.

Dino is unsure how he feels about Banks now. But the one word that pops into his head is *betrayed*. Banks made himself out to be a doting family guy, which made Dino feel inferior at times. It was disappointing to discover he was a fake as Dino had admired him in so many ways. Banks is forgotten though when one of the female joggers he frequently sees in the park comes into view.

'Hi.' She smiles his way, while slowing down to take a breather.

'Hey.' Dino waves.

He observes her wrestling a water bottle from her bum bag only to find it empty. He jogs over, holding out his bottle.

'I don't have any germs or diseases that I know of,' Dino jokes.

'Oh, thank you,' she replies, as she takes the bottle from him and wipes the top before putting it to her mouth.

Dino watches her drink greedily, thinking that she's petite like Tara but incredibly fit, unlike his late wife. She's also attractive in the Julianne Moore, the actress, mould. He's always been partial to redheads.

'Do you always run alone?'

She's to the point. Again, like Tara.

'Do you?' he counters.

'Touché.' She squints her eyes at the sun and chuckles.

Their pale green colour reminds Dino of the Fountain brothers. He shakes the thought away as quickly as it entered his mind, focusing instead on her damp hair, which is tied back in a ponytail. He imagines how it might appear loose around her pale, white shoulders. Then he tells himself to get a grip. He's probably frustrated without realising it. It's something he should work on. Increase the weightlifting. Spend more time in the gym.

'If you ever run out again there's a café not far from here where you can top up for free.'

'Really? I haven't seen it.'

'It's about a half mile away, by the lake.'

'That's worth knowing. Thanks.'

'I hear they also serve chilled prosecco.'

'Now you're talking.' She breaks into a freckly grin.

Dino considers whether he should offer to take her there right now. Buy her a drink.

'What makes you think I'm a prosecco girl anyway?'

'I'm told it's a particularly good one.' Dino lifts a playful brow. 'You'll like it. All girls do.'

CHAPTER 56: TARA

The denial

As I race down the driveway, my footsteps pounding the block paving, my breath coming in rapid gasps, I hear Brianna yelling my name from inside the house. Dana's sobs and howls echo her mother's screams. Clasping my hands over my ears, I block out their hateful, incriminating sounds but I can't escape the lies that chase me, outrun me, and overtake me.

If you really want to know who our rapist is you should try looking closer to home. It's a small world. Imagine my surprise when I turned up at your wedding reception to discover that my rapist was the groom.

Why would Brianna fabricate such lies? How could she possibly say such things? What did I ever do to her that she despises me so much? She is plainly out to destroy me. My life. My marriage. My family. But I won't let her. I'll show her that I'm much stronger than that. *We're* much stronger than that. Dino is the best of husbands. A fantastic father. He would never hurt anyone. Never mind force himself on a woman. He's too soft for that.

And I'd know if the younger version of my husband had raped me, wouldn't I? I'm not sure what Brianna hopes to gain from her false accusations but I have to assume she's mentally ill. No healthy person would make such ludicrous claims. This means I'm back to not knowing who my rapist is. If Brianna is telling the truth about Sean, which I still can't be certain of now I know how much of a liar she is, that makes Christian the prime suspect again. Is he the one who raped me? Was he mocking me for being naive enough to agree to go for a drink with him? I can't stand the thought of him having fun at my expense.

When I barge through the side gate, one of its fancy metal crooks catches my jeans and as I fight to free myself from its grip, I cast a quick, panicked glimpse back up the drive, in case Brianna is charging after me. But it's empty. When I whip my head around to look the other way, I see a young man standing in the middle of the road staring at me and I become conscious of how I must appear — a furious, red-faced, emotionally distressed woman impaled on a gate trying to escape a multi-million pound mansion. This time, when I attempt to wriggle my way loose, I'm successful and when I check out the road again, the young man has mysteriously vanished. He must have disappeared into one of the other houses.

I dash into the road, relieved to be away from Brianna's toxic home. I'd take my rented semi to Holywell House any day of the week. Brianna can keep her money and her expensive cars. Dino and my children are more than enough for me. I can't wait to be at home with them. To see their faces. It's a relief to know I'll never have to set foot on this posh person's street again. I wish that I'd never met Brianna Grant. That when she first said those words to me on my wedding day, *My name is not Brianna and I don't have a daughter called Dana*, I'd had the sense to listen.

Why, oh, why had I persisted in stalking her? Of being insistent that she speak to me. Why couldn't I just leave it be? Is Brianna right about me? Am I clingy and intense? Is that why I have no real friends? And do I make everything about me as she implied? *My rape. My baby. My life.*

But while I am certain that Dino is innocent of what Brianna accused him of, I'm aware that something doesn't add up. Why would Brianna scream such lies at me and risk Dana hearing them, as she clearly had in her out-of-control rage. She now has a lot of explaining to do. But how can she unpick such a massive lie? Why had she put herself in that situation in the first place? She was so insistent that she didn't want Dana to discover that Edward was not her actual father but she then went ahead and opened the can of worms herself. Her desire to hurt me had taken precedence.

As I've got my head down, hands dejectedly in my pockets, muttering under my breath, I don't look where I'm going so when I trip on a protruding part of the pavement, I can't stop myself from tumbling into the road. I hit the ground with a thud. My hand is grazed and bloody, my body unwilling to pick itself up right away, but I'm otherwise unharmed. There's nothing broken. Except for my pride. I'm about to check out the street to see if anybody witnessed my humiliating fall when a hand drops on my arm. I look up, startled to find the same young man I spotted earlier on the road.

'Are you okay? Can I help you?' he asks with concern in his eyes.

I know it's impolite, but I shrug him off overly harshly, forcing him to back off. He may be a harmless teenager, but I don't want to feel any masculine hands on me today. He keeps a safe distance away from me while I scramble unaided to my feet and dust myself down so that particles of the asphalt fall off me. One of my nails is broken to the quick and my hand is still bleeding. I'm about to apologise for my rudeness, thinking he didn't do anything to deserve it, but nothing comes out of my mouth when I look at him properly for the first time.

It's Dino. A much younger, incredibly good-looking Dino. But . . . I must be mistaken. Concussed, perhaps, without knowing it. Did I land on my head when I fell?

But the young man's chocolate eyes are just like my husband's. His dark hair has the same unruly curls as Dino's. His skin is the same olive shade. They match in height. They are identical in every way possible.

My hand flutters to my heart as I ask, 'Who are you?'

'My name is George,' he replies solemnly, 'but I believe you know me as Ryan.'

'You can't possibly be,' I gasp, taking a step back from him.

'Why not? Because that would make you my mother?'

His words have me reeling and my hand flies to my mouth. This cannot be happening and he cannot be my son. Not now. Not today. Not ever. Not looking like that. Like my husband.

'Sorry,' he says quickly, as though scared I'll fall back into the road. 'I shouldn't have sprung it on you like that.'

'What are you doing here?' I look around the street of luxurious homes as if I'd just woken up from a nightmare and found myself transported here. I feel like this is happening to someone else and that I'm just a casual observer. It's as if I'm conversing with a ghost. 'How did you find me?'

'I've been following you.' He pulls an apologetic face. 'And I've spent the last few days trying to figure out when the best time would be to introduce myself.'

'Have you been watching me the whole time?' I ask incredulously, but when I recall that I'd felt someone's eyes on me throughout the last few days, it makes sense.

'Sorry.' He apologises once more, his mouth tugging into a helpless smile, another of Dino's gestures.

I feel like I'm drowning as it becomes clear to me what this means. Brianna was right all along. She didn't lie. She'd actually been trying to protect me from the truth the whole time. Dino was the third boy in the park that night. Without my knowing he'd been the one who followed me. Who raped me. This means the young man standing in front of me with sorrowful eyes and a rejected hunch to his shoulders is our son. And a grenade that's about to be thrown into our lives.

He's live ammunition that nobody will recover from. Not me. Not my children and certainly not my husband — the rapist — and the father of my eighteen-year-old son. Sometimes the things you wish for in life come back to haunt you. Hadn't I wished for years that Ryan would one day come and find me? And now he has. I also recall wishing that each of my children would look more like Dino than me. This has also come true. And it's killing me. Ryan will be devastated to learn that his father is a rapist. Dino could go to jail as a result of this. The De Rosas could lose everything.

I've never stopped loving my son and a part of me wants to take him in my arms and hold him, telling him to stand up straight and stop apologising because he's worth more than that, but another more selfish part of me sees him as a threat to my other children and my way of life.

My heart hardens in my chest and I pray that God will forgive me as I say to him, 'You've made a mistake, George, or whoever it is you think you are, because I'm not your mother, and *you are not my child.*'

CHAPTER 57: THE CHILD

He doesn't move. He can't. Neither does his mother. Except she's not behaving in a very motherly way. She rejected him once before, eighteen years ago. He can't believe she's doing it again. It could just be the shock of meeting him but either way he's at a loss for words and doesn't know how to feel. Should he be angry? Sad? Disappointed? Maybe all three.

Her green eyes are wide with terror and she's starting to back away from him. But he's not about to let her get away that easily. He's waited a long time to meet her and he's got a lot of unanswered questions. *Like, who is my father and why did you abandon me?* When he told her he'd been following her for a few days he had lied. It's been going on for much longer, ever since he turned eighteen. He's been lurking in the shadows all this time watching her as she watched Dana Grant's house.

He first met Dana at Peterborough college and they hit it off immediately, having loads in common, even though she's an art student and he's studying psychology. He's been to the Grant's home several times before, but only when the mother wasn't around. Dana explained to him that her mum was very protective over her, especially around boys, but agreed to introduce him after six months of dating. He was cool with that.

He has no idea what the connection is between Tara and Mrs Grant but he'll add it to his list of questions. He didn't expect Tara, as he refers to his mother, to recognise him straight away but she clearly had. This implies that he resembles his father. He supposes it's something to be proud of.

When the electronic gates behind them abruptly open, they each jump as if shot with a gun. Like mother. Like son. Ryan notices Tara tilting her head to one side, listening to the sound of a car speeding down the driveway. From where he's standing at the side of the road, he glimpses the white Land Rover Discovery first. It's going too fast. He wonders who is behind the wheel. Mr or Mrs Grant? He knows it's not Dana because she drives a spanking new Mini Cooper that was given to her on her eighteenth birthday. Ryan had received a letter with his mother's name and address, and his birth name, on it for his. He wouldn't trade it for anything.

'You should move out of the way.' He motions with his chin to the oncoming vehicle but Tara doesn't seem to notice or hear him. Her attention is drawn to the approaching car and the woman inside. Mrs Grant. He only has a second or two to observe her, but it's clear she's in a terrible state. Crying. Screaming. Pounding her fist on the steering wheel. Not looking where she's going. The car shifts into a higher gear and accelerates again. It's getting closer but Tara is still frozen in the middle of the road.

'Tara. Move,' Ryan shouts and waves his arms to grab her attention. Yet all she does is stand there with her eyes closed as if she wants to die.

'Mum,' he screams at the top of his lungs. He can smell the diesel fumes. Feel the heat of the engine. See the panic in Mrs Grant's eyes as she tries too late to brake. They scream louder than he does. He darts forward in an attempt to save Tara, but it's too late. Her body is thrown into the air and lands on the bonnet as the car comes to a screeching standstill. Ryan imagines he hears her bones crushing as her body suddenly rebounds back into the road, landing in a crumpled heap as if it were roadkill.

'Mum,' he sobs as he races around the dented bonnet of the overheating car to find her, ignoring the howling woman inside it.

'Mum,' he cries again, throwing himself onto his knees beside her. Unlike before, when she stood in the middle of the road as if she wanted the car to mow her down, her eyes are now open and her gaze is fixed on him. He notices dark stains on her clothes and it takes him a minute to realise it's blood. Her chest pumps up and down as if an invisible medic were already carrying out CPR on it and when she opens her mouth a trickle of blood escapes it.

'Don't go, Mum. Don't leave me again,' he begs, squeezing her small, bloodied hand in his.

'Ryan,' her voice rattles with the effort of breathing. 'I'm sorry.'

* * *

It wasn't anybody's fault. Until it was. It was an unfortunate accident. Until it wasn't. The aftermath of what happened to Tara that day has sped up in Ryan's mind to make him think that his resulting actions had taken minutes rather than hours and that he may have reacted impulsively, driven by shock and a desire to please. As soon as Dana arrived on the scene searching for her mother, Ryan had taken charge. If he didn't help them, Mrs Grant would go to prison. But first, they had to get her to stop screaming. One look at Ryan's face had started her off and she wouldn't stop, until Dana slapped her hard across the cheek.

At breakneck speed, Ryan then drove Mrs Grant and Dana back to the house in the Land Rover that was streaked with his mother's blood. He left them alternatively crying and screaming at each other in the kitchen while he parked the car inside one of the garages and locked it.

He'd already learned from Dana that Edward Grant wouldn't be returning home for another two days, giving Ryan plenty of time to get rid of the vehicle. His adoptive parents owned a smallholding in Wisbech. There were plenty of old buildings he could hide it in where no one would think to look for it. The car was a recent purchase and not known to any of their neighbours. Even the DVLA paperwork hadn't been finalised yet. The plan was to tell Mr Grant it had been stolen a few days before but that they hadn't reported it to the police for fear of it being linked to the death of the woman outside their house.

Mrs Grant, whom Ryan found manipulative and self-serving, seemed confident that she could convince her husband to go along with the lie. Dana, on the other hand did not seem to want to go along with this, saying her father had a right to know, but Ryan sensed they were having a different conversation to the one he thought he was having with them. He was starting to wonder if Mrs Grant crashing her car into Tara was deliberate, rather than an accident, but as far as he could tell, she had no motive for doing so.

The worst part was abandoning Tara's smashed and bloodied body in the road while they waited for her to be found. It was too risky for any of them to call the police. When Ryan asked himself why he was protecting his mother's killer, he admitted that he was doing it for Dana. He loved her. He'd do anything for her. When it dawned on him that he'd finally tracked his mother down only for her to die rejecting him and that he was partly responsible for her death, *he'd acted too late and then covered it up for the Grants*, he'd chewed on a knuckle and screamed silently.

Over the next two days, it became evident that something other than the accident and subsequent police investigation into his mother's death was going on between Dana and her mother but they refused to confide in him. They walked on eggshells around each other. The two women whispered and hissed at each other like venomous snakes and would stop talking whenever he approached them. Mrs Grant couldn't be in the same room as Ryan, wouldn't make eye contact with him and wouldn't talk to him unless she was forced to, even though he'd saved her skin. She treated him like he was some kind of devil. As his mother had done.

Even his lovely Dana cooled towards him. She wouldn't let him touch her and shrugged him off every time he went near her. She appeared to see him with new eyes as if he'd done something wrong when all he'd wanted to do was protect her. It seemed unfair to Ryan at a time when he was going through so much. Losing Tara was killing him on the inside. He couldn't tell Dana or Mrs Grant that he was Tara's son. What would they think? He had stood by and done nothing to help his mother and the shame of admitting that she had rejected him for a second time was too much to bear. There was nothing to do but remain silent.

He was asked to leave Holywell House before Mr Grant returned home. Dana explained to Ryan that his presence was upsetting Mrs Grant although he couldn't understand why and felt she should be grateful to him, but when Dana went on to say that mother and daughter needed some time alone to come to terms with what had happened, he got the impression this had nothing to do with his mother's death. He felt used by Dana and her mother but it was too late by then to have second thoughts. He was an accessory to manslaughter. He knew he wouldn't see Dana again when he left the house that day, feeling rejected all over again.

As he let himself out of the gates of Holywell House, he had paused to stare at the spot where Tara died. The police had done a reasonable job of clearing up the scene of the accident but hadn't been able to completely erase the dark blood stains from the road. His mother's words boxed him around the ears as tears filled his eyes. *You are not my child.*

CHAPTER 58: DINO

Now

The young man standing on Dino's doorstep, who he estimates to be around eighteen or nineteen, is in no hurry to
leave it. He wonders if he's all right. He appears detached and
lost as if he's in difficulty and in need of assistance. But he
could just be another young hoodlum. The type who would
sell their grandmother for a tenner and a pack of cigarettes.
Then he takes that thought back. The teenager's hands are
noticeably trembling. He seems terrified. But of what?

'Are you okay, son?' Dino feels suddenly old. He's never
used such an expression before in his life. He's turning into
his papà.

'Yes. I mean, no. Sort of,' the young man stutters in an
apologetic tone, his face flushing acne red as he digs deeper
into his jean's pockets.

Dino notices that there's something remarkably familiar
about him. The brown eyes and hair. Something about the
smile. The tilt of the chin. He recognises him from somewhere, but where? He's about to ask him outright what he
wants when his papà appears besides him.

'Your mamma sent me to find you. The steaks are burning,' his papà complains in his irritable saved-especially-for-Dino voice, while tutting like a budgie on cocaine. When he spots the visitor at the front door, his grey, sagging face lights up in a rare smile, making him appear years younger.

'There you are my boy,' his papà exclaims, grabbing hold of the young man's hand and pulling him into the house. Dino catches the teenager's side-long look of alarm but his papà isn't taking no for an answer and whisks him inside before he can even think of protesting.

His papà must be deteriorating to do such a foolish thing. They have no idea who this young man is. For all they know, he could be a thief. A teenage serial killer. But if his papà believes he knows him, convincing him differently is going to be extremely tough. When it suits him, he can be as stubborn as a mule. And that has nothing to do with Alzheimer's.

'Papà, what are you doing?' Dino exclaims in panic, following them through the house and out to the garden.

The children are already there. They must have gone back outside while Dino was answering the door. They're in the inflatable pool, splashing each other with cold, grass-strewn water. Their nonna supervises their play but keeps her distance since she doesn't want to get her homemaker's apron wet. Her eyebrows scale her head like mountain climbers when she sees they have a guest. Dino shakes his head and shrugs his shoulders, which is sign language for *Papà's having one of his confused moments.*

Dino can tell that she's accurately interpreted the glance because her mouth twitches into a solid line of displeasure. His mamma doesn't like strangers or surprises. Tara was the same. He watches his mamma take off her apron because in her world it's not seemly to be seen in it when they have company, but her hands suddenly stop and the hardworking piece of material falls to the ground.

There's something wrong with his mamma. She looks like she could be having a heart attack. Her eyes are on stalks.

She has one hand clasped over her heart and the other one covering her gaping mouth.

'Mamma?' Dino swallows nervously, not liking the way her gaze is darting between him and the young man. Something is going on here that he doesn't understand. Meanwhile, his papà has taken the teenager over to the barbecue and is instructing him on how to cook the perfect steak. The teenager isn't looking at the sizzling meat though. He's staring at Dino, in exactly the same way that Dino is glaring at him. With shock. Horror. And recognition.

'Dino, what's going on here?' his mamma demands, looking visibly shaken. 'Am I seeing what I think I'm seeing?'

'Dino,' his papà interrupts in an insistent voice.

Dino's attention is tugged away from his mamma and directed back to his papà. Flames flicker dangerously close to the old man's arms. The steaks are on fire.

'Be careful!' Dino warns, hurrying over to his papà, only to be thrust off.

'I didn't ask for your help, mister. My son, Dino, can sort it.'

When his papà's gaze slides back to the young man, his elderly watery eyes resting proudly on his chocolate brown ones, Dino is overcome with envy. His papà has never looked at him that way. Nor is his papà confused. He saw what Dino did not when he first opened the door — the young man is a carbon copy of him. This can only mean one thing. Dino has a son he never knew about. This is why the teenager is here. He wants something from him. *What the fuck is going on*? Life had been going nicely up until this point. Dino's first selfish thought is that he doesn't need this right now.

But hold on. What is his papà saying to the boy now?

'Your mamma will be so pleased to see you, son.' His papà informs the teenager excitedly.

This definitely makes no sense. Dino's ears begin to ring and there's a jabbing finger in his head. He realises he hasn't finished piecing together the puzzle of why this young man is in his garden, disturbing their family barbecue. There's more to it than he first thought.

The barbecue is back under control. Someone, most likely the young man, has rescued the steaks and turned them over. They continue to spit and hiss like a cornered cat, which is exactly how Dino feels.

'What time is Tara getting here?' his papà calls out to no one in particular, before returning his attention to their visitor, around whom he now has a paternal arm. 'Let's hope she brings one of her homemade tiramisus. She knows I like them, and they're better than your mamma's,' he continues in whispered tones that everybody can hear.

The kids are squealing in the water, oblivious to what is going on. They pay no notice to the unexpected guest. A dog barks in a nearby garden. The barbecue continues to sizzle. Dino's lips taste of cold beer. The sun powers down on them. Radio 2 bounces across from the fence next door. The air smells of freshly cut grass. A garden hose is abandoned on the lawn, its sprinkler open in a snarl. It resembles a long yellow snake slithering through the grass. These are the sights and sounds Dino has grown accustomed to throughout the summer. He has a feeling those days are over. That family life, as he knew it, will never be the same.

'Dino,' his mamma snaps, clicking her fingers loudly in the air, like an impatient customer in a restaurant.

Dino awakens from his trance-like state. He's back in the garden where he doesn't want to be. Throat constricted. Knees buckling.

'Who is this young man?' his mamma demands, fixing Dino with accusing eyes. 'Do you know anything about him?'

'No. I . . .' Dino is at a loss for words.

'I'm George. But you can call me Ryan,' Dino hears the young man say.

Dino watches Ryan gently peel himself out of his papà's embrace, patting him on the back almost fondly, before crossing the badly mowed lawn to stand in front of his mamma.

His papà seems to have forgotten about Ryan by this point. He crouches like a much older man over the barbecue, clouds of black smoke billowing in his face, unsure where he is.

Dino's mamma avoids shaking Ryan's extended hand. Instead, she wrings her hands nervously, as if they must be kept busy at all times. Her eyes continue to dart up and down his thin frame as if she were bidding on an animal for meat at auction. Her gaze softens as it reaches Ryan's eyes. She has that soppy look on her face that Tara used to despise because it was typically reserved for Dino. 'Cringeworthy,' she called it.

'You have told us your name, son. But who are you exactly? And what are you doing here?' His mamma inquires quietly and calmly, realising that the children have stopped playing and are now paying attention to their visitor with their ears pricked. They've reached the age where they enjoy listening in on adult conversations.

Don't say it. Don't say it. Don't say it — is all Dino can think, biting on his bottom lip until it draws blood. He can't be the boy's father. It's not possible. And yet—

Ryan scrapes his chin with nibbled-to-the-stump fingers, grimaces, and then swallows, as though readying himself for the most important speech of his life.

'I'm Tara's son.'

CHAPTER 59: THE CHILD

Ryan has looked forward to and dreaded this moment for most of his life. He's imagined various different outcomes of his visit, including the impact it would have on the family that should have been his. Would he be accepted? Or called out as an imposter? But in no scenario did he imagine his mother would be absent from it. It's been nine months since she died. That's how long it's taken for him to come back to Peterborough. He feels nine months is rather appropriate because that is how long Tara carried him in her womb before giving him away to a couple who never loved him.

They're all staring open mouthed at him. Even the children. The old man has moved away from the barbecue to join them, a frown on his already deeply furrowed face. The old woman is scrutinising every inch of Ryan's face as if hunting for proof that he is who he says he is. Dino has flopped onto a deck chair, looking stunned and relieved at the same time. For a brief moment, Ryan was convinced that Dino was . . . . They look so alike, yet he knows it to be impossible . . . he files away the thought that his mother's husband had felt the same. He could see it in Dino's veiled eyes.

Ryan's gaze is drawn involuntarily to the children. For a long time, he's wanted to get a good look at them. He can see

Tara in the little girl. As for the boy, he is Dino's double, but he and Ryan could also be full brothers. Ryan's back spikes and his chest pounds on that thought. Why is he overcomplicating things? He should be focusing on his half-brother, who looks like he could be a lot of trouble, but in a cute way. Who cares if Ryan also looks like Dino? It's a coincidence, nothing more.

Ryan was brought up as a lonely only child and when he first found out he was adopted, at the age of seven, he'd imagined what his biological family were like and this is exactly how he'd pictured them. Close. Protective of one another. Loving.

The fear of them rejecting him, as Tara had done, was what had kept him away for so long. He'd wanted to come sooner but first he needed to grieve, not only for his mother's death but also for the end of his relationship with Dana. He'd never heard from her again, just as he'd predicted that last day at Holywell House. Not once. Despite calling and texting her hundreds of times. He'd heard recently on the grapevine that her dad had killed himself, and so he'd pinged her one last message telling her how sorry he was, but she never responded. He wonders now if Dana had confided to her dad everything that had happened that day, and he'd been unable to live with himself, knowing what his wife had done. Ryan will never know the truth, of course. They were a secretive bunch. He's finally over Dana though and she's now as dead to him as he is to her. But he's also a different person as a result.

Will Dino forcibly remove Ryan from the house when he gets over his shock? Tell him never to return. Dino's expression had been soft and forgiving when he first opened the door which caught Ryan by surprise. He'd conjured up a red-blooded, alpha-male version of his mother's husband in his head. Don't ask him why.

Will the old woman gather her grandchildren, his half-siblings, to her bosom and warn him to stay away from them? Her liquidly dark eyes are at a loss what to do. They dart all over the place. But she says nothing. None of them does. They know that anything they say in anger cannot be taken back later. And he's Tara's son. A part of her. Only the old man, whom Dino refers to as Papà, has so far been accepting of Ryan, but that's because he's confused him with his own son. Ryan decides that he must have dementia. There can't be any other explanation, can there?

His herding sheepdog gaze circles the children again. It no longer bothers him that they have never known a day of suffering in their lives, as Ryan has, except for the sudden loss of their mother. They can't help who they are. Nothing is their fault. Tara isn't even to blame for how things turned out for him. She was only fifteen when she had him. She had no way of knowing that things would not go as planned for Ryan with his adoptive parents or that they provided him with the basics, a roof over his head and food in his belly, but never kisses, cuddles or love. He's devastated that he'll never know who his real father is now that she's dead, but even as he considers this his eyes are drawn to Dino.

'Are you our brother then?' Fabio asks boldly, wrinkling up his nose and folding his arms across his chest in a menacing manner that makes Ryan want to playfully toss him up in the air.

'I believe I am,' Ryan tells him, holding back a mountain of emotion in his chest.

'Cool.' Fabio grins, while rocking on his feet. 'Do you like soldiers?'

'He's my brother too.' Bella possessively stamps her foot, before commanding, 'Come and play on the trampoline with me, Ryan.'

Ryan's heart melts as she extends a freckly trusting hand to him. When he glances at their nonna for permission, she nods sharply. Three times.

CHAPTER 60: DINO

They can hear Fabio's and Bella's excited squeals from inside the bedroom as they jump up and down on the trampoline in the garden outside. They've come upstairs to escape the children so they can talk privately with lowered voices but every so often Dino and his mamma can hear the deeper voice of Ryan, as he encourages the children to 'be careful,' and warns them, as an older brother would, and should, 'not to jump so high.'

The reminder that the life he knew is over causes Dino's shoulders to slump. He crosses the room with heavy-lidded eyes to close the window, drowning out their voices, but he can't help but peer down at Ryan. A sick feeling rolls around Dino's gut as soon as he sets eyes on him. Ryan glances up, sensing he is being watched, and his eyes spark with surprise. Panicking, Dino shuffles back, out of sight and sinks onto the bed.

'What's going on, son?' His mamma lifts dubious eyes as she sits on the bed next to Dino, not as close as she normally would.

'God knows, Mamma. I'm still struggling to get over the shock of seeing him.'

Mouth grim, his mamma states: 'He's yours, isn't he?'

'I swear to you I didn't know.' Dino fumbles around with the edge of the bedspread, its purpleness hijacking him with memories of Tara.

His mamma's body jerks in response. 'So why is he claiming to be Tara's son when he's clearly yours? Any fool can see that.'

Dino steels himself for further censure from his mother, whose face is clouded with confusion. 'Because he must also be Tara's son.'

'What? How is that possible, Dino?' Her voice is no more than a breathless rasp.

Memories mixed with regret swirl through Dino's mind as he travels back in time to when he was younger when they used to refer to him as the Italian Stallion. He'd considered himself to be a stud and the girls had felt the same way. Back in the day, he'd had a lot of them. Too many to count. Nameless girls mostly, a blur of faces who never meant anything to Dino. He has never been able to clearly recall those days, but before Tara, he assumed that every woman wanted him.

Dino struggles to maintain his composure under his mamma's razor-sharp gaze. For the first time, he wonders if he's misremembering how things had really been. He'd been high on pot throughout the majority of his adolescence. He'd even taken crystal meth and the odd line of cocaine. Had the drugs shrouded him in a blanket of darkness, concealing the truth?

Fear and disbelief still Dino's restless body as memories come back to torment him, of girls underneath him, squirming and struggling to escape, while he laughed. He'd convinced himself in his aroused drug-hazed state that they would enjoy the sex as much as he did. He never once considered that they were actually saying no. That he was forcing himself on them. Nobody ever said no to Dino. Certainly not his mamma.

But what of Tara? Is it possible that he had sex with her without him realising it? That they got together and married years later without either of them remembering. What kind of God would allow that to happen? And if it's true, does that mean he raped Tara? Is that how Ryan came about?

Dino closes his eyes, futilely attempting to fight the past. A vague memory stirs of a girl in an enormous hoody with electrifying eyes. A tangle of frizzy hair. Could that have been Tara? The so-called love of his life? There's a lingering taste of vodka, weed and cigarettes in his mouth. And the smell of semen and dog piss. A wet patch forming under him. *You'll like it. All girls do.* When Dino's eyes reopen, they are dark with grief.

'I raped her, Mamma. I raped Tara. I must have done. There were others too. I told myself they wanted it as much as I did but I've been lying to myself all along. Papà knew though. He's known the whole time.' Dino pauses to draw in panting gulps. 'That's why he was always so protective of Tara. He claimed to have followed me one night. Told me he saw what I'd done, but I never imagined it was that. He might not have turned me in to the police but he's never forgiven me. That's why he hates me, Mamma.'

Dino's mamma remains still for a full minute until he hears the faint tread of her footsteps on the carpet as she comes around the bed to wrap her soft, doughy arms around him. As he buries his face in her comforting bosom, heart-wrenching sobs shudder through him.

'I don't know what to do. Should I tell Ryan what happened and what I did to his mother? Doesn't he deserve to know the truth?'

His mamma remains silent for a long time before abruptly saying, 'No one deserves to know that sort of truth.'

Dino's head twists to follow his mamma's gaze which is fixed pointedly on a photograph of him and Tara on their wedding day. His jaw sags and his mouth twists into a self-hating grimace. 'Do you hate me, Mamma?'

'We'll love that boy as our own, as indeed he is,' she says, ignoring his question. 'That's the only way you can make things up to Tara. And God.'

'Are you saying we can't tell him? That we should keep it a secret?' Dino cuts across her protests.

'Imagine how he'd feel if he knew his father was a—'

'Go on, say it, Mamma,' Dino stammers. 'A serial rapist. A monster,' he finishes bitterly as images of Tara and other girls pleading for him to stop, flash through his mind. Caroline Roberts is there too, tucked away in the furthest corner of his warped brain. Her eyes wide with shock when Dino accidentally on purpose brushed against her body.

'I'm not judging you, son,' his mamma whispers, placing a hand on his forehead.

'Well, you should.' Dino lurches to his feet, cursing silently. Darkness seems to follow him everywhere he goes. He can't live with himself for what he's done. But he also doesn't want to die. 'You absolutely should. I don't deserve to be protected. No mother should ever have to do that.'

'You're just a man. What do you know?' His mamma is suddenly ferocious. 'Only a mother understands how far she would go to protect her son. Tara would have felt the same way about Fabio.'

'So, you're suggesting we pretend he's not my son? He must see that I'm the spitting image of him. If he hasn't already, he'll figure it out for himself in the end.'

'These things are easily explained. It's nothing new. Not to my generation anyway. We'll say Tara went for a certain type. Tall, dark, and handsome. And that's why you look so alike.'

'Even if he believes that, what about Papà? He knows.' He gives her a desperate look.

His mamma is dismissive. 'He only thinks he does. He'll have forgotten everything by tomorrow. That's how it is with him. No. The way I see it, Dino, is that Tara has given us something of herself back in that boy.'

'You'll be telling me it's a blessing in disguise and part of God's plan next,' Dino accuses her unjustly.

Her face registers surprise but she doesn't falter. 'Look, Ryan needs a home if ever a boy did. You can see it on his face that he's desperate to be loved. He's ours, Dino. Whether you like it or not. And that means protecting him from anything that could further harm him. Don't you think he's been through enough?'

Dino casts his eyes around the room, pondering why women are the wisest and strongest of the human species, and then he lets out a long, surrendering breath. His mamma knows best. She always has.

'And you'd better be prepared to love him as if he were one of your own, or I'll take a slipper to your backside like I did when you were little.' His mamma smiles faintly, but it doesn't reach her clouded-over eyes.

'I'm going down now to get to know my new grandson better,' she adds, dragging herself to her feet. 'And I suggest you do the same.'

Dino knows she means business when she purses her lips at him, but he pans over her shoulder to take in the rest of the room which still has traces of Tara in it. The purple duvet. The picture of her in her wedding gown. The photograph of her taken shortly after she'd given birth to Fabio in the hospital. Dino wonders whether every time she looked at it, she was reminded of her other son. Tara was never his, he realises brokenly. There had always been a piece of her missing from their lives. He doesn't want to, but he almost hates Ryan for that.

He sighs. 'I just need a few minutes to myself.'

'Okay. No longer than that,' she replies, eyes hardening.

Once he's alone, Dino curls forward in grief and puts his head in his hands. In the pit of his stomach, a scream is gathering.

Dino realises he knew Ryan was his from the moment he saw him, but shock and disbelief hid that awareness from him at first. Because it was so unexpected, he'd been blind to it. There's no disputing that secret number two has returned home and that there's nothing Dino can do about it. Where was Tara when he needed her?

Dino returns once more to the night when his papà followed him. He hadn't known there was someone in the shadows watching him as he was watching *them*, the girls. How many attacks had his papà witnessed? He only admitted to spying on Dino the once so perhaps he only knew about Tara. Not the others. Had his papà suspected there was something wrong with his son all along? That he was born bad? Was his DNA faulty? Is that why his papà was so strict with him? He'd failed miserably at keeping Dino out of trouble. Why hadn't he tried to stop Dino or help Tara? Shock perhaps? And instead of reporting Dino to the police, as his papà should have done, he kept quiet knowing his wife would never forgive him if their only son got sent to prison because of him. Was it his mamma's fault for being too lenient? Too forgiving? She had let Dino get away with murder when she should've let his papà horsewhip him as he'd wanted to.

What was Dino doing? He couldn't blame his parents for how he had turned out. It wasn't their fault he was a monster. He was born one. By the age of twelve he was already addicted to porn and masturbation. Yet he remembers his mamma hadn't let him attend sex education classes at school, thinking him too young. The irony wasn't lost on him, then or now. Could the porn and the attacks on the girls have gotten mixed up in his drug-induced stupor? Is that how he blocked them out?

When Dino was going through his rebellious adolescence phase, he used to hang around with a group of teens who believed they knew everything there was to know about girls. Like the girls in the porn films, they honestly thought they enjoyed sex as much as boys did, but liked to pretend otherwise so they didn't get called slags. In other words, they said "no" when they meant "yes". As an impressionable young man, Dino must have kept that conviction buried in his mind, even when he knew it to be wrong. Now that he's a man, with feelings of deep love and respect for the women in his life, including his late wife, his mamma, and his daughter, he knows better. Dino would be the first to jump to a woman's aid and he'd take on any man who dared to lay a harmful hand on his daughter. But when men claim to be protecting their women, what they really man is they're protecting them from *other men*. Men like Dino.

He'd never considered himself capable of inflicting pain on his wife but that's exactly what he'd done, along with God knows how many others. On top of being raped at the age of fifteen Tara had to give birth on her own before giving up her, *their*, baby for adoption. All because of him.

His mamma had suggested the boy was a gift from God and that they were regaining a part of Tara by welcoming him into their family. She must be insane to believe such a thing. As far as Dino can see, he has only one option. He would never be able to love a child who constantly reminded him of what he had done to the woman he loved. So, he must keep on telling himself that the boy is not his. He's Tara's. If he can convince himself of that, he will at least be able to act as if he cares for the child for the sake of his mamma and Ryan, since none of this is their fault.

Ryan is *not his child*.

THE END

ACKNOWLEDGEMENTS

The De Rosas in this story appear to be an ordinary family who had extraordinary things happen to them. My task, as their creator, was to treat their pain and trauma with empathy and respect. I hope I have accomplished this. It broke my heart that I allowed such terrible things to happen to them, especially to Tara, but, as usual, I had no say in how the story developed. For readers who may have found the storyline distressing or triggering in any way, please accept my apologies and know that I had my own very personal reason for wanting to write it.

The main characters felt very real to me, like extended family, and I feel their loss even now. As I begin my next story, I like to imagine that Dino is self-reflecting on his past offences, of which there are many, and that Ryan is coming to terms with his mother's rejection and subsequent, tragic death. I hope he never finds out who his real father is and that they can somehow get beyond the secrets and lies that tie them together as a family.

I'd like to dedicate *Not My Child* to the man in my life, Hero, my big-bellied, flat-faced cat, who sat with me while I wrote it. Hero rescued me at a time in my life when I needed it most, and, although he believes I kidnapped him from his old home he has turned out to be my bestie who thinks I live rent-free in his house. He's been on his own journey and it's been a pleasure to be a part of it, watching him transform from a posh Persian, who never once set a paw outside and would only drink filtered water from a fountain (I make do with tap), to a regular tom cat (without the naughty bits) who now roams the surrounding countryside hunting mice. When he's not bringing me worms (as presents) he follows me everywhere, like a dog, and we play hide and seek as if he were a kitten and me a child. Who knew I'd become cat woman?

I also want to say a massive thank you to everyone at Joffe Books for all their hard work in getting this story ready for publication. They have been an absolute pleasure to work with and I'm both proud and pleased that they took home the prize of Trade Publisher of the Year in 2023. A well-deserved win. Go Team Joffe. Special thanks go to Kate Lyall Grant, Joffe's publishing director.

Since I've lived and worked in the Peterborough and Stamford areas for years I decided, once again, to use them as a backdrop for this story.

Those of you who are familiar with the city of Peterborough will know that it has a large population of Italian immigrants based in Stanground. This is where one of the main characters, Dino De Rosa, who is English-Italian, grew up.

If you are not from the UK, please excuse the English spelling. Oopsy daisy, it's just the way we do things across the pond. Apologies also for any swearing but this is down to the characters and has nothing to do with me. Lol. The same goes for any blaspheming.

Now for the best bit where I get to thank my lovely readers for all their support, especially my ARC reading group. You know who you are!

Your loyalty and friendship mean everything. As do your reviews. ☺

THE JOFFE BOOKS STORY

We began in 2014 when Jasper agreed to publish his mum's much-rejected romance novel and it became a bestseller.

Since then we've grown into the largest independent publisher in the UK. We're extremely proud to publish some of the very best writers in the world, including Joy Ellis, Faith Martin, Caro Ramsay, Helen Forrester, Simon Brett and Robert Goddard. Everyone at Joffe Books loves reading and we never forget that it all begins with the magic of an author telling a story.

We are proud to publish talented first-time authors, as well as established writers whose books we love introducing to a new generation of readers.

We have been shortlisted for Independent Publisher of the Year at the British Book Awards three times, in 2020, 2021 and 2022, and for the Diversity and Inclusivity Award at the Independent Publishing Awards in 2022.

We built this company with your help, and we love to hear from you, so please email us about absolutely anything bookish at: feedback@joffebooks.com.

If you want to receive free books every Friday and hear about all our new releases, join our mailing list: www.joffebooks.com/contact

And when you tell your friends about us, just remember: it's pronounced Joffe as in coffee or toffee!

ALSO BY JANE E. JAMES

HER SECOND HUSBAND